Second Debt

INDEBTED #3

PEPPER WINTERS

Second Debt (Indebted #3)
Copyright © 2015 Pepper Winters
Published by Pepper Winters

Published: Pepper Winters 2015: **pepperwinters@gmail.com**
Cover Design: by Ari at Cover it! Designs:
http://salon.io/#coveritdesigns
Proofreading by: Jenny Sims:
http://www.editing4indies.com
Images in Manuscript from Canstock Photos:
http://www.canstockphoto.com

This story isn't suitable for those who don't enjoy dark romance, uncomfortable situations, and dubious consent. It's sexy, it's twisty, there's colour as well as darkness, but it's a rollercoaster not a carrousel.

(As an additional warning please note, this is a cliffhanger. Answers will continue to be delivered as the storyline resolves. There are six in total.)

Warning heeded...enter the world of debts and payments.

If you would like to read this book with like-minded readers, and be in to win advance copies of other books in the series, along with Q&A sessions with Pepper Winters, please join the Facebook group below:

Indebted Series Group Read

Jethro

I'D TAKEN HER, but ultimately, she'd taken me.

I'd tried to destroy her, but serendipitously, she'd destroyed me.

This was the beginning of the end.

Not the end of my feelings for her but the way of my life, my world.

Something would have to change.

Something would have to give...

. . .

Someone would have to die.

Nila

I EXISTED WITH a brain full of betrayal, schemes, and plotting.

Living with the Hawks was utterly exhausting. Every day was a challenge to figure out the truths from the lies. But no matter how hard I worked, I could never seem to unravel reality from fiction.

He'd won.

And with a winner came a loser. One triumphant and one depressed. A trophy over misery.

Two days had passed since Kestrel had granted the truth to one huge mystery. Two days in which I hadn't been able to think of anything else.

I wanted to hate Jethro for duping me—for stringing me along like an idiot.

But whenever my anger boiled over, needing desperately to confront him, I remembered one thing.

One important, vital thing.

He'd initiated contact before he was told.

He'd communicated with me almost as if it were a cry for help, rather than a plot to deceive.

If this were another trick, then so help him, I'd find a way to castrate him.

But, somehow, I didn't think it was.

I had a horrible feeling this was the one way that he would let me in. An avenue of truths that he felt comfortable enough to continue, because a silent written word didn't have as much weight as a loudly spoken one.

Which brought me back to my vitally important conclusion:

Jethro wants to be honest.

He wanted to stop playing charades and show me everything he kept hidden.

He wanted to talk to someone. Perhaps, for the first time in his life, he wasn't satisfied with the hand life dealt him and...

Stop fabricating excuses.

All day, I'd been coming up with theories on why he was how he was and reading too far into things that he'd done.

It could be as simple as: he'd been told to get in touch. Told to initiate contact in a way that could potentially mould me into a more submissive captive, especially if I were to believe he was on my side.

I wanted to believe he'd acted against his father. But no matter how much I wished it, it didn't make it was true.

How do you explain the knowing then?

I slouched against my pillows in bed. That was true. A part of me just seemed to *know*. Call it either sheer idiocy or feminine intuition. I believed he'd texted me because I was the first outsider permitted into his world—the only one not a Hawk.

My brain hurt.

When we were alone, when we weren't arguing or fighting, there was an enchanting calmness. A *connection*.

Closing my eyes, I let my mind skip back to Kes's unwilling promise. The way his eyes had darkened with secrets as I'd collapsed into his arms from the vertigo spell two days ago.

"Nila?"

A crushing headache appeared from nowhere. It was the most I could do to stay present and not permit my mind to relive every text Jethro had sent to see the hidden agendas now that I knew it was him.

"I'm—I'm okay. You can let me go." I struggled out of Kes's embrace, my skin humming from his touch. I needed some space. I needed a world full of space to get over the treachery and lies.

"You didn't know? You hadn't guessed?" Kes crossed his arms, never taking his golden eyes from mine.

I glowered. "How could I know? I thought the messages were from you!"

He flinched. "Yes, that was the plan. To make you believe it was me, so he could continue on with whatever little mind games he was playing." Leaning closer, he added, "I haven't been privy to any of the messages he sent you or you sent him—so don't feel like I've intruded on details that I shouldn't."

Anger infused my blood. "If you were both in on it—why didn't he show you the messages? Why were you so nice to me? What does all of this mean?"

Kes moved away, reclining against a sapling. "I was nice because that's just who I am. Yes, I come from a family with twisted up morals and I'm loyal to those twisted up morals, but I also did it out of loyalty to my brother. If you're pissed, direct it all on him. Not me."

"Oh, believe me. I'm pissed. Beyond pissed." My hands balled as my mind filled with crazy ideas of retribution and revenge. I would make him pay.

"I'd cool down before you spring it on him. Best to keep it quiet. Cut doesn't know. It was just me who knew Jet had been in touch with you before he was given the go-ahead to collect you in Milan."

I froze. "Why did he initiate conversation with me almost five weeks before he could claim me?"

Kes shook his head. "The day I understand my brother is the day I'll gamble my entire inheritance on the stock market. I can't work him out. The only thing I can do is be there for him. And I only found out 'cause he changed pretty much around the same time he started messaging you. Something was different—we're close. So, I saw it before the others."

My brain throbbed trying to figure out just what had changed in Jethro. He'd seemed the perfect Hawk when he'd come to collect me. Cold as ice and deadly as a sword.

Now that I knew his secret, I had power. And I had no intention of *giving that power back. Jethro had been playing me for far too long. He'd successfully screwed with my head. It was time for payback. "Don't tell him that I know."*

Kes's eyes popped wide. "Pardon?"

"You heard me. Don't tell Jethro about today. Let him continue to think I'm clueless." My heart frothed with rage and unhappiness. I was so stupid to believe I'd gotten through to him on some level. The sex between us left both of us stripped bare. Something more than family feuds and hatred existed when he slid inside me and sent both of us shattering into dust.

I'd let him inside me. In so many ways. It was my turn to do the same.

"You know I can't do that, Nila. As welcome as you are in our household, and as much as I like hanging out with you, I can't betray Jet. Not after everything he's been through."

I pounced on the small thread of truth about my tormentor. "What has he been through, Kes? Tell me and I'll march back to the Hall right now and tell him myself."

Kes shifted uncomfortably, refusing to meet my eyes. "Slip of the tongue. Forget it."

Crossing my arms, I hissed, "Fine. Seeing as you're so capable of keeping secrets, keep this one for me."

Kes scowled. "Keeping my own flesh and blood's issues hidden isn't the same thing as helping out a Weaver."

My heart raced. If Jethro hadn't taught me how to stand up for myself, I would've cowered at the thought of being so pushy with a full-grown man all alone in a forest. Now, I was raging and fully intended to get my own way. "Give me two weeks. Two weeks before you tell him that I know. Do that and I'll be forever grateful."

His shoulders slumped in defeat. "How can you be forever grateful when forever isn't something anyone has."

Especially me, seeing as my lifespan was destined to be significantly shorter than his.

"Just...please, Kestrel. One favour."

It took him a while to give in. His allegiance to his brother was strong.

Finally, he huffed. "Fine. But it won't save you from his temper when he finds out."

However, I had no intention of suffering Jethro's wrath. I had every right to deceive him after he did it to me. My revelations were safe—for now. I trusted that Kes wouldn't say anything. I didn't know why, but on some level I *did* trust Kes—just enough to use him in my plans. And I was fully committed to tripping Jethro up.

It was his turn to divulge things he might not have if he'd known the truth. Hiding behind the pretence that Kite was Kes had made him softer the past few weeks. I would use that chink to make the crevice I'd been trying to form since I gave him a blowjob after hunting me down.

I couldn't think about anything else. I couldn't focus on sketching, sewing, reading.

Nothing.

My brain was a whirly-gig of Jethro. Kite. Jethro. Kite.

And I'd had enough.

Throwing myself out of bed after another sleepless night, I wrenched back the curtains and glowered at the dismal weather.

The watery dawn did nothing to inspire either anger or contentment. The sky was grey. Fog looked like haunting ghosts, threading its ghoulish tentacles over the lower woodland of the estate. No birds chirped or sun shone.

Summer had truly abandoned us. The bite in the air shouted 'go back to bed where it's warm' but my brain had no such intention.

I hadn't relaxed for two days. I'd stared at my phone, determined to text Jethro and trip him into revealing everything he kept secret, only to stare blankly at an empty message.

Now that I knew it was him, my willingness to show so much had gone. Knowledge was power and he had too much of mine already. How could I dig deeper into his mystery while maintaining all of mine?

The answer—I couldn't. And that made me incredibly nervous. To find out who he truly was, I had to show everything that made me real. And despite the emotional growth spurt I'd endured at the hands of the Hawks, I wasn't ready to evolve again. I'd lost so much of myself already—how much was I prepared to leave behind before I became a perfect stranger?

"Ah!" I dug my fingers into my hair. I needed a reprieve from my racing thoughts, and I knew exactly how to do it.

Mother Nature's sudden urge to switch seasons from summer to winter couldn't stop my itch.

I needed fresh air, and I needed it now.

Racing around my room in the new Weaver quarters where Jethro had made me beg and come apart with his cock deep inside me, I found my black spandex shorts and highlighter pink sports bra. Pulling the clothing on, followed by my sneakers, I quickly smoothed my hair into a bun, and shot from the room.

I hadn't worn my exercise gear since the morning of the Milan runway show. I'd sprinted until I'd collapsed off the treadmill at the hotel, hoping I could dispel my anxiety enough to hide my stupid nerves and prevent a vertigo spell in front of the press.

It had worked—mainly. Until Jethro arrived, of course.

The moment when I'd set eyes upon him, I'd been done for. He'd been so dashing with his suit, tie, and diamond pin. So perfectly refined with his elegant haircut, chiselled physique, and sculptured lips. Even though his soul was dark, his body had summoned me.

He'd called to me, and like the stupid Weaver I was, I'd followed him blindly.

Now, it's his turn to follow my whims, my rules.

Jogging down the corridor, my racing mind and temper eased, already reacting to the stress relief I'd sought all my life.

I need him out.

It wasn't fair. I was supposed to seduce him and make him care for *me*—not the other way around. I wasn't supposed to fall for my own games.

Lust was as dangerous as love. Only it was worse because it had the power to make even the worst ideas seem plausible—and even recommended—when a sexual reward was given.

The moment Jethro gave in and kissed me, I'd betrayed more than just myself. I'd betrayed my entire family line and all the Weaver women who'd died before me.

I had feelings for him.

A dangerous softness toward my would-be-killer.

It has to end.

I had to find a way to seduce him...to make him love me, all while I kept my heart frigid and locked away in an ice fortress.

I laughed under my breath. *You sound just like him.*

Only, ice wasn't impervious. Ice melted and succumbed to fire.

I'd proven that over the past month.

The house breathed around me with gentle heartbeats only ancient dwellings could have. Spirits of past generations lived in its walls, revenants danced in the drapery, and figments of long forgotten lovers floated through the tapestries.

A grandfather clock tick-tocked as I jogged past, showing the time at six thirty a.m.

After being privy to the business meetings with Kes and the Black Diamonds, I knew the men never got up this early. They worked late, dealing with shipments and the transportation of stones worth more than any dress I could sew. Darkness was their asset, the sun their foe.

At least I could run and be back before anyone tried to stop me.

I didn't want them to draw the wrong conclusion that I was trying to escape again. I blinked as I ran head first into a horrendous conclusion.

Even if you found the boundary this morning, you wouldn't leave.

My heart thumped harder at the tangled web I lived.

Freedom was something I wanted more than anything. But even if I escaped the Hawks, I would only run back into the trap of pity and vertigo. I wanted more than that. I *deserved* more than that.

If I found the estate edge, I wouldn't disappear. I *couldn't.*

My captivity wasn't just about me anymore. It was about the future. It was about Jethro.

Admit it...

It was about *living.*

The passion, the intensity, the blazing ferocity of existing with enemies and plotting beneath their noses was a much worthier cause than sitting at home sewing for the masses.

This was about me. Me standing up for myself, and for a future I wanted, not a future already planned for me.

This was about so many twisted things.

I wrenched open the French doors at the end of the corridor and stumbled into the foggy dawn. Fresh air welcomed me and I found a reprieve from my scrambled thoughts.

I can't forget my ultimate plan.

No matter how Jethro endeared himself to me—giving me glimpses of someone barely coping inside his wintry armor—I wasn't going to forget my goal.

Freedom.

Not just for myself, but for the rest of my legacy. My children and their children and their children's children would never have to go through this. I intended to be the last Weaver stolen.

It's time for a new debt—one that owes us life, not death.

Sucking in lungfuls of crisp air, I steeled myself in what I had to do. In order to win, I had to guard my soul. I had to play along with Jethro's mind games and hope to God I won first.

A cool breeze whistled through the trees, sounding like haunted laments. I shivered, wishing I'd brought a jacket.

You'll be sweating in ten minutes. Ignore it.

Gritting my teeth against the cold, I bent over and stretched my quads. The tug and slow release of muscles was heaven after the stress of the past few days.

My body hummed with the knowledge it was about to run.

And run.

And *run.*

For fun this time, not for survival.

Bouncing on the spot, I rolled my shoulders, eyeing up the sweeping lawn before me. If I went right, I'd loop around the stables. If I went left, I'd cut through the sprawling rose garden and orchards.

Go straight.

Down the meandering path that disappeared over the horizon.

I switched from bouncing to jogging.

"And just where do you think you're going?" a cool voice whispered through the silver fog.

I wrenched to a stop, peering behind me.

No one.

"I thought you'd realised running wasn't a viable option, Ms. Weaver."

His icy voice sent a strange mixture of hot and cold desire down my spine. Jethro morphed into being, seeming to solidify from the mist like a terrible poltergeist. He leaned against one of the pillars holding up the portico, crossing his arms.

My heart collapsed, unable to untangle the maze of hypocrisy between us. My skin begged for his touch. My lips tingled for his. Every inch of me *craved* what he could deliver.

Heat. Passion. An eruption that I felt in every cell.

But none of that was real.

And I refused to believe in trickery any longer.

Mirroring his body language, I crossed my arms. "I realise *escaping* isn't a viable option. But I'm not escaping. I'm running. Running is my *only* option to escape the mess you've made."

His jaw clenched. "The mess *I've* made?"

"Yes." I took a step backward as he advanced. "You're messing me up, and I'm done playing whatever it is that you're doing." I sucked in courage and embraced honesty. It seemed to work around him, and I needed him to see how serious I was. How hurt I was with his deception.

He's Kite.

Bastard.

Baring my teeth, I said, "It seems I have a weakness for you, but I changed my mind. I don't—"

A low growl escaped him. "A weakness? You call what happened between us a fucking weakness?"

My breathing ratcheted as if I'd already run two miles. "The worst kind of weakness."

He smiled, but no mirth entered his gaze. If anything, his golden eyes were luminous with anger. "You're the one who started it...*Nila.*"

I gasped at the delicious decadence of my name on his lips. The sound echoed in his mouth, shooting straight to my core. *Shit.*

Jethro advanced again, his body trembling with barely veiled lust. "*You're* the one who created this problem." His hand came up, fingers slinking through my tied-up hair, tightening around the back of my skull. "I can't hear the name Weaver without getting fucking hard. I can't even think of you without boiling with need."

His nose brushed against mine, his lips so damn close to stealing all my scrambled plans and sending me headfirst into a life of debauchery.

"You should never have said those two words, Ms. Weaver. I told you. We're both fucked now."

My mind was blank, every synapse focusing on his fingers in my hair and his mouth only millimetres from mine. "What two words?"

He chuckled. The sound was self-deprecating and almost morbid with dark intensity. "Kiss me."

I shivered in his hold. "You're reminding me of what started this mess, or you're asking me to kiss you?"

Ask me. And I will. God, how I will.

I'd kiss him until I'd stripped him of his arctic armor and destroyed it, I'd lick him until I tasted his truth, and I'd bite him until I'd eaten every morsel of his soul.

I'd do all that so he had nowhere left to hide.

We stood wrapped in foggy silence. The drawn out anticipation of a kiss turned my legs to jelly. If he pressed his mouth to mine, I wouldn't be going for my run. I would climb his body and sink onto his cock.

Fakery be damned.

Kite's messages and deceit be damned.

I just wanted a raw connection—with this man, who made my soul whimper for wrongness.

Jethro's tongue slipped between his lips, hypnotising me. Then…he let me go. "No, I'm not asking you to kiss me. I won't ever ask anything from you."

I flinched as if he'd slapped me. "Why not?"

"Because I own you. Everything I want will be given, not requested."

Double shit.

I should hate him. I should smite him. So, why did his every word seduce me, even while I knew his morals were chauvinistic and heartless?

Forcing my body to obey, I shoved the weakness I had for him as far away as possible. My eyes trailed down his front. He wore tan jodhpurs, black riding boots, and a tweed jacket. The bulge between his legs looked heavy and far too dangerous to be legal.

"You've been riding."

A gentle gust of early morning air blew his scent directly into my nose. I inhaled, soaking my lungs in hay, horse, and all things Jethro.

He nodded, crossing his arms once again. "You run. I ride. Seems we have something else in common."

Something other than being forced into this debt and finding each other irresistible, you mean?

"Oh, what's that?"

Jethro stepped closer, seeming to bring shadows into the smoky light of dawn. "We both need time alone to hide from the things that chase us." He stiffened, his eyes churning with things he refused to voice. A five o' clock shadow decorated his strong jaw, his lips parted while his gaze was pure brimstone.

Swiftly, he cupped my cheek.

Oh, God.

Electricity instantly sparked beneath his fingertips.

Would I always suffer the rhapsody of his touch?

My skin smouldered; pinpricks of light, of fire, of hell, all burnished beneath his hold. I swayed, pressing my face harder into his palm.

He sucked in a breath, his fingers digging harder against my cheekbone.

The chemistry and need to devour each other thickened with every heartbeat.

One beat.

Two beat.

Three.

We stood there, frozen on the stoop of Hawksridge Hall just waiting for the other to move. The moment we did, our clothes would disintegrate and I would willingly let him drag me into a bush and fuck me.

Lust and tension swirled.

I had so many questions and doubts; so many reasons to hate and fear him. But when he touched me...*poof.*

I no longer remembered, nor cared.

We swayed closer, drawn against our will to close the aching distance.

I couldn't breathe.

Kiss me. Please, kiss me.

The moment stretched until it hummed with overwhelming possibilities.

Then, it snapped.

Loudly.

Painfully.

Shattering around our feet.

"You're too fucking dangerous," Jethro muttered, removing his touch and stepping away. Dragging his hand through his hair, he commanded, "Wait here. Don't go anywhere." His hands went to his jacket buttons, undoing them with nimble fingers.

I blinked, struggling to shed myself of heavy need and focus on the true reason why I stood barely dressed in the freezing morning. "I'm not escaping. I'll be back in forty minutes or so."

He shook his head, slipping out of his tweed and revealing a black long-sleeved jumper.

My mouth went dry. Even in clothing, I could make out every ridge of muscle in his stomach, every ripple of energy as he breathed in and out. He was designed straight from my fantasies, and I hated him for being so splendid.

My core clenched, sending flutters of wetness between my legs.

I hadn't seen him in two days, yet I'd panted after him as if he'd been missing my entire life.

If he suspected I knew that he was Kite, he hadn't let on. After Kes had told me the truth, I'd waited for Jethro to barge into my room and swear me to secrecy.

But he hadn't.

He didn't look at me any differently; he gave no outward sign that his lies had begun to unravel. As much as he confounded and frustrated me, I couldn't help admiring his perfection at hiding.

I wanted to be like him. I wanted to protect my secrets so damn well that whatever I did next would come as a surprise.

I wanted to *rule* him.

"I'm coming with you. Don't leave." He disappeared into the house, leaving me abandoned and covered in chills from both the morning air and his departure.

Jogging on the spot, I deliberated ignoring him and leaving. *Just go.*

What was the worst that could happen? He'd have to chase me again. My tummy coiled at the thought. I liked that idea way too much. I liked the thought of what would happen after he found me.

The power I'd felt giving him that blowjob. The awe and attraction that'd glowed in his eyes.

I want that again.

Screw waiting like a good little captive.

Make him hunt.

And then I would make him explode.

I bolted.

Jethro

OF COURSE, SHE ran.

I fully expected her to.

Unlike last time when I expected her to cower by my feet, I'd had the last month to get to know my charge. Through getting into her mind via text messages, and getting into her body by sheer insane passion, I'd come to understand her— more than she knew.

And unfortunately for her, she'd lost the ability to surprise me.

She'd lost the ability because I'd been inside her body and mind. I'd traded my soul for hers—no matter how much she would deny it. No matter how much *I* would deny it. We were linked.

Connected.

Bound.

Somehow, she'd crept inside my barricaded heart. She'd weakened me—but that weakness worked both ways.

I *felt* her. I heard her fears, tasted her tears, and somehow knew how she would react.

I hadn't permitted anyone to have that control over me since Jasmine. Even Kes and I didn't share such a strong connection.

That strange bond had a name.

I called it my disease.

And it only got worse the more I was around Nila.

I craved her so intensely; I would break both of us before any more debts were paid.

I didn't think she believed me when I said we were well and truly fucked. And not just because of my father and what he would do. But because of what I *was*.

Because of my...condition.

The moment I left her on the porch, I knew she'd go. The knowledge echoed in my bones, making it fact rather than speculation.

In the time it took to jog back to my room and trade my riding attire for all-black workout gear, she'd gone.

Balling my hands in the cool morning air, I smiled. A genuine smile. It'd been forever since I'd let myself relax enough to be genuine about any emotion.

Just like empathy and compassion were banned from my repertoire, so too, was feeling something so purely that it became a spark in my dead heart. I didn't want to be genuine about anything because it could be used against me.

It was best to hate everything and everyone. To hide my true desires even from myself.

The anticipation of another hunt sent my blood flowing thick and hot.

Her tiny footprints led a trail, like enticing crumbs. The dew-damp grass flattened from her path.

I'm coming, Nila.

Just like before, I took off after my prey. But the difference between this chase and the previous one was I *knew* she wanted me to hunt her. I knew she wanted to be found. And I knew she fed off this cat and mouse idiocy as much as I did.

My legs spread into a large stride as I left the Hall behind.

I preferred to perch on the back of Wings when galloping fast and far. I wasn't a jogger. It wasn't quick enough for me. I missed the power of a large beast between my legs, responding to the commands to race and outrun everything that I was.

Every footfall caused me to wince from what I'd done to myself in my last 'fixing' session. The pain radiated up my legs. I supposed I should be grateful for the agony—it helped me in so many ways. And I needed all the help I could get with Nila wreaking havoc on my world.

You know it's no longer working, so why still do it?

That was true.

Pain no longer held the comfort or fortress it used to. Jasmine was right. It was time to start looking at other methods, or, if I was brave enough, let everything that I'd been hiding emerge.

I snorted at the reaction that would get me. Not to mention the complications with my father.

No, I wasn't ready. Not yet. Besides, I had more important things on my mind.

Such as hunting.

Leaping over the rock wall and tearing down the path, I put my head down and ran after my little Weaver.

A pitiful six minutes later, I gained on her.

Her stride and pace were impressive, and I had to appreciate her wily ways of trying to throw me off her trail by cutting across the driveway and disappearing into the woods on the other side.

But I was an experienced hunter.

Her clues littered behind her, leading me directly to my prey.

Her hair bounced, tendrils coming loose from her hair-tie. Her sculptured legs led to the firmest arse I'd ever seen.

My mouth watered.

I wanted to bite it. Bite her. Lick her. Fuck her.

"This seems all too familiar," I muttered, pulling up beside her with a burst of speed.

She jumped, clutching her heart. "Shit, I didn't hear you creeping behind me."

"Creeping? I did nothing of the sort."

She rolled her eyes, settling back into the punishing pace she'd set. I matched my stride to hers. Companionable silence fell as my attention turned inward again, focusing on the agony in my feet.

I really shouldn't have chosen that part of my body—especially if running with her became a frequent occurrence. I'd have to find a new place in which to fix myself. The soles of my feet had been used for years—when I needed the extra buffer. No one could see the marks, no one would know, and the pain was constant whenever I moved.

A perfect place for secrets.

"Do you run?" Nila asked. Her breathing was heavy but even, her fitness level higher than mine.

I shook my head. "No. I prefer exercise where a horse does the hard work, or perhaps a punching bag that takes my fists."

"You do that often?"

"What, ride?"

"No, assault an innocent punching bag." Her dark eyes landed on mine, diving deep into my complexities before I slammed up my walls and prevented her from seeing any more.

"No more than usual," I said, pulling ahead of her.

With a small grunt, she matched me, not letting me disappear. "I know you have issues, Jethro. But I'll keep my speculations to myself...for now." Running for a while, she finally asked, "What time did you wake up today?"

I frowned, gritting my teeth against the pounding pain in my feet. "What?"

"It's dawn, yet you've already been for a ride. Are you an early riser?"

I snorted. *You could say that.* "I'm not good at sleeping. Wings is used to me."

"Wings?"

"My gelding." I threw her a glance. "The horse I was riding when I tracked you. Remember?"

Nila's face shadowed. No doubt thinking of the hunt and the consequential amazing blowjob.

Sexual tension sprang harder between us, itching my skin, making my cock swell.

My voice turned gruff as I added, "Ever since he was broken in, Wings has been used to me sneaking into the stables and going for a ride in the dead of night. He got a small sleep in today. I didn't saddle him up until four a.m."

Nila nodded, soaking up my confession as if I'd announced the epicentre of why I was fucked up.

"You didn't have any shipments to take care of?"

I narrowed my eyes. "How do you—" I cut myself off. Kestrel. Of course. The weeks they'd spent together meant she would probably have a good idea of the sort of wealth we smuggled and the amount of shipments completed since she'd arrived at Hawksridge.

"Why can't you sleep?" she asked. We ran side-by-side, leaving the gloom of the forest and trading mud for the gravel of a pathway.

I looked up. My heart clamoured.

Shit, we're on the wrong track.

I didn't want her to see what was up ahead. Not yet. I was sure my father had some sick agenda to show her when she fell out of his good graces, but I didn't want to break her again. Not so soon.

I'd avoided the place most of my life. It held only terror. So, why the fuck were we running toward it? It was almost as if she'd been summoned by forces outside my comprehension.

A chill darted down my back at the thought. I slowed my pace.

Nila looked back, decreasing her steps to match mine. "Are you going to answer me?"

What, why can't I sleep?

"No."

I had no intention of answering. There was no easy response, and she knew far too much about me already. Trying to distract her, I said, "Why do you have to run?"

She ran a hand over her forehead, wiping away glistening sweat. "To re-centre myself. At home, it was the only time I had to calm my mind. The deadlines, the demands—it all stole something that I only found again when I was alone with just my frantic heartbeat to keep me company."

Shit.

Her answer was fucking perfect.

I swallowed hard as a glow of more than just lust washed over me.

She understood. She dealt with the same pressures, the same expectations. Only her flaws were visible to everyone, while I hid mine as best I could.

Admit it. The moment you saw her on the catwalk in Milan, you knew.

I fisted my hands, trying to stop the conclusion from forming.

But it was no use. My mind delivered the crushing knowledge with fanfare and barely hidden relief.

She's the same as you. You could tell her.

No fucking way would I ever tell her.

I didn't want to feel anything for her, but I did care. Enough to stop her from seeing what existed ahead. I might not want her in my brain, but I didn't want her in pieces, either.

I slammed to a halt. "Nila. Stop."

Locking her knees, she bounced in place and turned to face me. Her chest rose quickly, panting for breath. "What? Why?"

My eyes involuntarily went to the break in the trees up ahead. Damn sunshine broke through the fog at the exact same moment, spotlighting the one place I didn't want her to see.

Nila followed my gaze. Her shoulders hunched, feeding off my nerves. "What's up there, Jethro?"

"Nothing."

"If it's nothing, then why are you determined not to let me see?"

My temper fed off her nervousness, creating a sick

sensation in my gut. "Because it's time to get back. You've wasted enough of the day doing something as pointless as running." I snapped my fingers. "Let's go. Now."

Her eyes filled with rebellion. She looked back to the hill, chewing her lip.

I moved forward, ready to pounce and drag her back to the Hall. "Ms. Weaver—" I inched closer.

Hesitation flittered over her face.

I tried to grab her. But I was too late.

Darting away from me, she said, "I want to see what you're hiding," then bolted down the path.

"Fuck!"

Her hair flew free from her hair-tie as she sprinted faster up the gravel and onto the moor that I wished didn't exist.

Shit, she's fast.

I tore after her, wishing I had Bolly and the foxhounds to swoop in and cut her off before she reached the crest.

My feet burned and my socks became slippery as old wounds opened. My lungs were pathetic in delivering enough oxygen as I sprinted the final distance and skidded to a halt.

She'd turned from super-sonic to a statue, staring dumbfounded at what existed before her.

Goddammit, why did she have to be so determined to uncover what I wanted to keep hidden? The truth never helped—it only made things worse.

Her hands flew into her black hair, fisting tightly. "Oh, my God…"

I sucked air, hating the sensation of trespassing on such a sacred site. I wasn't welcome here. None of my family was welcome, and if I were superstitious, I would admit there was a stagnant force that howled with hatred and pain.

"No!" she whispered. Her strong legs that'd sent her flying into hell suddenly collapsed from beneath her.

Her fingers dove into the dirt, clutching at grass and mud. "This can't be real. It can't."

She bowed with disbelief, kneeling on the grave of her

mother.

Her anguish joined the storm of revulsion that never seemed to leave this place. Goosebumps darted down my arms as a gale whipped her hair into a frenzied mess.

"Ms. Weaver—" I moved forward, fully intending to pluck her from the earth and hurl her over my shoulder. I couldn't be here another fucking second.

Goddammit, this isn't supposed to happen.

Her eyes met mine, but they didn't swim with tears—black hate glittered instead. "Is this true? All along, my father said she'd run off. All along, he told us stories of her leaving us for a better life. My brother understood that meant she was dead, but not once did Tex take us to her grave. After what your father said...about what he'd done, I still held onto those childish stories that she was alive. But this..." Her voice sliced through me. "Is. This. True? All this time my mother has been buried, cold and lonely, in the ground of the men who murdered her?!"

I swallowed, rapidly diving into the safety net of my snow. I couldn't stand there and hear her horror. I couldn't let her grief infect me. I refused to fucking listen.

"I didn't do it."

As if that makes it any easier to bear.

Nila shook her head, staring at me as if I were some grotesque abomination. "*You* didn't do it? Do you think I care if it wasn't your hands who severed her life? It was your family, Jethro. Your bloodline. You're a monster—just like them!"

The cuts on my feet no longer protected me. I was so fucking close to losing control.

I itched with the need to shut down. To hide from everything snowballing inside. "Let's go."

"I'm not going anywhere with you!" Nila spun to face the burial place of her mother.

My eyes rose to read the inscription on the simple marble headstone looming over her trembling form.

In here lies payment for debts now paid.

Rest fitfully Emma Weaver wherein hell you may face another toll.

Nila looked over her shoulder; her eyes widened until they were as black and as soul-sucking as an eclipse. "Jethro—"

The pain and hatred in her voice sliced me better than any cut on my foot. I took a step backward, placing distance between us. "I can't give you what you want."

She shook her head. "You can't or you won't?"

I knew she wanted answers. An explanation. Facts on why her family was buried on Hawk land and how we circumnavigated the law to do things no one else could.

But what could I say? I was bound. Muzzled. Shackled, not just by Hawk blood, but the very condition that made me a reject in my own family.

The truth hurt. Fuck, everything hurt.

Her panic. Her grief. The throbbing pain in my feet.

I had to get away.

This was why I'd remained cold. Why I did what I did.

This was why I never let anyone get close to me and embraced my duties as a son over the cravings of my heart.

My disease meant I couldn't let things like this happen.

I couldn't handle it.

"I told you I didn't want you to see this place but you fucking defied me!" Hot anger gave me somewhere to hide. "I refuse to indulge your feelings of self-pity." Rage coated my veins, granting sanctuary.

I backed away, distancing myself from the raw fury glowing on her face. "Come here. We're leaving." I snapped my fingers again. "Now!"

Nila stood. Her eyes darted to the semicircle of death surrounding us. An unlucky horseshoe of tombs.

Her chest rose as a silent sob escaped her. Waving her hand at the other graves, she shook her head. In one motion, she asked a lifetime of questions.

How could you?

How did you get away with it?

Why has no one stopped you?

I had no answers.

My eyes fell on the graves.

Six in total.

All with a diamond chiselled into the remembrance of their tombstone and the ultimate mockery of all: a hawk perched on the top, its talons dripping blood down the face of the eulogy.

"This—it can't be real. No one could be this diabolical."

You're wrong. The Hawks can.

I pinched the bridge of my nose. "Quiet." Looking back up, I demanded, "Say goodbye. We're leaving, and I doubt you'll be allowed back up here."

Her mouth twisted with black amazement. "You...I don't have any words for what I think about you. How sick you make me."

"Good. I don't want words. I want to leave." Storming forward, I grabbed her elbow, yanking her away from the cemetery.

"No!" she screamed, scratching my hand and backpedalling. A huge wave of anguish buffeted me. Everything she felt poured from her like a tsunami. I stood, unable to move as it drowned me.

Apart from knocking her unconscious and carrying her back to the Hall, I had no way of making her leave. I couldn't handle carrying her kicking and screaming.

I'd break.

She rattled with the pieces of her broken heart, and just once, I wanted to give in to the benevolence that others enjoyed.

But I couldn't.

I couldn't stand there while she grieved.

It just wasn't possible.

Not for a man like me.

Sighing, I said, "Fine. Stay. Pay your respects and worship the dead, but you'll do it alone."

You'll do it alone, so I don't lose the rest of my soul.

This wasn't a good place for a Hawk, but in a way, it was

home to a Weaver. She might find whatever she was missing by conversing with her past.

"I'll—I'll leave you alone."

Nila balled her hands, looking as if she wanted to strike me. "Disappear, Mr. Hawk. Run like you always do. Good fucking riddance. Leave. Get the hell away from me and don't come back!"

I paused for a fraction. I should do something about her outburst—teach her that I wouldn't permit her to raise her voice, but I was done here.

Taking another step away, I said, "I'll see you back at the Hall."

She didn't reply.

With a black-laced heart and thundering headache, I backed away, faster and faster. Her arms wrapped around her body and her hair danced in the turbulent breeze. She looked like a witch placing a curse upon my house. Then she collapsed at the base of her mother's tombstone, bowing in the dirt. I left her with only ghosts for company, kneeling on the grave of her ancestors.

Shuddering once, I turned and didn't look back.

I GOT MY wish.

My wish to become as cold and as merciless as Jethro came true as I huddled on my mother's grave. My sweaty skin turned to ice with renewed hatred for the Hawks. I struggled with rage so damn strong I was sure the earth would crack beneath me and swallow me whole.

How could he?

How could they?

How could devils live so blatantly amongst us?

My teeth ached from clenching; my eyes bruised with unshed tears.

I breathed revenge. I ate vengeance. All I saw was hate.

I felt invincible with rage, as if I controlled the tectonic plates and had the power to summon a catastrophic earthquake to devour this disease-riddled place forever.

How could any goodness live inside me when all I wanted was four graves—one for each of the Hawk men? How could I believe in right and wrong when all I wanted was their blackened hearts bleeding at my feet?

Morning turned to noon.

Afternoon turned to dusk.

Twilight turned to midnight.

I stayed vigil, moving slowly between the six graves. My

bloodless lips whispered as I read aloud their horrific epitaphs.

Farewell to Mary Weaver

Long ye may rest in solitude and reap the havoc in which you sowed

My heart broke at the thought of my grandmother and great-great-grandmother enduring such a life.

Herein rests the soul of Bess Weaver

Her only redemption was paying her debts

The oldest looking tombstone had the simplest carving but the one with the worst desecration of a dead soul.

The corpse of the Wicked Weaver who started it all

Wife to a traitor, mother to a whore

I couldn't forgive. I couldn't forget. I couldn't even comprehend how I could ever set eyes upon the Hawks again without wanting to slaughter them with my bare hands. My rage fed me better than any material sustenance.

I wished I had magic; a potion to strike them all dead.

Every murmur that escaped me, every incantation and promise, worked like a spell.

My whispers wrapped around me like a cocoon—turning my tenderhearted naivety into a chrysalis where I rapidly evolved into a monster as bad as them.

I threw myself into darkness. I traded any goodness I had left for the power to destroy them. And with each chant, I chained myself deeper to my fate—cementing me forever to my task.

I didn't want food or water or shelter.

I didn't need love or understanding or connection.

I wanted retribution.

I wanted *justice*.

No one came to get me. If they cared I was missing, no Hawk came to corral me back to my prison.

In a way, I wished they *would* come. Because then my removal from my dead family would've been a justified struggle. I would've screamed and cursed and fought so hard, I would've drawn their blood.

But they never came.

So, I had to swallow my bitter resentment and plod back to purgatory on my own accord. I couldn't fight. I couldn't scream.

I had to deliver myself willingly back into the devil's clutches.

By the time I entered my quarters, I shook so hard I was sure my teeth were chipped from chattering so badly—from cold and from horror.

I didn't recognise the woman inside me. Something had switched permanently and any facet of the little girl—the twin who'd always believed in fantasies—had died upon that patch of earth.

I'd been destroyed, yet my eyes remained dry. Not one tear had been shed. Not one sob had come forth.

I'd become barren. No longer able to display emotion or find relief from the pounding terror of seeing proof of my ancestor's demise.

The diamond collar around my neck disgusted me and the weight seemed to grow heavier with every breath, sucking me deeper into hell.

Struggling to remove my sweat-dried exercise gear, I barely managed to crawl into the shower. Gradually, I turned my blood from snow to spring—thawing out the phantoms that now lurked within.

I stayed beneath the hot spray for ages, curled upon the floor with my arms wrapped around my knees. Mud and soil from the graves siphoned down the drain, swirling around like dead souls.

So much had happened, so much that would've broken the old Nila.

But this was just another hurdle—another obstacle to clear in my quest for victory. My essence had been infused with the lingering spirits of my ancestors. They lived within me now, wanting the same thing I did.

The clock hanging above the fish tank in my sewing room announced the witching hour as I climbed exhausted into bed.

Three a.m.

The time when ghouls and demons were thought to roam the passageways of homes and terrorize helpless sleepers.

I'd always been superstitious about keeping my wardrobe doors shut against night monsters. Vaughn used to laugh at me, saying beasts and night creatures didn't exist.

But now I knew the truth.

They *did* exist, but they didn't come out when the witching hour opened a portal from their world into ours.

They weren't called werewolves or vampires.

They were called Hawks.

And I lived with them.

The next morning, I woke to a text.

A single message from the crux of my annihilation.

Kite007: *I feel what you feel. Whether it be a kiss or a kick or a killing blow. I wished I didn't, but you're mine, therefore, you are my affliction. So, I will feel what you feel, and I will live what you live. You won't understand what I mean. Not yet. But it's my best sacrifice. The only thing I can offer you.*

I waited for my heart to spike.

I held my breath for a sparkle of desire.

Jethro had just shown me the truth. In his cryptic, almost poetic message, he'd torn aside the mysterious curtain of who Kite was—fully admitting something that only he would know. There was no way a message like that could come from Kes. I doubted the middle Hawk was deep enough to pen such a complex riddle.

If such a message had come yesterday, I would've tripped from lust into love. I wouldn't have been able to stop my heart from unfurling completely and letting my enemy nest deep inside.

But not now.

Not now that I'd seen the heinous truth.

With steady hands and an even steadier heart, I sent a

single message to my brother.

Needle&Thread: *I'm living a nightmare, V. I...I can't do this anymore. I miss you.*

Once it had sent, I deleted Kite's message and turned off my phone.

A NEW MORNING, yet I felt older than I'd ever been. Every part of me ached.

I'd left Nila at the cemetery—I'd had no *choice*.

But when she didn't return after dusk, I went back for her.

She'd sat beneath the crescent moon, arms wrapped tight around her ribcage as if to prevent whatever meagre body heat she had from escaping. Her white skin glowed in the darkness, etched in shadow, making her seem part wraith, part woman.

I'd waited in the blackness, obscured by trees. Waited for her to either fall asleep or fret herself into unconsciousness. I wanted to wrap her in warmth and take her back to her chambers where she could find some resemblance of living…with me.

I wanted to kiss her frigid lips and run my fingers down her icy arms. I wanted to be *warm* for her and forget all notions of being a glacier.

But powerful waves of hatred and disgust rolled from her delicate form, lapping through the trees and around my ankles. As much as I wanted to go to her, I couldn't.

For the same reason I needed to see Jasmine so often.

For the same curse I'd lived with my whole life.

So, I'd waited.

I'd sacrificed myself by feeling her pain.

I'd shared the cold with her.

I'd hoped she sensed my presence and it offered a shred of comfort.

And when she'd finally retreated to the Hall, I'd followed discretely. Shadowing her every step, determined she wouldn't see me.

It wasn't until she'd stumbled from her bathroom in a cloud of steam and wearing a towel that I'd left the security hub and the constantly recording cameras and returned to my own quarters.

As I lay staring at my ceiling, thinking how disastrous my life had become ever since I texted her over two months ago, I felt another stirring inside my broken heart.

One that gave me a small blaze of hope that there might be *some* way to salvage this nightmare.

For the first time in my life, I wanted to talk to someone. Fully confess. And not just to my sister.

I wanted to unload and spill everything to my sworn enemy. To the woman I wanted but could never have.

If I stepped off that ledge and took a leap of faith, I had no doubt I would end up dead when I fell. But I'd left it too long to fix myself and no longer had control over my impulses.

I'd regret it.

Shit, I already did.

But it couldn't stop me.

With a rabbiting heart, I'd messaged her the first shred of truth.

I began the journey that would pulverize me.

Cut looked up from his newspaper, his eyes narrowing. "Where were you yesterday?"

Torturing Nila. Torturing myself.

"Nowhere. Not important." I strode toward the dining table, glaring at Daniel. He was the only other man indulging in breakfast. Everyone else must've eaten and split.

Daniel smirked, smearing butter onto a fresh croissant. Keeping eye contact, he stuffed it into his mouth.

The idea of eating with my two least favourite people turned my hunger into repulsion. Grabbing the back of a chair, I made no move to pull it out. "Where's Kes?"

Cut pursed his lips, folding the newspaper sedately beside him. "How would I know?"

I cocked my head in acknowledgement. Fine. If he wanted to play hard-arse, I could play. Squeezing the back of the chair, I nodded and made my way back to the exit. I had something to discuss with Kes, and wasn't in the mood to deal with my father and his mind manipulation.

Reaching the door, my fingers wrapped around the doorknob, but before I could escape, Cut said, "We haven't finished. Come in. Sit. Eat."

I turned, finding it no hardship to find the snow that protected me. I vibrated with icicles, just waiting to use the glittering tips as weapons. "We have finished. I have things to do."

Daniel snickered. "That's what you think."

"Shut up," I snapped. "Eat your damn food and mind your own fucking business."

Cut raised an eyebrow, pushing back his chair to stand. Moving to the buffet table where Nila had collected the trays to serve the Black Diamond brothers, he used a pair of tongs to place a raspberry Danish and some fresh grapes onto his plate. "I'm not convinced you're coping with the pressure of what is required of you, Jethro."

I swallowed, fisting my hands. "I'm coping just fine."

"Then why have you been making almost daily visits to see Jaz?"

"Oh, someone's been caught sneaking," Daniel chuckled.

I threw him a death stare before focusing the rage on my father. "Jasmine is our flesh and blood. I'm permitted to see family. Or is that against the rules now, too?"

If he took Jaz away from me, I would go fucking rogue.

Cut clucked his tongue, turning to face me. "Your temper and wisecracks have been steadily getting worse for weeks." Tilting his head, he added, "In fact, it's become so bad no amount of bullshit from you can convince me that you're coping. You're losing control, Jet. Losing it all thanks to that little Weaver Whore."

My heart thundered. Words flew and collided in my head.

She's not a fucking whore.

Don't fucking talk about her like that.

Stay the fuck away from her.

But I swallowed every syllable and forced myself to stay stoic.

When I didn't respond, Cut glowered and made his way back to the table. Sitting down, he waved at a chair. "Join us."

"No. Whatever you have to say, say it. I have somewhere to be."

Someone to see.

"I do not like this side of you, Jet. I thought we'd turned a corner with you a few years ago. Don't make me regret what I promised you."

My heart switched from anger to anxiety. I hated that he had such power, such sway over me. "I've done everything you asked."

Cut popped a grape into his mouth. "Ah, see, that's where you're wrong. I know more than you think, and you haven't been following the rules."

Shit.

Sweat dotted my brow at the thought of him seeing me come undone while thrusting into the woman I was meant to treat like filth. "Name one thing."

My father's eyes twinkled.

Shit, I shouldn't have said that.

Cut took a bite of his pastry, never taking his gaze off me. "You're in fucking trouble," Dan sneered.

My head tore up, locking eyes with my psychotic little brother. I didn't think it was possible to hate someone as much as I hated him. I didn't want to be anywhere near him. He wasn't good for me. *Healthy* for me.

Snapping between clenched teeth, I said, "Watch your tongue, Buzzard."

Daniel growled, "Don't use that nickname, *Kite*."

"Shut it," I hissed, glaring behind me just in case Nila had arrived for breakfast. I'd given her the truth in my last message, but I wanted her to come to me and ask. I wanted to stare into her eyes as she waged between anger at being tricked and acknowledgement that in some way, she'd known all along.

"Enough. Both of you," Cut ordered, pointing a spoon at us. "Stop being a twat, Dan, and, Jet, he's right. You're in trouble."

I trembled with pent-up aggression. The pressure of competition and testosterone in the room seemed to drip down the damn walls. "Why, exactly?"

My father relaxed into the chair, believing he was in complete control.

And he was. As much as I hated it.

"What didn't you do after the First Debt was paid?"

My mind charged with all sorts of things. There were so many instructions I hadn't kept. I struggled to recall one that he'd caught me out on. Did he know that I hadn't dropped her core temperature before the whipping? Did he know I'd fucked her and in turn fucked myself?

Keeping my face blank and cold—just like I'd been taught—I snarled, "I tended to her injuries, as per the custom, and left her to heal."

Cut sighed. The weight of his disappointment and annoyance crushed me. "You didn't do the tally, though, did you?"

My heart clenched. "Fuck."

He nodded. "Fuck, indeed."

How did I forget that part?

My body filled with thick resentment. "I'll fix it."

"Damn right, you'll fix it." Cut lost his smooth edge,

showing his jagged temper beneath. "I don't know what you're playing at, Jethro, but I'm not fucking happy. Get it done. Today. Now, in fact." Grabbing his napkin, he wiped his fingers. "Go grab her and meet us in the solar."

My soul twisted, feeding off his blackness, his darkness. Every moment I spent in his presence, I slipped back into the man he wanted me to be. I became infected with whatever madness lurked within my family tree.

"I'll get it done. I don't need an audience."

They could trust me.

All my life, I'd lived with these men, and all my life, I'd drank their poison. I was one of them. It didn't matter that I'd had a weak moment yesterday. *This* was who I was.

I'm a Hawk.

Before Nila, my family was all the company I had—their morals all I'd been taught.

And up until two months ago, I believed Cut loved me—cared for me—that was why he gave me a system to follow.

Another thing Nila and I had in common: we blindly followed our elders, naively believing they had the answers to our problems.

No matter who Cut groomed me to be, he failed. I might want to obey. I might crave to be happy in the boundaries he'd set, but I never lived up to his expectations.

Cut broke into my thoughts. "You're right, you will get it done. And you'll have witnesses to ensure it happens correctly." His eyes bored into mine. "Unless you'd rather hand Nila over to Kes and spend the month working on your disposition?"

My teeth clenched at the thought. "No. I'm fine."

The spike of possession and desire overrode my frosty heart, showing me once again how thin the ice was that I skated upon. It was no longer solid and strong. The surface was breakable, just waiting for me to step into its trap and drown me.

I'd suspected for years that there might've been another

43

way to 'fix' me. But whenever I attempted to revert to my true nature, Cut would notice and stop me.

I knew what it did to me. I knew how to survive with the sessions, but ever since Nila had arrived, it hadn't been enough.

Nothing was enough anymore.

"You're not fine, Jethro, but I'm willing to give you the benefit of the doubt. One more chance, son. Don't make me regret it." Striding past, he ordered, "Go fetch your Weaver. It's time to fix your mess."

Nila looked up as I entered her quarters.

Her onyx eyes cleaved right through my heart. I slammed to a stop as she glowered. Words flew between us, but none were spoken aloud.

I don't want you here. You disgust me.

I want you to obey. You terrify me.

I understood her temper, but it didn't mean I had to take it. It wasn't me who'd slaughtered and buried her family.

I fumbled for my ice and strode into the room.

Nila looked away, cutting me off from her thoughts. She sat in the middle of the huge oblong table, surrounded by material and brightly coloured pins.

She's sewing.

I didn't know why that comforted me, but it did. She'd returned to her craft because it was a part of her. She'd found a way to stay fundamentally true to her family, all while I drifted further and further from mine. Where I was melting and losing myself, she was forming into a defiantly stronger person.

You're doing that.

It was because of me that she'd grown. Because of who I was and what circumstances we found ourselves in. I shouldn't take such perverse happiness from that, but I did. It wasn't her father or twin who'd made her grow and see her own potential.

It was her sworn enemy.

The man who'd tasted and fucked her.

The man whose heart thumped uncomfortably alive whenever she was near.

I couldn't work out the complex mess inside. One moment, I hated her for dragging me from where I'd existed all my life, but the next, I wanted to kiss her for showing me an alternative to how I'd been living.

My ice couldn't compete with her.

And what was worse, I didn't want it to.

"What are you doing in here?" Suspicion, lust, and anger buffeted me in her stare, turning me to stone.

Before she'd arrived, I'd been a ball of twine—carefully packaged with no loose ends in sight. But Nila, with her needles and scissors, had somehow found a thread and pulled. Every tug undid the tightly wrapped nucleus of who I was, and I battled with fighting against the change or just giving up and letting it happen.

I couldn't remember the last time it got this bad. But it was my own fucking fault. I shouldn't have let myself slide so far from my safety net. Who knew if I could find my way back?

When I didn't move or speak, Nila placed the swatch of turquoise cloth onto the table and narrowed her gaze. "Either speak or leave, I can't be around you right now."

She couldn't be around me? How about *I* couldn't be around *her*?

Silence granted me a reprieve. I stood taller, locking my muscles against the haunting memory of her yesterday.

My eyes fell to her hands. Her index finger had a bright pink plaster on the tip—no doubt from pricking herself with a needle while working.

Needle.

What would she do if I were to suddenly call her Needle? What if I just admitted I was Kite? Would she hate me for the deception or be grateful that she no longer had to pretend?

Why had she not confronted Kestrel? And how much longer would she continue to avoid my text last night?

It fucked me off that I couldn't drop my guard, knowing

whatever she felt toward Kite transferred to my brother. He was winning, even while I stripped myself bare in the hopes of achieving the impossible.

Her eyes glinted. "Dammit, say something or go!"

Her voice jolted me back into the present. "I need you to come with me."

"Why?"

"Why? You belong to me, that's why. I don't have to have a reason."

Her knuckles turned white as she fisted the material. "Carry on being delusional, Mr. Hawk, but disappear so I don't have to look at you." She turned around, showing me her back.

Temper frothed in my gut. How dare she turn her back on me? I snapped my fingers, growling, "I won't ask again. Come here."

"You didn't ask the first time. And don't snap your fingers. I'm not a dog and I will not heel." She wore a gypsy cream skirt and black sweater. With her spine ramrod straight, she looked haughty and as chilly as any sovereign.

My mouth watered to kiss her.

My cock twitched to fuck her.

My heart thumped with desire.

An argument brewed between us, gathering force until the curtains twitched with an animosity-storm.

"You're right, you aren't a dog. A dog is much easier to train."

"Believe me, if I was a dog, my fangs would be buried in your arse, and you'd be pleading for mercy. I definitely wouldn't be well-trained."

My hands balled. A stupid flippant comment but it spiralled us deeper into a quarrel.

Just knowing she had the guts to stand up to me made me fucking hot. I wanted to bend her over the table and fuck her, hard and ruthless.

Were all Weavers like her? Strong willed and contentious or was she unique—a once in a lifetime adversary?

"Turn around. Look at me."

If she did, I'd give into the throbbing in my cock and make my father wait.

"No. I don't want to look at a Hawk." Her voice was sharp and cutting. Whatever liveliness she'd had before had disappeared—almost as if she'd left her soul where her family lay on the moor.

Her dismissal and obvious unaffectedness of our pointless argument tensed my muscles.

Didn't my desire for her mean anything? Didn't my text help her see me? The *real* me? Surely, the truth granted me some leeway for forgiveness.

I stepped forward. I wanted to curse her for making me this way. This *weak*. "Last night—" *I gave you more honesty in one text message than I've given anyone.* Who was I kidding? She didn't fucking care. She *shouldn't* fucking care.

Grow a pair, fuckwit, and forget about whatever connection you thought you had.

Nila spun around; her cheeks dotted red with rage. "Last night! You dare talk to me about last night? Where I spent the evening mourning family members that were subjected to the likes of you?"

The weakness she conjured inside switched to fury. I stormed forward, towering over her. "I told you not to go up the path, Ms. Weaver. Whatever you're feeling is your fault, not mine." Moving fast, I snatched her elbow and jerked her from the bench. "Enough. I'm done reliving something I had no part in." Shaking her, I dragged her from the puddle of fabric heading for the exit.

My fingers tingled from touching her. My lungs eagerly inhaled the unique scent of cotton, chalk, and Nila. If I wasn't so damn angry, her smell would've entranced me. It would've granted a tiny oasis from everything else I dealt with.

"Let go of me, you arsehole!" She squirmed in my hold.

"No, not until you learn how to behave."

"How about you learn to behave, you cold-hearted-emotionally-screwed-up-jerk!"

I slammed to a halt. "Careful, Ms. Weaver."

She stabbed me in the chest with her fingertip, a maniacal laugh escaping her perfect lips. "God, you're—I don't know what you are. I think your rule of not letting people call you mad or insane is because it isn't a slur, but the truth. You're bonkers, Jethro Hawk. And you can hit me for saying it—but it's about time someone pointed out the obvious." Her voice dropped to a murmur. "You're a nutcase. Completely cuckoo."

I'd never suffered a barrage of words so fucking painful.

Grabbing her by the diamond collar, I shoved her backward until her spine hit the wall. Dropping my head so my mouth lingered above hers, I whispered, "And you're the Weaver who let a psychotic Hawk between your legs. You're the one who's damned, not me. I have an excuse for what I am. You? You have no excuse but getting wet all over—what did you call me—a nutcase Hawk."

Her lips twisted into a snarl. I tensed for her barrage.

Our eyes locked with fury.

Then something happened.

Something switched.

Fury became desire.

Desire became insanity.

I couldn't withstand the command.

"Fuck this."

I kissed her.

She cried out as my lips slammed down on hers. In a seamless move, I pressed my entire body along Nila's twisting one, pinning her unforgivingly against the wall. My leg jammed between hers, opening her wide, crushing my thigh against her clit.

Her mouth hung slack for a second as her hips involuntarily rocked on my leg. My stomach twisted and everything I'd been trying to hide rose up completely out of control.

Heat.

Wetness.

Hardness.

An ache so fucking brutal in my chest it almost brought tears to my eyes.

Then pain.

I reared back as Nila's sharp teeth punctured my bottom lip. I licked the tender flesh. She'd broken the skin.

Blood.

Metallic.

Life.

Her chest rose and fell; her eyes wild and sending messages that tripped and conflicted. She felt what I did. But she hated me for it.

Too bad. I had to have more.

I grabbed her, smashing our bodies together and reclaiming her mouth. Offering my blood, forcing her to drink my injury and share my bone-deep pain.

She wriggled and fought, but beneath her rage echoed the same mind-crippling desire that turned us from enemies into something *more*.

"Stop—" she moaned before my tongue danced with hers, stealing her curses. In her arms, feeling nothing but heat and passion, I could pretend life was simpler. There were no debts, no arguments, no families, no hatred.

Just us.

Just this.

Nila stopped fighting and kissed me back. She vibrated in my arms, her hands pushing and pulling at once. Her lips opened to scream or beg, but I silenced her by tangling my tongue deeper with hers.

She fought me.

She encouraged me.

She confused the shit out of me.

My mind roared and instinct took over reason. I thrust against her, grinding my aching cock, seeking relief from the annihilating greed to consume her.

Her back arched as I shoved her against the wall—harder and harder. I wanted to crawl inside her. I wanted to own her every thought.

Agony erupted in my balls.

"Fuck!" My stomach swooped and my gut roiled as if to vomit. Stumbling away, I clutched my cock, willing the blistering pain to ebb.

She kneed me!

Over the stupefying pain, I barely noticed Nila encroaching on me. Her breath was ragged, her cheeks flushed, and her eyes blazed with an odd mixture of lust and hate. "Don't touch me, Jethro Hawk. You might have been between my legs. I might've let you inside my body, but I will never let you inside my soul. Not now."

I hissed between my teeth, riding the waves of torrid agony. I couldn't stand straight.

Nila bent over to whisper in my ear. "I might not have fangs, but I do have a sharp knee." With infinitesimal softness, she brushed away the hair that'd flopped over my forehead. Her touch was tender, loving, but beneath it lurked the truth.

Something was missing inside her.

Something that drew me to her and made me believe.

Once again, my family had destroyed any hope of me finding salvation by breaking the one woman who might've been strong enough to help me.

Nila murmured, "I don't kiss men who I find abhorrent. Whatever happened between us is over."

Gritting my teeth, I unfolded. "Quiet!"

She froze.

My outburst sliced through our bullshit, granting a smidgen of clarity. "Don't lie to me. You *will* let me inside you. And you *will* let me own you." Snatching her wrist, I jerked her close. "You will because we don't have a choice. You're inside me. Don't you get it? *You're* inside *me*. And it's only fair that I'm inside you."

Silence.

Breathing hard, I growled, "You know as well as I do the dangerous game we're playing. I won't retaliate from what you just did, but don't push me any further. And don't you dare fucking say it's over." Pressing my nose against hers, I hissed, "Because it's not."

Her eyes flared. "Believe me, it *is* over. I have no intention of ever touching you again."

My temper boiled at the thought of her denying me more of this—whatever this was. I'd tasted her; I refused to believe we were through.

Cupping her jaw, I murmured, "The moment this morning is done, I'll show you how wrong you are. I'll show you how deep I am inside you. How fucked both of us are." I pressed my lips against her cheekbone. "You want to win? What if I told you it would be better if you lost? Better for both of us if you submitted and stopped fighting for a change."

She laughed. "Stop fighting? That's all we have. Don't you see? If I don't fight you—then what am I supposed to do? Am I supposed to be okay with all of this?"

"Yes."

She snorted, anger sharpening her features. "Delusional as well as insane." Shoving me, she demanded, "Tell me why you're here before I knee you in the balls again."

God, I wanted to strike her.

I wanted to antagonise her to the point of giving in just so I could fuck her again. My blood was lava; my cock rock hard.

Trying to get myself under control, I snapped, "I forgot to complete a part of the First Debt. My father just reminded me."

She stiffened. "Didn't I pay enough for that monster? Twenty-one lashings complete with scars that will last a lifetime. Or did he find out you didn't freeze me before making me bleed?"

Resentment radiated on her face.

How could I handle her like this? This belligerent?

"No matter what you think of me, I'm doing my best to

protect you. I told you I would be in equal trouble for disobeying. I have no intention of explaining the truth."

Despite herself, some of her temper dispersed, leaving resigned tolerance in her gaze. "If it's not that...then what?"

My fingers curled tighter around her wrist. I winced as something sharp dug into my thumb. Holding up her arm, the glint of metal winked through the black fabric of her jumper. "Are there needles in your cuffs?"

She tried to jerk her arm away. Unsuccessfully.

"Hardly safe, don't you think?"

She looked at the sharp pins as I pulled them free and dropped them onto a side table.

Her lips curled. "A hazard of the occupation. It's convenient to have them there—I misplace them if I'm knee deep in material." Her black eyes met mine. "Careful where you touch me, Jethro. You'll never know if a needle will stab you to death."

I froze. Everything she said came layered with hints and metaphors.

A chill scattered down my spine. "You're beginning to piss me off, Ms. Weaver. If I didn't know any better, I would take that as a threat."

"Maybe you should."

"Maybe you should say what you mean and be done with it."

"Oh, I'm sorry. I thought I just did. I hate you. There, that blatant enough?"

Oh, my fucking God. This woman.

"You don't hate me."

She snarled. "Believe me. I do."

"You don't know me."

"I know more than I need and I don't like what I know."

My heart lurched. "You're just like them. Judging me before you understand me." The moment the words were free, I panicked. *What the fuck?*

My fingers twitched to wrap around her throat, to squeeze

the knowledge of my secrets from her ears. She'd cut me out. She didn't deserve to understand.

I moved forward, closing the distance between us, unable to ignore the twinges of cuts on my soles. "Stop punishing me for what happened yesterday."

She laughed coldly. "Yesterday? You think my repulsion of you is from yesterday?"

I frowned. "Of course, it is. Before you saw what was on the moor, you liked me. You kissed me. You wrapped your legs around me while I fucked—"

"And you fell for it, didn't you?" Her smile was nasty. "I made you kiss me. I made you fuck me to prove a point."

The fire in my blood suddenly snuffed out, leaving my heart blackened and charred and eager for the creeping icicles in the dark. My voice dropped to an emotionless void. "What do you mean?"

You used me.

Same as them.

You lied to me.

Same as them.

"I told you to kiss me to prove you have a soul. You have one. I see that now. But I don't like it." She sucked in a breath, cocking her chin with a haughty dismissal. "I slept with you because I was weak and because I believed you were different. But you're not different. You'll toy with me, hurt me, and ultimately kill me. And then you'll bury me with the rotting corpses of my slain family."

Her blood pumped thickly beneath my touch. A headache brewed from nowhere. I'd only been here for ten minutes, yet it felt like an eternity. An eternity where all my dreams had just vanished, transforming into nightmares. "What do you want from me? An apology? A fucking—"

"That's the thing. I don't want anything from you. All I want is to have nothing to do with you or your bastard kin ever again. I intend to stay in my quarters until each debt must be repaid. I don't care how long it takes or what you do to me, I'm done playing your stupid games."

My muscles locked.

Stupid games?

She thought my texts were stupid games? She thought everything that I was going through was a *fucking game?*

Ice turned to sleet, raining upon my soul. "What are you saying?"

Her eyes glittered with cold-hearted conviction. "I was wrong to think I had any power in this fate. I'm done. Seeing those graves made me grow up."

"So, you're just going to lock yourself away and wait to die?"

She nodded. "Having free roam of this place, receiving gifts, and enjoying people's company undermines my right to feel wronged. I won't play along anymore. I'm a prisoner and I refuse to forget that."

I wanted to slap her. I wanted to throw her onto the bed and fuck her. Whoever this woman was in front of me, she wasn't the Nila who'd made me unravel.

She thought she couldn't change my family? Maybe she was right. But she sure as fuck changed me.

"Everything you just said is bullshit."

She shrugged. "Believe what you want to believe."

I searched her gaze, delving as deep as I could, trying to see the truth. Something about this entire exchange felt fake.

She stared right back, hinting at nothing.

We'd run out of time. Extracting the truth from her would have to come later.

"Enough melodramatics. We're leaving," I muttered. "Time to go."

She scoffed. "Do what you have to do. I'm sure there's a special place reserved for you Hawks in hell."

"Goddammit, Nila!"

She flinched.

I didn't have the strength to have another fight, especially when I needed to concentrate and get through what was about to happen. "Behave. Just once if your fucking life trust without having to understand."

Yanking her forearm, I pulled her toward the exit.

In a magical twist, she somehow dislodged my grip and stalked to the door on her own.

My jaw locked as she threw me a cold glare and disappeared into the corridor.

Bloody woman.

Catching up to her, I captured her hand.

My heart skipped at the simple touch. Up until now, I'd always grabbed her elbow or arm—keeping our roles perfectly clear. So, what was I doing grabbing her hand like an equal?

Her fingers twitched then looped purposely through mine.

My cock hardened and I slammed to a halt. Christ, I wanted her.

Her nails were long and the tips suddenly sliced into the back of my hand.

I hissed between my teeth. The pinpricks of pain sent me reeling into a memory of her clutching my back as I thrust deep inside her.

Her fingers turned white as she tightened her grip. I didn't jolt as two fingernails broke my skin and drew blood. This was a perfect example of her undoing. She didn't understand me. Didn't understand that she'd just given me a gift better than anything. With pain, came relief, and with relief, came snow.

My heart slowed its beat. My temper faded. Any remaining fire dwindled to nothing. "Thank you for reminding me of my role in your life, Ms. Weaver. What just happened won't happen again."

I won't be so weak as to kiss you again.

I won't be so stupid to believe you can see me.

She tilted her chin. "Good."

I slipped into the dutiful firstborn son. "Kindly remove your claws."

A coy smile played with her lips. "My claws?" She blinked innocently. "I don't know what you mean."

Lowering my head, I murmured, "You know exactly what I mean."

Your claws around my fucking heart.

Untangling our fingers, I snagged her elbow. The throb where her nails had punctured helped me focus. I'd been blinded by her. Hypnotised by a promise of more—of a connection I never dared dream of.

It was a lie.

And I was sick of being used.

Striding down the corridor, dragging my prey through the house, I said, "No more, Ms. Weaver. No more games. We're through."

The solar.

A room hidden on the second floor located down twining corridors. Glass cases lined the hallways displaying ancient crochet and needlepoint. Black Diamond brothers and visitors were prohibited from this floor.

It was feminine territory—housing only my grandmother and sister, along with my father's study and private rooms. His bedroom was up another level in one of the turrets. Fortified and armed, ready for a war that never came.

Nila didn't speak as I guided her up the massive spiral stone staircase in the east wing. She'd gone peculiarly obedient but lagged behind me; I practically had to drag her.

"Where are you taking me?" Her eyes darted around the second floor as we stepped onto the landing.

"You'll find out soon enough." Gritting my teeth, I pulled her forward.

"Did a Weaver do those?" she asked, jerking me to a stop to stare at an embroidery of Hawksridge Hall bathed in golden sunlight with wild horses prancing on the front lawn.

"No."

Her eyes met mine. "Who did then?"

"No one you need to know about." We moved in testy

silence to the large double doors at the end.

"Is this where you sleep? Upstairs, I mean?"

My head whipped to face her. "You're asking where my quarters are?" Dragging her close, I whispered hotly in her ear. "Why? So you can sneak inside and fuck me? Or perhaps murder is more on your mind."

She vibrated with anger. "Like I would tell you."

My palm itched to strike again. I'd never been a violent person, preferring to intimidate with winter rather than with fists, but goddammit, she made it hard to remember just who I was and what was expected of me.

I'd lost myself.

I'm fucking floundering.

"Stop asking questions." Splaying my hand on the doors, I pushed them open.

Her gaze went wide, sweeping around the large space. The solar was masculine in both use and décor, and frankly, rather drab. Heavy oak panels, with carved hawks and feather wreaths, covered the ceiling. The walls were gold-gilded leather, oppressing the space with dark brown while the carpet was blood red.

Slouchy black couches rested in clusters, some by the huge fireplace, and others by the lead-light window. An oversize coffee table took centre place with thick glass imprisoning the bleached bones of my father's old dog, Wrathbone.

A slow clap filled the space. Daniel smirked, his eyes locking onto Nila. "You didn't get lost after all. Pity, I'd just volunteered to be the search party."

My spine locked. Shit, not only had my father decided to be present for this, but he'd invited Kes and Daniel, too. The thought of Daniel seeing me around Nila both enraged and terrified.

He'd always seen how different I was and used my flaws to hurt me.

Nila subtly moved closer to me, never taking her gaze off my younger brother.

So, she hates me but still expects me to protect her.

I wanted to pull away and leave her on her own. She deserved it. But no matter what just happened, she was still mine and with ownership came responsibility. Her welfare was my concern.

"About time you two arrived." Cut leaned against one of the embossed walls, his posture relaxed. In his hand was a tumbler of cognac. Not even midday and he had hard liquor in his belly. My father wasn't a drunkard. He would never give up control enough to be under the influence. He just indulged in things he wanted, when he wanted them.

Cut's gaze went to Nila. "Pleasure to see you, my dear. I heard you've recently relocated to the Weaver quarters. How are you finding your new accommodations?"

Her arm jerked beneath my hold, her fingers curling into a fist.

Nila sniffed. "I appreciate a place to work and equipment in which to do it, but if you think I'll find happiness anywhere in your home, you're mistaken."

Cut laughed. "I would suggest you stop lying to yourself. I've seen you smiling. I've witnessed your contentedness these past few weeks."

Nila growled low in her chest. "Yes, that was a mistake. And before I saw what I did yesterday."

Cut pushed off from the wall, throwing back the rest of his cognac. "And what did you see yesterday?" His eyes flickered to mine, glowing with annoyance.

"Nothing to concern you about," Nila snapped.

I glanced at her out of the corner of my eye. She could've told him about the graves. She could've told him all manner of things that I'd sworn her not to tell. If she wanted me punished, my father would ensure I would pay.

My heart thundered, waiting for her to announce my weakness. The secret of what it meant to both of us when I'd slipped inside her and felt her come around my cock.

She felt it, too.

I know it.

I sucked in a breath, holding on to the faint connection still between us—not ready to submit to our fight—to believe that whatever existed was gone.

"Jethro, are you going to permit your charge to speak to her elders so disrespectfully?"

Shit.

My forehead furrowed at the challenge, the command.

If I was anything like the son Cut had taught me to be, I would force Nila to her knees and teach her better manners. I would hurt her, scold her, and deliver her heartbreak at his feet.

But if I did that, she might reveal my darkest secret. The fact that I'd fucked her. And that it'd destroyed me.

Cut grunted, "Jet—"

Embracing the cold, I shifted my hold on Nila and grabbed her around the back of the nape. My fingers dug into the tender column of muscle, holding her firm. "Be polite, Ms. Weaver. Drop the insolence and be grateful for all that my family has given you."

She flinched but didn't try to break my hold. Glaring at Cut, she said, "Forgive me, Mr. Hawk. What I meant to say was thank you for welcoming me so cordially into hell. I'm so happy to live so close to the devil."

"Why you—" Cut grabbed a handful of Nila's long black hair, jerking her from my grip. "I'll make you pay for—"

"Gentlemen, surely there are more interesting things to be done than tormenting the poor little Weaver Whore?" Kestrel inched closer; his ability to guard his emotions and true feelings were a gift. He glowered in my direction, warning me not to move, to obey his unspoken help.

And like so many times in our past, I listened. I forced my heartbeat to regulate and latch onto the projection of calmness he oozed.

Nila hung in Cut's grip. Her tiptoes kept her balanced, but her face screwed up in obvious pain. Despite her agony, she didn't look away from my father's challenge or cry out.

Kestrel sidled up to them. "Father, we have a shipment arriving today and one of the brothers said a rival MC plans to ambush us. Save your wrath for those who deserve it. Not a guest who will be here for a long time to come."

My heart raced. My fists locked.

I closed my eyes so I wouldn't have to see my father holding my woman so possessively.

A moment ticked past. Sometimes Kestrel's reasoning worked. Sometimes it didn't. And if it didn't, it only made Cut worse—making him feel manipulated and eager to prove dominance over his sons.

The room held its breath; the air hovered stagnant and poised.

Then Cut let Nila go, rubbing his hands as if he'd touched something foul. "Next time you address me, my dear, make sure it's with respect, otherwise I won't be so lenient."

"That goes for me, too, Nila," Daniel said. "Don't forget we own your life; best to treat us like gods if you wish to survive longer."

Striding forward, I looped a fist in Nila's long hair, tugging her firmly but not cruelly, reminding her that as long as she obeyed me, she would be safe from other Hawks.

Don't you see I'm bad, but I'm not the worst?

"I'll remember," Nila snapped, moving backward until her shoulder brushed my bicep. That small point of contact sent tendrils of heat licking through my blood.

Kes grinned, hiding the fact that he'd just controlled the situation. "So, are we going to just stand around glaring at each other or what?" He moved forward, nudging me out of the way and slinging an arm over Nila's shoulders.

She sucked in a breath but didn't fight his guidance as he moved her away from me. He pecked her on the cheek and whispered something into her ear.

My jaw clenched as she willingly went with him, drifting away.

I hated their bond. The bond I'd made happen by letting

her believe Kite was Kes.

She hated me for what she'd seen at the cemetery. Therefore, she should hate my brother, too. He wasn't innocent. Not by a long shot.

I took a step forward, intending to steal back what was mine. But I stopped as Kes squeezed her and laughed at something he'd said. She didn't respond. Just like she'd shut down around me, she tolerated Kes's touching. But the moment his hold loosened, she ducked from his arm and placed distance between them.

Her attention was divided between the men surrounding her, but mainly, it was turned inward, barely acknowledging her predicament of being in a room full of Hawks.

What had she done? And how did she turn off so successfully? I wanted to know her trick. So I could do it.

Kes beamed, gathering Nila's willowy frame and tucking her firmly against him again as if she'd never left. Raising his voice, he asked, "Where's the party? And when does it start?"

Cut scowled, pouring himself another finger of cognac. "You always were too jovial, Kestrel. Tone it down. You're getting on my nerves."

Kes's gaze met mine for a second.

"Don't want to be on Daddy's nerves now, do you?" Daniel cackled. His attention never left Nila as Kes manhandled her to a black couch and sat down.

Her dark eyes flickered between me and my family—never locking onto one of us for long, hiding her thoughts.

"Enough, Daniel." Waving his now empty glass, Cut added, "Retrieve the box."

Daniel shook his head, inching toward Nila. "In a moment, Pop."

Nila sat up straight, her nostrils flaring in fear and repulsion as Dan squatted before her. "Hello, pretty Weaver. Just say the word and I'll steal you from my brother. I'm sure you're bored of him by now." He placed a hand on her knee, gathering the material of her skirt. "I'm the one you want, admit it."

I couldn't stand by and tolerate this bullshit.

"Fuck off, Dan." I prowled forward, fists clenched. I wanted to throw him across the room. With every step I took, I was exceedingly aware of Cut watching me.

My father said, "Jet, don't interfere."

It took everything to obey, but I ceased and stood still.

Nila didn't flinch, nor look in my direction. Her lips curled in distaste. "Stop touching me, you arsehole." Her voice was just a whisper, but it echoed dangerously in the room. "I'm not yours to toy with so do me a favour and leave."

My mouth twitched.

The atmosphere thickened, fizzing with intensity like a fuse on a bomb.

"I rather like touching you." Daniel's fingers tightened.

I stomped forward, unable to stop myself. "Hands off, Dan." *Don't show too much*. I squeezed my eyes for a second, trying to find some sanity amongst the animosity between us. "She's mine."

Daniel chuckled, making eye contact. "Just 'cause you have a plaything doesn't mean you're better than me. She belongs to *all* of us."

"Not until I say—"

Cut slammed his glass onto the coffee table, rattling the bones of his deceased pet. "Must I mediate every time my sons are in the same fucking room?" Running a hand over his face, he growled, "Kes, seeing as Daniel won't listen, you go get the box. Dan, shut the fuck up. Jet, control yourself and sit down."

Kes gave me a look. I knew what he thought, but now was not the time to discuss our family issues. He rose from the couch and headed toward the sixteenth-century sideboard by the entrance.

Moving forward, I kicked Daniel out of the way and took Kes's spot beside Nila.

Daniel stumbled from my boot before rising in a fit of fury. "One of these days, brother."

I stood up, towering over him—willing him to raise a fist.

"One of these days, indeed, *brother.*"

Dan breathed hard through his nose. I waited for him to punch me, but he had enough control to snicker and retreat.

"For God's sake," Cut muttered. "I raised a bunch of idiots."

Dan moved to his father's side. "Only one, Pop. And pity for you, he's the firstborn."

My nostrils flared. Fuck, I wanted to knock him out.

Something warm and soft touched the back of my hand. I jumped, looking down at Nila. Her hair cascaded over her shoulder in a wash of ink. Her eyes wide and gleaming with a silent request.

Sit down.

Do what you're tasked to do.

Protect me.

Her message filtered into my soul, switching my irritation to protection. My legs bent, depositing me beside her. A small gap existed between us, but it didn't stop my skin from prickling with awareness or her chest from rising when I placed my palm next to her hip and touched her once with my pinky finger.

Her eyes shot to mine, holding the fierce whip of connection.

The blackness of her eyes reflected my lighter ones, showing the strain and anger I couldn't contain. These wordless moments seemed to happen frequently between us.

Sucking in a breath, Nila broke eye contact and shifted away.

"Got it," Kes said, moving back toward us.

I risked another glance at Nila. She refused to look at me, her attention split between my father and Kes, who carried a smallish box in his hands.

"What's going to happen?" Nila whispered, her body swaying a little toward me.

Forcing myself not to inhale her scent, I shrugged. "The

tally. It should've been done the same day I took the debt."

Kes set the box before us on the coffee table. It clunked into place with the finality of pain.

This would hurt. For both of us.

"I forgot to do it that day."

I'd forgotten because I'd permitted myself to feel her grief and pain while I washed her back and wrapped her in bandages. I'd forgotten because I'd shamed myself by masturbating all over her while she'd hung whipped and bleeding.

Nila's eyes bounced around the Hawks towering over her in a ring of authority. "Do what?"

Could others hear the trace of terror hidden beneath her snappy anger or was I the only one? The only one cursed to listen to her fears and feel her confusion?

No one was laying a hand on her. I didn't care if I had to draw Hawk blood to make that a reality. She would stay mine until the end.

With a smirk, Daniel leaned over and opened the lid of the Tally Box. "Ready, brother?"

I looked at Cut, but he just crossed his arms, watching to see how I would proceed. Bastard.

I swallowed. I would forever wear these marks. When Nila paid the Final Debt and was dead, I would remain alone and without her. Cursed by her presence every time I looked at the tally.

My father wore his from what he did to Nila's mother on his ribcage. I'd seen it over the years—the marks of coming of age—of being a full-blown Hawk worthy of inheriting the legacy.

"Tell him where you want it to go, Nila." Cut looked at my charge.

She trembled with tension. "Want what?"

Daniel shifted closer, his eyes slithering all over her. My skin crawled at the thought of him touching her. Hurting her.

Fucking arsehole.

Closing the distance between Nila and me, I pressed my

thigh against hers—hoping she'd understand that we were in this together. Just like I'd told her. Her life was my responsibility and I wouldn't fail.

"I'll pick," I said.

"You aren't allowed, Jet," Cut muttered. "It's Ms. Weaver's decision."

Cut moved around the back of the couch, and ran his hands through Nila's hair. She bit her lip as he kept her still, hemming her inside the barricade of his fingers. "Time to choose, my dear. Where do you want to wear the mark?"

"The mark?"

"The mark of the debts."

WHAT THE HELL is happening?

Ever since I'd crawled out of bed after seeing my ancestors' graves, I'd been different. Remote, cold. To be honest, I didn't recognise myself.

I'd tried to work, to drown my thoughts with patterns and sewing, but I couldn't stop thinking of the past. How did the other Weaver women cope? How did they justify their captivity and pay the debts in full?

In one month, I'd made more progress with Jethro than I'd hoped, yet now, I wanted nothing to do with him. I'd lied when I told him I'd only slept with him to prove he had a soul. I'd lied to myself, hoping I would believe it. But nothing could sway the truth or hide the tingling connection that stitched us together—for better or for worse.

As much as I needed him on my side, I couldn't come to terms with what his family had done.

His text kept repeating inside my head; the words making no sense but somehow holding a promise of understanding if I only gave it time to unriddle.

Somehow, I had to do the impossible by pretending to care all while hating his guts. It was easier said than done when face-to-face with the evidence of his family's crimes.

Seeing the tombstones of my ancestors hurt me deep,

terrified me of my future, but worse than that—it showed me just who I'd become.

I was a deserter. A betrayer to the Weaver name.

How could I wield my heart in a battle that I wouldn't win? And how could I ignore the fact that by letting Jethro into my bed, I'd let him turn me into a Hawk?

Cut tugged hard on my hair, snapping my attention back to my current predicament. His alcohol-laced breath sent fumes into my lungs as my scalp burned from his hold. "The marks of the debts must be done. Chose a place. Quickly, my dear."

I squirmed on the black couch. Cut wrapped his fingers deeper into my hair, flaring worse pain. "I don't understand what you want."

I had no idea what they were talking about or what they expected. Being surrounded by four men—all of whom I despised—would've given me a heart attack when I first arrived. Now, I only drew deeper into myself.

Even vertigo had lost its power over me. I'd stumbled a little as Jethro had dragged me up the stairs, but he hadn't noticed. If Vaughn ever saw me again, he wouldn't recognise me.

Daniel tapped the box, its contents shielded by a lid engraved with birds of prey and the Hawk family crest. "Don't have all day, Weaver. Pick."

I tried to shake my head, but Cut's fingers clutched my skull, keeping me prisoner.

"Pick what? I have no idea what you're saying."

Jethro tensed, his body tight and unyielding. "You paid the First Debt. A mark has to be made to acknowledge that fact." His golden eyes landed on mine and for the first time since I'd asked him to kiss me, I didn't give into a flutter or tingle. I'd slipped too many times this morning. When he'd kissed me before, he'd poured so much passion down my throat I couldn't help but respond.

It made me hate myself.

I couldn't deny that I appreciated him beside me. He was

my only salvation against his father and younger brother. But I refused to let him manipulate me.

He's Kite.

Liar.

Con artist.

Deceiver.

He swallowed hard, feeding off my refusal to give in to him. His emotions were locked away, sparkling with snowflakes rather than desire. But it didn't stop the lashing of awareness binding us together.

"Choose, Ms. Weaver. Then we can leave," Jethro said.

"I—"

Cut let me go, moving to perch on the couch arm. He loomed above. "You have to select a place to wear the marks. In this decision, you have full control. Each debt that you repay is recorded. On video, in the ledger, and...on skin."

My heart plummeted into my feet. "What?"

Cut snapped his fingers, ordering Daniel to produce whatever was in the box. The carved wooden lid opened, revealing its treasure.

I leaned forward, trying to glimpse what was inside. My mouth hung open at the glint of needles, vials of ink, and alcoholic wipes.

Oh, my God.

"What—" I swallowed. "You can't mean—"

Jethro said, "The tally is a tattoo. Permanent, and for all intent, non-erasable." His black t-shirt and dark jeans made it seem as if he bristled with bleak acceptance. "After every debt, you earn a mark."

My stomach twisted. "So, it's not enough to take pain from me in way of debts—you have to drill me with ink, too?"

Cut replied, "It isn't just you who has to wear the tally." Pointing at Jethro, he added, "My son will wear the mark, too. And it's entirely up to you where it goes on your body. But bear in mind that it will match on Jethro. A mirror image. Like for like."

I shivered. "Excuse me?"

Jethro leaned closer, granting comfort from a body that'd been in mine. "Pick a place, Ms. Weaver. Just pick. I have things to do and want this over."

His sudden temper left my mouth hanging open. Everything he was and pretended to be filled me with rage. "I hate you."

Jethro's jaw twitched. "Doesn't change anything. Now...where do you want it?"

Daniel smirked, gathering the tattoo equipment and installing a small cartridge of black ink into the hand-held gun. "I suggest you pick, or I'll just mark you where I think it would look best." He rubbed his chin. "Your forehead, perhaps."

I sank into the couch, wanting to run from this madman. Kes smiled softly, standing beside his moronic brother. "It doesn't hurt, Nila." He pointed at his bird tattoo on his forearm. "A few stings and then you get used to it. But in your case, the mark will take a few minutes, instead of a few hours."

I stared coldly in his direction. When he'd hugged me before, I'd had the overpowering urge to push him away. To slap him. To scream at him to drop the act and show the truth. If Jethro struggled to hide his true self, then Kestrel was a genius at it.

I had no clue who he was.

The thought that any of these men were on my side or understood what I faced was laughable after seeing my family's graves. I wanted nothing to do with them.

Not anymore.

Instead of seducing Jethro to make him care enough to free me, I now just wanted him dead. I could see the allure of martyrdom. If I had a bomb, I would willingly strap it to my chest and press the trigger if it meant I could take out these men when I died.

Kes lowered his voice. "I've seen the scars on your back. I know the pain you endured from the First Debt. If you can survive that—you can definitely survive this."

I couldn't breathe. Not only had they taken everything, but now they wanted to mark my body—yet another reminder of my fate.

When I didn't respond, Kes tried again. "You don't have to say anything, just point to where you want the mark then you can go."

Go? Go where? Home? To the nearest black market and buy a bazooka to destroy them?

Kes moved closer, crowding me so I had a Hawk in every direction. "It won't hurt. Much."

Jethro snapped.

Soaring upright, he shoved Kes away and snatched the Tally Box from Daniel. "You're fucking suffocating us. Give us some space, for Christ's sake."

My heart twitched.

Jethro's temper was lethal, his position in the family high up the ranking pole, but the passion underlying his command sounded suspiciously like he'd picked my side over them.

I should've been overjoyed.

I should've done everything in my power to thank Jethro and encourage him to fall for me.

But I had nothing left but hate.

Kes chuckled. "Don't worry, Jet. Just trying to make it easier on Nila." He planted his hand on Jethro's shoulder, squeezing tight.

I expected Jethro to shrug him off and punch him. Instead, he relaxed slightly, nodding as silent communication ran between the brothers.

What the hell does Kes know about Jethro? And how does he use it so effortlessly to keep his brother calm?

Daniel stole my hand, running a sharp fingernail along the centre of my palm. I jumped, gasping in pain and surprise. I yanked my hand back, trying to dislodge the crazy creep.

No way did I want him infecting me.

A hand was the one part of a person's body that touched so much. The first point of contact for new experiences. A five-fingered tool to get through life.

"Stop touching me."

Jethro slapped his brother's hand aside, allowing me to tuck my palm between my legs.

Cut growled, "Stop chitchatting and get it done. You have five seconds to decide where the tally will go, Ms. Weaver. Otherwise, I shall decide for you."

Jethro sucked in a harsh breath, watching me from the corner of his eye.

Your fingers.

What? I shook my head at the idea. It was a stupid place for a tattoo.

It makes sense.

My reasoning laid out my conclusion in crystal clarity.

I intend to use my hands to slaughter them in the future.

If my fingers wore their mark—bore the signs of pain extracted at their whim—it was only fair that they extracted pain in return. My hands were currently virgins in murder, but soon they would smother in their blood.

It's only fitting to wear their tally while I steal their lives.

My eyes fell on Jethro.

Even him?

I steeled my heart against whatever desire existed between us.

Even him.

Sitting straight, I announced, "My fingertips."

Jethro scowled. "Out of anywhere on your body, that's where you've chosen?"

I nodded. "Yes." I spread my hands, silently cursing the shake in them. "One fingertip per debt."

I just hope there aren't more than ten to repay.

Daniel smirked again. "Not a place I would've chosen, but it does leave your body open for more marks in the future."

I narrowed my eyes.

"Put your hand on my leg, palm up."

"I'm not touching you."

Lightning quick, Daniel snatched my wrist, twisted my arm until my palm was as he requested, and slammed it against his thigh.

"Keep it there," he ordered.

My skin crawled. I went to pull away, but Cut said quietly, "Do as you're told, Ms. Weaver."

Jethro sucked in air, his ire buffeting me. "This isn't how tradition states." His head shot up to face his father. "Cut, I should be the one—"

Cut's features blackened. "There are a number of things you should be doing, Jethro. Yet you don't do any of them. What makes you so eager to do this one?"

I looked between the men, all the while trying to forget my hand rested on Daniel's thigh. Apprehension bubbled in my chest as he pressed a button on the side of the tattoo gun. Immediately the machine hummed with life.

Vertigo swirled in my blood at the thought of being permanently marked. I'd never had a tattoo, nor did I want one.

Jethro leaned forward. "This is my right."

His eyes met mine.

My tummy twisted.

My skin ached to be touched, to be kissed, to be bruised with lust.

Gritting my teeth, I shoved away those treasonous thoughts. I forced myself to focus on my mother's tombstone. Instantly, every desire fizzled into ash.

Daniel tore open an alcoholic wipe with his teeth, and swiped the disinfectant across the tip of my finger, breaking our connection. He grinned, holding up the buzzing gun. "Ready?"

"Cut!" Jethro growled.

I squeezed my eyes, biting my lip in preparation of the pain.

"Stop."

My eyes tore open at Cut's angry command.

"Enough, Daniel. Make Jethro do it. Can't break tradition, after all."

Daniel threw a disgusted look at his father. "You were never going to let me do it, were you?"

Cut glowered at his youngest offspring. "Watch what you say."

Jethro shifted to the edge of the couch. "Give me the gun." Daniel ignored him.

His father snapped, "Daniel, give the gun to your brother."

A glaze of inhumanity and insanity flickered across his eyes. Without permission, I stole my hand back, grateful it no longer had to touch his horrible leg.

I'm living in a madhouse.

Jethro snatched the gun. The vibrating equipment settled between his fingers.

Twisting to face me on the couch, he raised an eyebrow, looking between my hand and his leg.

Ugh.

Obediently, I placed my hand on Jethro the exact same way it'd been on Daniel. The moment I touched him, he sucked in a breath. I tried to ignore the awareness snapping between us. I tried to fight the lashing heat.

I no longer wanted it—not after yesterday.

But it seemed Jethro couldn't control it, either. He bowed over my hand, unsuccessfully hiding the thickening hardness between his legs.

Licking his lips, he focused on my hand. His cool fingers imprisoned my index—the one without a Band Aid on from pricking myself while measuring out material—and pressed the tattoo gun against my skin.

Ouch.

I gasped, trying to control my flinch as the tiny teeth tore through my skin, layering me with ink.

"Don't move, unless you want a sloppy tattoo," Jethro muttered. His concentration level hummed along with the gun as it razored across the pad of my finger. I tried to see what mark he drew but his head was in the way.

Kes was right, though.

The pain started sharp but swiftly faded to an intoxicating burn. And no sooner had I relaxed into the metal teeth, it was over.

Five minutes was all it took.

The gun turned off and Jethro reclined, letting me steal my hand.

Nursing my new brand, I eyed up my fingertip. My flesh was slightly swollen and red; a new black sigil glowed like sin.

JKH

This time I couldn't stop my heart from tangling with my stomach.

He'd marked me. Owned me. Controlled me.

"Your initials?"

Jethro pursed his lips. His eyes hooded, trying unsuccessfully to hide what he truly wanted to know. If his text wasn't blatant enough, his initials were a slap in the face with honesty.

His gaze shouted it.

Ask me.

Am I Kite?

I looked away, following the flourish of his old-fashioned handwriting. He wanted me to admit it. To confirm what he'd guessed. I had feelings for Kite. Feelings that I thought were safe being given to a nameless stranger, only to find out that nameless stranger was my nemesis who'd charmed both my body and heart.

The ink glowed black, forever etched into my skin. With evidence like that, I no longer had to ask.

Jethro Kite Hawk.

I looked up through my eyelashes, transmitting a silent message of my own.

I already know.

And I hate you for it.

He stiffened, understanding. "Unless you ask, I won't say

what the letters stand for."

Secrets shadowed his eyes. Secrets his family weren't privy to but I was. What did that mean? What did any of this mean?

Deciding this wasn't the time nor the place to discuss something that would no doubt end in another fight, I tilted my head and played dumb instead. Taunting Jethro was too rewarding to let it go. "You want me to ask? Fine. What does the K stand for?"

Jethro frowned.

Kes chuckled. So far, he'd honoured my request for him to keep my knowledge a secret. Turned out he didn't need to keep it, after all.

"Your turn." Jethro deliberately avoided the question by handing me the gun.

I took it, my mouth plopping wide. "What do I do with this?"

Jethro unfolded his hand and carefully rested his knuckles on my knee. The submissive position of his hand and the gentleness in which he touched me sent unwanted pinwheels sparking in my blood.

We both gasped at the contact. My vision went grey on the edges as I fought the overwhelming urge to forget what I'd seen yesterday and give in to him. To trust in my original plan that I had the power to make him care. To trust in my heart and permit it to enjoy this blistering lust.

Jethro's voice was low and full of gravel. "You have to mark me in return."

To brand him. Own him. Command him.

It would be a wish come true. Perhaps, if I tattooed him with my name, I could cast a spell over him to become mine, not theirs. To use him once and for all.

Cut jumped in. "Each firstborn involved in the Debt Inheritance must wear the tally. It's been that way for generations. I must say I'm enjoying watching Jethro be so obedient. I thought his unwillingness to be marked by a Weaver would mean I'd have to strap him down."

Jethro threw him a black look.

Waving at Jethro's awaiting hand, Cut added, "Do it, Nila. Mark him with your initials so even when you're no longer with us, he will remember his time with you."

I blinked, unable to stop my heart from squeezing in pain.

No longer here.

When Jethro takes my life.

I wanted to hurl crude threatening insults but held my tongue. We would see who would die by the end of this.

Bending over Jethro's fingers, the very same fingers that had been inside me, I hexed the heat in my cheeks and twisting desire in my core.

Looking up, I caught Jethro's gaze. It glowed with need, mirroring mine. How could I hate this man? Positively hate him for doing what he did to my family, yet still want him so badly?

Bastard.

Even now, even in a room full of his flesh and blood amidst talk of murder and debts, he still managed to invoke uncontrollable need from me.

I wanted to stab him with the tattoo gun, not mark him.

Taking a deep breath, I turned on the button and jumped at the powerful vibration of the tool. "How hard do I press?"

"Just like a pen, Nila. There's no trick. Not for something as simple as this," Kes said. He hadn't stopped standing over us, watching everything, saying nothing.

Brushing wayward hair from my eyes, I leaned further over Jethro's fingers.

The second I pressed the jumping needle against his skin, he locked his muscles. Instead of tensing against the pain though, I sensed he wanted more. He swayed into me, his lungs inhaling deep. I shivered to think he willingly breathed in my smell, imprinting not just my initials but my essence, too.

Biting my lip, I drew on his flesh. My hand shook and sweat dampened my palms. After ten minutes, I sat up and rubbed at the cramp in my lower back.

His index finger held the same torture as mine.

NTW

Subtly, I glanced at my burning tattoo. First, Jethro had made me sign the Sacramental Pledge, and then made me sign his body.

If we hadn't been bound by sin and debts and a lust that refused to be denied, we were now. Locked, joined, and forever linked until one of us died.

It was tragic to think I'd gone my entire life never finding anyone who interested me, only to find such chemistry with a man who I had to kill before he killed me.

Jethro cradled his hand, glaring at the black ink imbedded in his fingertip. He traced the pattern almost reverently. "What's your middle name?" he whispered. His question was too delicate and imploring for the room full of violence and Hawks.

I wanted to slap him and show him how much he'd slipped from the icy son he was supposed to be.

He looked up, waiting for my answer.

My heart panged. It wasn't a middle name. It was more than that. I missed the loving address that my father and brother called me. It was who I was. Who I'd been raised to be.

Threads.

"Doesn't matter."

Turning off the gun, I placed it back in the box.

Cut clapped his hands. "Perfect. I'm so glad the formalities have been completed." Glaring at Jethro, he added, "Don't forget next time, son."

Jethro scowled, climbing to his feet. "Are we dismissed?"

Dismissed? Not only was the word choice like an obedient child seeking approval to leave his elders, but his voice sounded odd. Strained, gruff—an explosive blend that seemed as if he'd detonate at any moment.

"Fine."

Without another word, Jethro stormed out, leaving me

alone with Cut, Daniel, and Kes.

What the hell?

I might not like him, but I was his. I needed him to protect me from his bloody family.

Instantly, the atmosphere in the room changed. It rolled thick and heavy: testosterone, possession, vileness. Why didn't I feel it as strongly when Jethro was by my side? And why had he left in such a hurry without me?

Daniel took the opportunity of my stunned state to lean forward and grab my hair. Whispering evilly in my ear, he said, "The way you watch my brother gives away your feelings, Ms. Weaver. I know you want to fuck him. I know you're horny living in a house full of men as powerful as my family. But you won't get to fuck him; not until we've all had our fill. He's the firstborn, but he'll be the last to stick his cock inside that sweet little pussy of yours."

Wrong, you arsehole. He's the only one who will touch me that way.

I struggled, trying to pull away. Cut watched us, neither interfering nor caring.

Daniel's tongue lashed out, licking around my earlobe. "I've seen you wandering around Hawksridge as if you own the place. Next time you're out for a stroll, you might want to worry about who's waiting. Because believe me—I'm not a patient guy. The minute you're alone and I find you—I'm fucking you. I don't care about the rules."

Pulling back, he stood with a horrible smile on his face. "Until then, Ms. Weaver." Tipping his head as if he had a top hat on his greasy black hair, he smiled at his father and Kes then disappeared out the door.

Oh, my God.

My heart was a fluttering mess. I'd been so stupid to believe I was untouchable. Believing the airs and graces of Cut and timelines of tradition.

I supposed I was grateful to the little creep for opening my eyes. I wasn't safe here—from anyone, at any time.

I need a weapon.

I needed some way to protect myself from that psychopath.

Ask Jethro to protect you.

I shook my head. Jethro wasn't the one in charge. Not yet. And besides, he was on my hit list as much as his family. I wasn't loyal to him. I could never be loyal to someone who made me despise myself.

I stood up, hissing as my new tattoo flared. Summoning whatever strength I had remaining, I glared at Cut and Kes. "Tell Daniel if he comes near me again, I'll make him bleed."

Without a backward glance, I left.

A weapon.

Find a weapon.

I could run to the kitchen and steal a knife. Or I could head to the library and swipe a sword hanging from the walls. Or, if I had any musket understanding, I could commandeer a gun and hide it beneath my covers.

What I really needed, however, was something deadly but also transportable. I never intended to be defenceless again. Not in these walls.

Dashing down the corridor, I plotted where I should go. Weapons existed all over Hawksridge Hall. I hadn't bothered to pilfer one because Jethro hadn't given me a reason to fight—other than verbally. Daniel, on the other hand, wouldn't touch me—not without walking away missing a few vital pieces of his anatomy.

The dining room would be my best hope at selecting something sharp and small enough to hide on my person. I'd seen a ruby-handled dirk there last time. It would be perfect and easy to conceal.

A flash of blackness up ahead wrenched my attention from scheming. I narrowed my eyes, moving faster to catch up with the blur that'd disappeared down the corridor.

Thanking the thick white carpet below my bare toes, I

tiptoed the final distance and peered down the hallway.

Jethro.

My heart rate picked up as he strode quickly and purposely, his hands balled by his side.

My gaze fell on the hand where he now wore my initials.

I brought my finger up, inspecting his impressive cursive and arrogant flourish of his name. Not only had we slept together, but we'd stamped ownership on each other, too.

Jethro stopped and knocked on a door. A moment later, he turned the brass door handle and disappeared.

The second the door closed, I darted down the corridor and pressed my ear against the ancient wood.

What are you doing?

I didn't know.

Eavesdropping never brought good news, but I refused to be in the dark any longer. Where did he disappear to when he struggled? Who or what did he run to when he slipped from ice to emotion?

A low murmur of voices came through the door.

I couldn't catch any words, but my heart raced at the sound.

Jethro didn't disappear to be on his own. He didn't run to Kestrel or a Black Diamond brother.

Of course, it wasn't that simple.

No, he came here.

He visited a woman.

A woman who spoke with a softly whispered voice.

A woman who'd lived all this time on the second floor of Hawksridge Hall.

Jethro

"WHAT ARE YOU doing in here, Kite?"

I slouched.

My nickname. The term of endearment that I allowed no one but my sister to use filled me with equal parts relief and annoyance. I should never have used it to message Nila. Now its meaning intertwined with the debts. It would never again just be a simple term of togetherness between Jaz and me.

I'd been so stupid to call myself after James Bond, too. Kite007. What a ridiculous name. It wasn't that I even *liked* James Bond. I just thought he had cool gadgets and deserved his kickass status for always killing evil bastards.

My fingertip burned with licking fire. My knuckles still tingled from resting on Nila's thigh. So many times, I'd had to brace myself so I didn't flip my hand over and slide my touch between her legs.

I'd been achingly hard the entire time I'd tattooed her. I'd wanted to see if she was wet while repaying the favour. There was something primal about knowing the woman who I'd fucked, who intrigued me over all others, was walking around wearing my brand.

A brand that marked her forever as mine.

Shit, perhaps I should've taken care of myself before coming here. The moment I let my thoughts drift to Nila, I grew hard again.

Jasmine smiled, waiting patiently like she always did for me to reply. There was no judging, no annoyance. Only acceptance and quiet companionship.

"I had to come see you."

Every second that ticked past in the solar had dwindled my defences until I had no reserves, no ice, no energy to fight against my family. The instant the tally concluded, I ran. A pussy move, but the only one to keep my sanity.

Jasmine shifted higher in her chair. She sat by the window, her embroidery threads and cross-stitch pattern spread out on the window seat where she had the most light to see.

Her rooms were the epitome of class. Dark grey walls with yellow coloured upholstery and linen. Archangels and fluffy clouds painted the ceiling while her floors drowned in multi-coloured rugs of different sizes and designs.

This was her world.

This was the only place I felt safe to let down my guard.

Jaz patted the window seat, folding up her pattern chart and moving aside some of the threads. "Want to talk about it?"

Did I? Did I want to admit the havoc Nila wreaked on me, or was it best not to talk about it and hope the power she had disappeared?

I shook my head. "Let me just hang here."

She smiled. "No problem. I'll just continue doing what I'm doing."

She knew me so well.

Her jaw-length black hair flicked at the ends in some fashionable haircut she'd recently adopted and her button nose and heart-shaped face was too kind to be around my brothers. Jasmine Hawk looked exactly like our mother. And only eleven months younger than me, she was practically my twin.

I wouldn't admit it to Nila, but I understood her connection with her brother. There was something to be said for finding a kindred soul in a person who'd been there right from the beginning.

I probably wouldn't have survived without Jasmine. I owed her everything.

"Relax, Kite. Let it go." Her small hands smoothed down her pretty woollen dress. She always looked immaculate in old-world fashions, which was utterly depressing as she never stepped foot off the grounds.

I'd tried many times to take her for a ride, on either Wings or my motorbike, but she claimed she was perfectly content looking through a window and watching others enjoy the world.

One of these days I would drag her out and show her how much she missed by playing Rapunzel in her tower.

Picking up her cross-stitch, Jaz gave me one last smile and continued to work on yet another masterpiece of our imposing monolithic home. Considering she didn't fit the Hawk traits like me, she was extremely patriotic to her heritage.

Threading her needle, she said, "Rest, brother. I'll watch over you."

I woke with a chill.

Gloomy dusk had replaced the grey morning. "Damn, what time is it?" I sat up, holding my head as a rush of nausea battered me. It was always the same. The sickness at the end of a long day. Especially if I'd been subjected to my family for long periods of time.

Jasmine was still in her chair, her legs covered in a blanket she'd crocheted. Her fingers flew, drawing a needle with orange thread through the hoop of her recent cross-stitch.

Not bothering to look up, she replied, "You slept through dinner again. But it's okay. I had the servants bring you up some cold cuts." She motioned toward the sideboard by her bed. Resting on the polished surface was a silver dome covering a plate.

I sighed, running both hands through my hair. Chuckling softly, I said, "You know me too well."

Her eyes met mine. "I know what you are but not who you're becoming."

I froze.

It wasn't uncommon for Jasmine to state such poignant weighty things. She was wise—an old soul. Someone who I leaned on far too much.

Knowing she had questions, I stood up wearily and went to retrieve the meal. Returning to my place, I sighed. "Am I supposed to understand that or is it a helpful way to ruin my sleep tonight?"

She giggled softly. "I think you've ruined your sleep by napping here all afternoon."

Even though she watched me with impatience and expectation, I felt nothing from her but love. Unconditional acceptance.

I sat back contentedly.

Finally, I could breathe again.

Nila tangled me into knots, drove flames through my icicle-ridden heart, and forced me to confront parts of my personality I wished were dead. But Jasmine…she soothed me. She granted me strength in her silence and a place to heal in her adoration.

Pulling the silver cover off, I picked up a piece of honey-cured ham and placed it into my mouth.

Jasmine reached for her glass of sour apple. She refused to drink anything else—water and sour apple quenchers—that was it. "So…you ready to talk yet?"

I ignored her, placing another piece of ham on my tongue.

She huffed, wrapping her tiny hands around her glass. Her fingers were almost as delicate as Nila's. They were both proficient at needlepoint and of similar build. Everything inside knew they'd probably get along.

But I wanted to keep the two women of my life separate. I had my reasons.

Nila couldn't know who I truly was and I wouldn't be able to keep my secrets if she met Jasmine.

Jasmine knew the truth. The whole truth. The truth that

could potentially cut my lifespan into pieces and steal my inheritance on the eve of it becoming mine.

My phone buzzed in my pocket. Pulling it free, I scowled at the screen. The alert on keywords surrounding my family and the Weavers flashed with new information.

My blood boiled at the latest leak online about our private affairs. I'd been watching him, just waiting for him to do something stupid.

That little shit-stirrer has gone too far this time.

"I have to make a call."

Jasmine shrugged. "I don't mind. Do what you need to do."

Gritting my teeth, I dialled the number and placed the phone against my ear. I did my best not to crush the device in my fingers. I was angry. Fucking pissed. If I had time to drive to London and tell him in person, I would. Only, I would invariably end up using my fists—not my voice.

"Hello?"

My heart thundered viciously.

"Hello, Vaughn."

"Uh, hi...who's this?"

I laughed coldly. "As if you don't know who this is. Listen, whatever you're doing, stop it. This is the only friendly warning you'll get. She's ours now. Not yours. And you can't win against us so don't even fucking try. Got it?"

Deafening silence came down the line.

"Last warning, Mr. Weaver. Tell the press to mind their own business and put a gag on whatever bullshit you're spreading."

Harsh breathing filled my ear. "Listen here, you arsewipe. Nila is my sister. I love her more than fucking anything, and I *will* get her back. She's not happy with you. If you think I'm going to sit back and let her be subjected to you maniacs, you're completely fucking nuts. Soon, everyone will know what you've done. Soon, every law enforcer and newspaper will understand how sick and twisted you are. And then you'll be ruined, and we will have won. Go suck on that, fuckface. Don't call me again."

He hung up.

I threw my phone across the room.

"Shit!"

Not only did I have to deal with my own fucking weaknesses, but now I had to find a way to stop Nila's brother from destroying everything, too. Christ, this day couldn't get any worse.

Jasmine looked at my phone as it bounced against the wall. "Well...I'm guessing that didn't go as you wanted."

"He's determined to kill himself."

"And take both our families' reputations down with him."

I nodded. "Exactly. He has to be stopped."

I didn't relish the thought of killing Nila's brother, but what else could I do? He couldn't be permitted to steal what was mine. He couldn't ruin what I'd found. And he definitely couldn't take the one thing that I needed to make it to my thirtieth birthday.

"Don't be too hard on him. We took his mother and his sister. He's allowed to be—"

"He thinks having a dead mother grants him compensation?"

Jasmine's face fell. "No, of course not. Just like we don't expect anything after what happened to ours."

Colossal pain howled in my chest. Memories of a woman who looked so like Jasmine filled my mind. I never let myself think about her because that one incident had scarred me for life. It didn't make me who I was, but it had taught me death and pain and horror—things I'd never be free of.

"Kite..."

I swallowed my agonising memories, glaring at my sister. "I know, Jaz. We agreed not to bring up that day."

She nodded. "You came in here to find peace, yet you brought anger and pain instead. Let it go."

I sighed, hanging my head in my hands. "I'm trying.

Just…give me some space."

She shook her head. "If you wanted space, you would've taken Wings for a ride. Don't bullshit me, brother. It's getting worse for you, isn't it? All of this…it's too much." She put her empty glass down, leaning forward in her chair. Her cherub cheeks were flushed from the roaring fire that a servant had set in the white marble fireplace. "You slept with her, didn't you?"

I choked. "Excuse me?"

She reclined, shoving aside all thoughts of our mother and focusing once again on my damn issues. "You heard me." Waving a hand in my direction, she added, "You're the worst I've seen you since you were fifteen. You're stressed and angry. You're *hurting*, brother." Her voice softened with worry. "It's been a long time, Jethro, and I hate to see you in pain. But I think…I think you finally need to learn to control it, rather than bury it. It's not helping anymore."

My heart thumped in horror at the thought of being denied freedom from the horrendous disease I battled. If Jasmine couldn't grant a reprieve, how could I get through the next ten months and finally take my place as heir?

It's so fucking close. I'll make it. I have to make it.

"You know that isn't possible, Jaz."

"You don't have a choice. It's eating you alive, and unless you face it, you're going to massacre your feet or lose your mind. Either way, both aren't healthy and both will only bring disaster."

I shoved away the food, no longer hungry. "Then what the fuck do you propose I do?"

Jasmine narrowed her eyes, conclusions and solutions already formed in her gaze. She looked at me as if all of this had an answer. Which it didn't.

After a moment, she murmured, "Use her."

I froze. Blood roared in my veins. "You know I can't do that. I'm risking everything by letting her get this close to me." I bent forward, resting my head in my hands. "I don't know what the hell I'm doing anymore."

I had too much on my shoulders. Worrying about what Vaughn was doing. Fearing what my father would do. Stressing about my feelings for Nila.

I'm done. Literally about to fucking snap.

Jaz ignored me, diverting my thoughts back to her original statement. "You'll have to. If you've let her in enough to sleep with her—"

My head shot up. "I didn't sleep with her."

Jaz raised an eyebrow, pursing her lips. "Oh, really? You forget I can see through your lies."

My forehead furrowed. "I fucked her, but I didn't sleep with her."

Even as I said it, my subconscious screamed the truth.

If I had fucked her, I wouldn't have let her affect me. It would've been purely physical and nothing more. She wouldn't have this hold over me—this damn fucking power.

"You're lying, Kite." Jasmine sighed, running a hand through her glossy hair. "And until you fess up and see that you're the one ruining the only thing that might work for you, I can't help you."

My blood ran cold. "What do you expect me to do? She's a Weaver!"

She didn't flinch at my outburst—completely used to me. "Doesn't matter. If you have to use her to cure yourself and realise you can be who you are, even after a lifetime of being told you can't, then do it."

Goosebumps broke out over my skin. "What are you saying?"

She stiffened, looking a lot older than her twenty-eight years. "I'm saying you need to find another way. If you don't, you won't survive, and I refuse to live in this family without you." Reaching forward, she took my hand, linking our fingers together. "In another few months all of this will be yours, Jethro. Don't let her destroy you—not when you're so close."

I squeezed her hand, wishing it were that easy. "I can't let her in."

Jaz smiled. "You don't have to. Make her fall in love with you. Do whatever it takes for her to ignore the reality of her circumstances and fall head over heels for you. Then deal with her brother and make peace with who you are.

"Only then will you find your salvation."

Nila

MONDAY MORNING.

I stood in the shower, letting warm water cascade over me.

The past few days had disappeared with no event and the weekend was a distant memory. Not that I had any reason to hate Mondays anymore. I had no deadlines, no runway shows to organise, or orders to fill. My new life was a constant holiday, interspersed with fabric sorting and designing that was a passion rather than a chore. Yet I couldn't stop my body from waking up and hurling me into work mode at dawn. I'd never been able to sleep past sunrise—a curse that Vaughn didn't share. He was a night owl where I was the morning starling.

Leaning my head back, I opened my mouth and welcomed water to trail over my lips and across my tongue. It felt good. Almost as warm as Jethro's tongue when he kissed me.

Ever since tattooing each other, everything turned me on. My bra rubbed against my nipples. My knickers whispered across my clit. I ached with the need to release but had no idea how to give myself an orgasm. I needed to come, but there was no way I would sleep with Jethro again.

I couldn't. It was too dangerous.

My finger, with its glowing *JKH*, had scabbed and

healed enough for me to bear the itch as my skin acquainted itself with the foreign ink.

What does he think of his tattoo?

After sneaking down the corridor and watching him disappear, I'd battled every night with the need to return to the unknown floor to investigate the unknown room and interrogate the unknown woman.

He'd gone into her room but didn't come out.

I hadn't waited long—I couldn't. After all, cameras watched my every move. But I needed to find answers, and I had a horrible feeling that everything I needed to know was in that boudoir on the second floor.

Just thinking of Jethro sent a spasm of desire through my core.

Dammit, what's happening to me?

A daydream of Jethro slamming to his knees before me and wrenching my legs wide stole my mind. It was so vivid, so real—a trickle of need ran down my inner thigh. I gasped as I imagined his tongue lapping at my clit, his long fingers disappearing inside me—the same finger that I'd tattooed with my name.

Would I come harder knowing he touched me with a finger branded by me? Or would I hold on as tight as I could and make him work for it?

Oh, God.

I needed to get rid of this satanic desire. I needed to be free.

My eyes opened, latching onto the detachable showerhead.

I could do it myself...

My heartbeat whizzed with need. I couldn't fight the churning demand any longer.

Reaching upward, I unhooked the showerhead and turned the water temperature down so as not to burn myself.

Feeling awkward and ridiculous and a hundred times guilty for what I was about to do, I braced my back on the tiled wall and spread my legs a little.

My teeth clamped on my bottom lip as the water pressure tickled my clit.

Oh. My. God.

My eyes rolled back as I grew bolder and pressed the stream of heavenly water harder against my pussy.

Water cascaded down my legs while my torso shivered from sudden cold. My nipples stiffened as I wickedly angled the jet down and down until water shot inside me. Every jet and bubble aroused sensitive flesh, sending my muscles clenching in joy.

I moaned.

Loudly.

My legs trembled as my neck flopped forward and I gave myself over to the exquisite pleasure conjured by an innocuous showerhead.

Starbursts flashed behind my eyelids; Jethro loomed into my mind. I pictured him shrugging out of his black shirt, prowling toward me while unbuckling his belt and unzipping his trousers. I moaned again as my daydream shed his clothing and stood proud and naked before me. He grabbed his cock, pumping himself hard and firm, while his eyes feasted on what I was doing. He didn't say a word, only watched, then crooked his finger and beckoned me closer.

My heartbeat exceeded recommended limits as I forced myself higher and higher, locking my knees against buckling as an orgasm brewed into being. I rocked the showerhead, biting my lip as the pressure spurted over my clit and then inside me. The rhythm I set was exactly like fucking and I daren't overthink how I looked or how depraved I felt getting off this way.

My daydream forced its way past my misgivings. My forehead furrowed as I trembled, both welcoming and fighting an orgasm.

Daydream Jethro crept closer, working his cock, a dangerous glint in his eyes. The moment I was within grabbing distance, he captured my waist. "I need to be inside you, Nila."

I put words into Jethro's mouth, but it was his voice I heard in my heart.

I moaned again, angling the showerhead harder against my clit.

"How do you want it?" my fantasy whispered in my ear as he spun me around and pressed me hard against the wall.

I swallowed hard, answering in my mind. "Fast and…"

"Filthy?" Daydream Jethro's nose nuzzled the back of my ear, sending shockwaves down my spine. "I can fuck you filthy."

I couldn't speak. But I didn't have to. My fantasy knew exactly how I needed it. Jethro bit the back of my shoulder, spreading my legs wider with his.

"Fuck me, Jethro Hawk," I whispered.

"Oh, I will. Believe me, I will." Without further warning, he dug his fingers into my hips and slammed inside me.

My fingers went numb as I slid the showerhead from clit to entrance. I cried out as water shot inside at the same time as Jethro thrust into me from behind, sliding deep and fast, stretching me deliciously painfully.

My heart exploded with bliss. An orgasm squeezed every atom, getting ready to hurl me into the stratosphere.

Jethro thrust again and I rode my new friend the showerhead.

"Oh, God. Yes," I hissed, rocking harder. "Yes, *yes…*"

A masculine cough sounded. "You continue to surprise me, Ms. Weaver; at least this time, I rather enjoy it."

Everything crashed into awareness. My daydream shattered, fracturing by my feet like broken glass. I squealed and dropped the showerhead. It turned into a water snake, spewing water left and right, wriggling like some terrible demon.

Jethro snickered. "You're using up the entire Hall's supply of hot water. Are you planning on saving some for the rest of the inhabitants of my home?"

I couldn't. *I can't.* The horror. The shame!

"What the hell are you doing in here!?" Embarrassment painted my cheeks. I wished I could curl into a ball and die. With trembling arms, I tried my best to hide my decency. Slapping one arm across my chest, I positioned a hand between my legs, exceedingly careful not to touch my throbbing pussy.

So close!

I was so close to coming.

So close, in fact, I wanted to scream.

One more stroke and I would've found peace. Now I was even worse—vibrating with tightly strung desire, fogging my every thought.

The showerhead continued to hiss and spurt by my feet, slipping me further into disgraced hell.

This can't be happening. Please don't let this be happening.

Jethro leaned against the doorjamb, his arms crossed, and a smile on his lips. "Don't stop on my account." He waved at my flushed skin. "By all means, finish. I can wait."

My daydream interlinked with reality and all I could think about was pulling Jethro fully clothed into the shower and impaling myself on his cock. I wanted him so damn bad. I wanted to be ridden, taken filthy and wrong.

My head throbbed as mental images of slippery bodies granting pleasure invaded my normally rational mind.

Jethro laughed quietly. "You look in pain, Ms. Weaver." He lowered his head so he watched me beneath hooded eyes. "Do you need help?"

I almost moaned at the thought of him filling me, fucking me. "I—" *Yes, I need help. Get in here and take me. Fix me so I can get over my horrible infatuation with you.*

I shook my head.

Dammit, Nila. Get a grip!

Jethro's jaw tightened; joviality disappeared, replaced with thick, thick lust.

My nipples turned from pebbles to diamonds, so hard I swear they would slice anything that touched them. I couldn't move as he continued to drink me in. With every second that ticked past, the air changed until the steam around us shimmered with barely veiled hunger.

Jethro's gaze drifted down my front. "Fuck," he breathed.

I almost puddled to the floor. I didn't trust myself to say anything—not one word. I'd betray everything I'd promised myself over the past few days. I would crash to my knees and beg him to put me out of my misery.

I would never be able to live with myself again.

We stayed silent, devouring each other but making no move to deal with what we wanted. My eyes fell to his trousers and his straining erection. It was so proud, so big.

Wait. He's wearing jodhpurs.

I blinked, trying to make sense in my sex-hazed brain. "Are—are you going somewhere?"

My voice snapped him out of whatever fantasy he'd been having. My scalp tickled as his golden eyes radiated intensity. "Yes. You're coming, too."

My eyes snapped closed.

Coming.

Yes, I'd love to.

He laughed softly. "Perhaps the wrong choice of words." In a rustle of clothing, he pushed off from the doorjamb. "Or the right ones, depending on how the next few minutes go."

A full body clench tore a small pant from my lips.

My eyes flew wide as he grabbed a fluffy towel and stalked toward me.

I pressed myself harder against the tiles. Shaking my head, I squeaked, "Stay there. Don't—don't come any closer."

His face darkened; a flash of temper etched his features. "It's not like I haven't seen what you're hiding, Ms. Weaver. Or are you forgetting that I've stuck my tongue in your cunt and driven my cock deep inside? I've tasted you. Ridden you. Made you moan."

Shit.

My core spasmed, greedily latching onto his words— seeking the final push for the orgasm living in my blood. It would be so simple to let go. To tell him what I truly wanted and to hell with the rest of it.

They're rotting up there while you fuck the oldest son.

Common-sense threw freezing water onto my overheated libido. With all the power I possessed, I ordered myself to ignore the tantalizing release and step back into the real world.

Seemed Jethro had come to the same conclusion as the aching awareness between us solidified into obligation. "Get dressed. We're late."

Swallowing hard and cursing my heavy body, I asked, "Late for what?"

With an unsteady hand, he held out the towel. He had the willpower of a saint or perhaps he was just as crazy as I feared because he didn't move to touch me.

Damn him.

His eyes narrowed as his fingers tightened around the towel. "Polo."

"Polo?" Images of men on horses whacking a ball around a field gave me something else to focus on.

"But…it's Monday."

Jethro cocked his head, chuckling under his breath. "You think the day of the week influences the crowd who play with us?" He shook his head. "If you hadn't have told me it was Monday, I wouldn't have known. Work days and weekends mean nothing when everyone obeys our schedule."

He's so damn arrogant.

Why do I find that so hot?

His eyes fell to my wet body. "Drop your hands."

"No."

"Obey me."

"Why?"

Because you'll end my anguish and give me what I need?

"Do it, Ms. Weaver. I won't ask again."

My tummy twisted. "Just because you've seen me doesn't mean you have the right to see me again."

He pursed his lips. "I can see and touch and do whatever

the hell I want to you whenever I want."

Temper slowly overrode my lust. I stood taller, glowering at him.

Fine.

He was back to being an arsehole. I could be a bitch.

Dropping my hands, I stood proud and defiant. I ignored the hissing showerhead and dared him to say something cruel. "Go on, look." I spread my arms, twirling in place. "Seeing as you control my fate, I might as well walk around naked so you can always drink your fill."

He growled, "Knock it off."

Snatching the towel from him and throwing it to the floor, I snarled, "No."

"What the fuck got into you?"

"What got into me? How about seeing proof of what my future holds."

God, I didn't mean to bring that up again. But if I wasn't thinking of sex with my mortal enemy, I was plotting ways to switch coffins from Weavers to Hawks.

"You knew that's what would happen."

"Knowing and seeing are entirely different things."

Jethro pinched the bridge of his nose, digging the tips of his fingers into his eyes as if seeking release from the rapidly building pressure in the room. "You're driving me mad."

"At least you finally admit it."

His head whipped up.

I froze. Shit, I'd gone too far. Again.

"What did you just say?"

The spurting showerhead faded; the rapid *thump-thump* of my heartbeat faded. All I focused on was Jethro's golden eyes—but more than that—I focused on his soul. The ragged, tattered soul that looked so completely lost.

Something inside him scared me to death but also called for help. I backed away—or rather, I tried to morph into the tiled wall behind me.

He glared, then…stepped into the shower.

Water instantly splattered his grey t-shirt and black jodhpurs as he stood over the wriggling water demon. His eyelashes sparkled with droplets as he coldly looked me up and down.

His hand came up. His lips twisted. A flash of violence danced across his features.

I did two things at once.

I cowered and suffered a vertigo wave.

Sickness slammed into me as I raised my arm above my head in defence. "Don't hit me!" The room spun and I stumbled against the tiles, desperately trying to grasp something to keep me upright.

My vision shot black and I flinched as harsh fingers captured my elbows, giving me an anchor just like Vaughn used to do so many times when we were children. The moment I had a sanctuary, the vertigo left me, depositing me firmly in Jethro's hold.

His eyes blazed with fury. "You couldn't hurt me any more than you just did, Ms. Weaver."

Why?

It's because you jumped to conclusions.

When I first arrived at Hawksridge, I would've been completely justified to cower and protect myself, but only because I didn't know who Jethro was. Now, I saw what he hid and violence was just a tool to him. A tool he didn't like to use. A tool he'd been made to wield all his life. But beneath his ferocity was pain. Deep, deep pain that spoke of a man far too immersed in this farce.

He won't hit me.

Not now. Not after what we'd shared—even after I'd tried to push him away, we were still intrinsically linked. He'd proven that when he'd remained on my side in the solar.

Shit, this is too messed up.

Blinking away the residual sickness, I tried to change the subject. "Stop using my last name."

He didn't reply, his face unreadable.

Something shadowed his gaze. Was it regret or annoyance? I couldn't tell. My heart lurched regardless. Sighing, I faced the true issue, hoping to grant him peace. "I'm sorry if I hurt you. I didn't mean to."

He let me go. "You thought I was going to hit you. Your fear...your loathing—you can't hide the truth. One flinch and you proved what you thought of me. I'm a fucking idiot to believe there was anything more between us."

Terror erupted in my stomach. Pushing *him* away was one thing. But having him push *me* away was entirely another.

Wait...fear and loathing?

He spoke as if he felt what I did. There was no way he could correctly feel my horror at what'd happened.

Glaring, I said, "What was I supposed to think? You raised your hand and expect me not to protect myself? You've told me time and time again to fear you." I should stop, but I couldn't contain the fire inside. "You should be happy you got your wish."

Jethro's jaw clenched. He stood so still, so regal, completely oblivious to the spurting showerhead by his feet. "I'm not happy with any of this, least of all you trying to provoke me."

"I'm not trying to provoke you."

He snorted. "Now who's the liar, Ms. Weaver? First you lie about the reasons why you slept with me, and now this." His lips twisted. "I'm beginning to think you are as lost as—"

His eyes flared, cutting himself off.

The words dangled between us. I throbbed to speak them. To see his reaction.

...as lost as me...

I was defiant and righteous, but I wasn't cruel. Holding my tongue, I let the moment pass.

Jethro visibly shuddered, holding up his finger. My eyes fell to his perfectly formed digit and my core clenched thinking of him pushing it inside me and granting me a release.

He sighed. "I came here, not to watch you pleasure

yourself or to summon you to get ready, but because I wanted to show you something."

My attention flickered between his raised finger and his glowing eyes. "Show me what?"

He sighed. "It's *your* initials that I bear. Your mark. Your brand. I may be born a Hawk, but I've been captured by a Weaver."

My heart exploded.

Jethro leaned closer, pressing his mouth against my damp ear. "You sewed a cage. You somehow managed to fabricate a web that I only seem to fall deeper into. And this mark is proof of that."

My chest rose and fell. Was this a proclamation of his feelings for me? It was too strange, too forward for Jethro.

Slowly, I wrapped my fingers around his raised one, running my thumb over the tattoo. "Proof of what?"

Jethro closed his eyes briefly before murmuring, "Proof that no matter what happened on the moor, and no matter the grief you feel at my family's treatment of you, we are in this together."

Breaking my hold on him, he bent and gathered the showerhead from the floor. His hair tickled my lower belly, his mouth so close to my core. Standing straight, Jethro placed the showerhead back in its cradle and together we stood under a stream of droplets, drenching both of us and thawing out my frozen muscles.

Without a word, he reached for the tap and turned the water off.

Silence.

We didn't move, dripping wet in a billow of steam. I was naked while Jethro's powerful form beckoned me closer. His clothes clung to his body in ways that were utterly illegal. His cock was rock hard, his stomach etching his t-shirt with ridges and valleys of muscle.

I swallowed as my need to come bombarded me.

My eyes drifted down his front to the hard length in his

jodhpurs. "You can't keep playing games, Jethro."

He ran a hand through his damp hair. "Where is the game or joke in any of this?"

"There isn't any."

"No, there isn't." Grabbing my hand, he pressed his fingertip against my own newly inked one. "This isn't a game—not anymore. The debts bind us together as long as we're alive. You're mine and I told you before not to throw away that gift before knowing what it means."

My heartbeat lived in my blood, stealing strength from my knees, making me wobbly. "I don't want to belong to you."

He shook his head, a few renegade droplets sliding down the locks of salt and pepper hair. His forearms were wide and powerful as he moved to cup my cheek. "It's too late for that."

"It's never too late for the truth."

Bowing his head, he pressed his forehead against mine. "You're right. It's never too late for the truth."

The way he said it sent my soul scattering for the nearest exit. *What is he hiding from me?* "If you say I belong to you, then, by rights, your secrets belong to me. They'd be safe with me."

He sucked in a breath, his eyes trained on my lips. "I know what you're asking."

"What am I asking?"

He smiled sadly. "You want to know why I am the way I am. You want to know where I disappear to when I need space and you want to know how to use my weakness for you against my family."

Yes. I also want to understand why I feel this way. Why, when faced with the graves of my ancestors, do I so quickly forget and seek what I cannot find?

His fingers tightened against my cheek, holding me steadfast. His head tilted, bringing his lips within a feather-frond distance from mine.

My mouth tingled, sparking for contact. The anticipation raised my blood until I needed a cold shower instead of hot.

"Pity for you, I plan on keeping my secrets." His minty

breath washed over me, grabbing me by the soul and tearing me into smithereens.

"Why? What's so terrible that you have to hide who you truly are?"

He swallowed, closing the final distance between us and pressing me against the wall. "Quiet."

I gasped as his lips suddenly sealed over mine.

The moment we touched, everything ignited.

The rage I'd nursed waned. My loathing and bitterness abandoned me. Even the images of epitaphs and graves couldn't stop me from betraying my family.

I wanted to drop my walls and bare everything. I wanted to forget about the past month, and pretend he was a simple boy with a simple offer. I wanted to believe he would save me and not ultimately kill me.

He groaned as I threw myself into the kiss, moulding my body along his.

I was already in hell. I couldn't fall any further. Might as well give up, give in, and just admit defeat.

Every dark facet of who I was, every spark and knowledge that made me human, wanted to be seen and understood. I wanted him to see me as his—not because I was a pawn in a game I didn't understand—but because I was a woman who he couldn't live without.

His delicious form pinned me harder against the tiles. His tongue broke the seal of my lips, diving in as if he had perfect right to be there.

And he does.

Over everyone, my body had chosen him.

Just your body?

I couldn't admit my soul might've chosen him, too.

Despite everything, I couldn't win against the truth.

As our tongues danced, my mind skittered from the present to a memory I never knew was there.

"Nila, this is Jethro."

I blinked through my bangs at the tall skinny boy who looked so dapper in a three-piece suit. I found his attire perfect for the beautiful teagarden I sat in with my nanny. She'd told me to dress up in my favourite ensemble—a white four-tiered dress with pink bows and ribbons—and she would take me for my seventh birthday to lunch.

The only stipulation was no one must know. Not even my twin.

My nanny nudged me. "Say hello, Nila."

I looked again at the boy before me. He had black hair, which was combed to the side. Everything about him spoke of stuck-up and resentful but beneath that lurked the same thing I felt.

Obligation.

A small butterfly entered my tummy to think he might feel the same stifling knowledge that we were already destined for a role—regardless if we wanted it or not.

"Do you have a strict daddy, too?" I asked.

"Nila!" My nanny spanked my behind. "Be polite and don't pry."

Jethro narrowed his eyes at my caregiver. He balled his hands and his cheeks turned red from watching her discipline me. I thought he'd run off, his feet shuffled to the teagarden's exit, but then he locked eyes with me. "I have a dad who expects me to be something I'm not."

My childish heart fluttered. "Me, too. I like clothes, but I don't want to be a weaver. I want to be the first girl to prove unicorns exist."

He smirked. "They don't exist."

"Yes, they do."

He shook his head, something cold and hard snapped over his features. "I don't have time for stupid kids." Spinning on his heel, he left me gawking after him. I didn't stop looking until a man with greying hair and black jacket stole his son's hand and disappeared into the sunshine.

We'd met.

How many times had we been introduced? Jethro had said I'd signed something in pink crayon. And now I remembered my seventh birthday luncheon.

Did I feel what I did because he'd been there in my past—like a stain upon my fate? Or was it because some part of me knew the kid I saw that day still existed?

Jethro pulled back, his gaze searching mine. "What? What are you thinking?" His lips were wet from kissing me.

A surge of need took hold of me; I pressed my mouth against his.

He tensed then opened, inviting my tongue to slink into his dark flavour.

I moaned as his hand moved from my cheek to the back of my skull, holding me firm. The moment he'd imprisoned me, his kiss turned into a meal. I was the main course and he did exactly like he'd said in his text as Kite. He kissed me so deeply I had no choice but to inhale his every taste, ensuring he lived forever in my lungs. He made drunken love to my tongue, driving me higher, higher with every silky wet sweep.

My blood raced with need, sending throbbing desire to my clit.

If he continued to kiss me that way, I might come from that alone.

"Truth does more damage than lies," he murmured between kisses.

I'd lost the ability to reply. My body craved his, and all I wanted to do was tear off his sodden clothes and sink onto his cock. I wanted to forget about hostility and death. "Then stop lying," I breathed.

He pulled away, stealing his heat and passion. "I've lied all my life. There is no other way I know." Tucking wet hair behind my ear, he added with finality, "However, you're a novice. You better become talented in the art of deception if you wish to survive my family."

Without a backward glance, he left.

I balled my hands as I stalked the length of the corridor to the French doors leading outside.

I was riled, pissed, and entirely on edge. The molten desire of my almost-orgasm had switched into blistering annoyance. How dare Jethro come into my room unannounced and see me doing something so private? How dare he make me feel embarrassed but also strangely aroused at being caught? And how dare he tell me I sucked at lying, all while I caught him out on every single one!

After he'd left me to get dressed, my mind had created a few snarky comebacks. If he hadn't have run—like he always did—I would've had the last laugh. I was sure of it.

I repeated my retaliation, committing them to memory so I could hurl them in his face next time we had a fight.

I'm already a better liar than you are.

Are you so stupid to believe I don't see you?

Congratulations on winning the hypocritical award.

It'd been too late to say them, but I wouldn't forget. It was time to tell him that I didn't believe in his icy shell anymore. I was still afraid of him—on some level—but it was nothing compared to the sick terror I felt toward his father and brothers.

Crap, did I put it on?

I was so in my head while dressing in a knee-length black dress with a silver mesh jumper that I didn't know if I'd attached my new favourite item.

My fingers moved fugitively to my outer thigh.

Thank God.

I relaxed when my fingers found the small garter I'd made out of Victorian cream lace and pearl buttons. Tight with elastic, it was used to hold up ladies' pantyhose back in the day.

Now I used it to keep my stolen weapon from sight. The holster I'd made suited dresses and skirts but would be no use if I had to wear trousers. No matter, that was what bras were for.

After trying to eavesdrop on Jethro and the unknown woman, I'd given up and snuck to the dining room. There, I stole the ruby-encrusted dirk and placed a bronze figurine in front of the now empty hooks on the wall. I just hoped no one would notice.

"Nila! He said you were coming. I'm so glad."

I spun around. My heart rate increased as Kes strode toward me. "Morning, Kestrel."

He beamed; the hazy air of the ancient Hall blurred his five o' clock shadow and neatly combed tinsel hair. I found it strange that the Hawks were so young, yet they were greying already. Almost as if time stole their youth in payment for their atrocities.

Kes took my shoulders and kissed first my right cheek then my left. "Pleasure to see you this morning. How's your tattoo?"

I pressed my thumb against my index finger, activating the remaining burn from the needle and ink. "It's good."

Kes held out his hand, waiting until I slipped mine in his. He ran a finger gently over Jethro's initials. "Lucky bastard gets to live on your flawless skin." He grinned. He also wore a t-shirt and jodhpurs. Not that the tight trousers fit him nearly as good as Jethro. Kes was too bulky—too rough for something so...refined.

"Guess it's official now."

"Official?"

Kes nodded. "Just between you and me, I didn't think my brother had it in him. He's not coping—in fact, I'd go as far to say he's the worst I've ever seen him—but he's still managing to win against Cut."

I peered at the small tattoo. "What do you mean?"

Kes laughed, brushing away the topic as if it was nothing. "Cut has watched and re-watched the video of Jethro whipping you for the First Debt. Apart from the footage cutting off before he untied you, Cut was pleasantly surprised at how vicious Jethro delivered the punishment."

My heart skipped a beat remembering the agony I'd been in. "He didn't hold anything back, that's for sure."

"Exactly. Which was the best thing for all. He's proven he can be trusted to carry out the remaining debts and that means he's still in the running for inheriting it all."

I stood gobsmacked to learn there was more than just me and debts at play. What else was Jethro fighting for behind the scenes? "Inherit what?"

Hawksridge?

A holiday house?

The diamond mines?

Kes shook his head, tucking my hand into the crook of his arm. "Nothing. We're late. Better head out there before they send in the stable lads."

He took off at a brisk pace. I had no choice but to trot beside him as we traversed the remaining distance and exited the Hall.

Unlike a few days ago, the sunshine was bright and determined. I squinted, raising a hand to shield my eyes in the glare.

Kes asked, "Where is he?"

"Where's who?" I looked around at the sprawling mayhem before us. Normally the large expanse of gravel at the front of the Hall was empty. Not so this morning.

Two large horse trucks blotted out the garden with their black sides and gold-gilded hawk crest. Three 4WDs dotted around, some with doors opened, others with their boots wide and being filled with equipment by quickly moving staff.

Kes snorted. "Who do you think? That brother of mine."

"Oh, him. I guess he had to change."

"Change?" His eyebrows shot up. Cut and Daniel stood off a little way, both dressed in suits with a black leather jacket. They looked so similar, so removed from the normal human race.

"Why would he have to change?"

"Because I took another shower quite by accident," a masculine voice said behind me.

I bristled, not looking over my shoulder. The hair on the back of my neck stood up having Jethro so close. I might've been able to push away my never-enjoyed orgasm, but I didn't want to be too near. "There, he answered your question."

Twisting my fingers from Kes's hold, I said, "Now, if you'll excuse me, I'll go see if the staff needs any help with that picnic basket." Without waiting for permission, I disappeared down the steps and beelined for the two women in white pinafores struggling with a hamper.

Up close, I noticed the 4WDs were the newest model Land Rovers, and the horse trucks were ridiculously glitzy. How many diamonds did the Hawks smuggle to afford all this?

I jumped as a large hand splayed on my lower back.

Jethro didn't look down, preferring to keep his attention on a stable boy carrying saddle blankets. "Did you finish?"

I flinched, trying to move away from his touch. "That's none of your business."

Jethro moved with me, his fingertips digging into the tense muscles at the base of my spine. "None of my business? I think it is." He lowered his voice, his eyes still avoiding mine. "You see, I need to know if the woman who belongs to me is wet and panting for a release. We'll be in public today, Ms. Weaver. Having someone who's as hungry to come as you were in that shower is a matter of public security."

His lips twisted as he finally bowed his head to look into my eyes. "So, tell me...did you finger yourself until your cunt squeezed, all while fantasising it was my cock riding you—my cock slamming inside you? Or did you pretend you weren't that sort of girl and stop playing with yourself?"

"Shut up," I hissed. My eyes darted to the staff who crunched across the gravel in front of us. Jethro wasn't exactly quiet—anyone could hear if they tried hard enough.

Hard.

God, even innocent words painted lewd pictures inside my head. Images of Jethro's hard cock consumed me, and my heart hurled itself against my ribs. All my efforts at pushing down the ache between my legs was in vain. In a few sentences, Jethro had made me sopping wet and trembling with lust.

Again.

Damn man has super powers.

"Answer me, Ms. Weaver."

My hands balled and I snapped, "No. I didn't. Satisfied? I was too angry at you for saying I suck at lying. You're the one who's terrible." I laughed, adding, "Congratulations on winning the hypocritical award." I mentally patted myself on the back for using my remembered reproach.

Jethro rolled his eyes. "How long have you been waiting to use that?"

Damn him, he stole any joy I might've had from one-upping him. His hand moved to clutch my hip, tugging me closer. "By the way, I believe if there is an award for such a thing, it would go to you."

Don't ask. Do not ask why.

It pained me to hold my chin high and not grab his bait, but I managed it. Just.

Jethro huffed, annoyed that I didn't play along. "Fine...if you're going to be like that." Letting me go, he turned to leave but brushed his lips against my ear. "If I'm rock hard and in pain after fantasising of fucking you; if I can barely see straight from imagining my cock sliding in and out of your heat, I'm sure as hell going to grab my dick and throttle it until I come so hard it looks like fucking snow."

Pressing a chaste kiss on my cheekbone, he murmured, "Think about that next time you're riding a showerhead and just call me. I'll put you out of your misery, but it won't come for free."

My mouth hung open. My womb ached in a way I hadn't felt before—heavy, tender—a call for more than just sex but the primal need to have a man fill me.

Jethro's lips twisted into half a smile, then he left, prowling toward his father and Daniel.

My heartbeat roared in my ears. I stood like an idiot as staff continued to load and look at me with an odd expression. Chagrin painted my cheeks, thinking they probably knew exactly what ailed me.

Sex.

I'd been debased to craving sex all while my life hung in some precarious balance.

Sex.

The monstrous need that made graves and debts and tally

marks insubstantial compared to the promise of finding heaven in his arms.

"Nila...you okay?" Kes asked, sidling up to me.

I blew out a breath. I wasn't in the mood to deal with him.

"Yes, I'm fine." Waving my hand at the dwindling chaos, I asked, "What is all this for?"

Kes grinned. "I told you a few days ago. Polo."

For some stupid reason, I thought it would take place on Hawk ground. I looked down at my black dress and thin mesh jumper. The garments weren't enough now the weather had lost its summer warmth and slid straight into autumn chill. "Am I still permitted to come, or—"

"Of course. I told you...staff, prisoners..." He nudged my shoulder in jest. "The more the merrier. Come on, it's time to go." He moved toward his family, leaving me no choice but to follow, regardless that I wanted to move in the opposite direction to Cut Hawk.

Jethro never took his golden eyes off me as I stopped before them. Kes clapped his hands together. "Ready to get this mayhem on the road?"

Cut rubbed his jaw, looking me up and down. "Would you care to ride with me, my dear?" He pulled free a black handkerchief from his pocket, dangling it between his fingers. His smile was cold and sadistic. "I'll have to blindfold you so you won't know the way off the estate, but you're welcome to the luxury of the vehicle."

I hated that he came across so cordial—almost grandfatherly.

Jethro muttered, "She'll be fine with Wings and me."

My eyes widened. "You're travelling with the horse?"

Jethro nodded. "Wings hates being confined. It kills him to be in the dark with no escape."

My heart flipped. How could he say something so caring about an animal, yet be so strange about everything else?

Cut laughed—it held an edge of warning. "I expected you to grow out of that stupid notion, Jet."

Jethro's hands fisted. "Sorry to disappoint."

Cut glared daggers at his oldest son. I stood poised to jump out of the way, just waiting for a fight to break out or some accusation thrown that might hint at whom Jethro truly was. It seemed his entire family knew and constantly used his weakness, condition—whatever he had—as a warning and an aid to heel.

Breaking the tense silence, I said, "I'd rather travel with the horses."

Cut stopped trying to kill his oldest by death stare and turned his blazing eyes on me.

I rushed, "Plus, I won't have to wear a blindfold as the truck doesn't have windows."

The thought of being cooped up in a dark space while weaving and swaying in traffic turned my stomach. The symptoms would be eerily similar to vertigo. But I would rather go with Jethro over Cut any day.

Cut nodded slowly. "Fine. We'll see you at the match."

Daniel shifted closer. "That's a pity." His unhinged soul glimmered in his eyes. His dark hair didn't have any of the silver tinsel that Jethro and Kes had, but all three of the Hawk boys had inherited their colouring from their father. Daniel's hair had thinned, whereas I knew from experience that Jethro's was thick and entirely too enticing.

I know because his head has been between my legs, licking me while I dug my fingers—

Don't think about that.

Once again, I had to shove away the wetness Jethro had conjured and shut down my bodily cravings.

Daniel smirked. His pristine suit, diamond pin just like Jethro's, and polished boots made him seem the perfect catch for any eager woman—until he opened his mouth, of course. "I rather enjoyed our car ride together last time."

A chill flash-froze my system. He meant the car ride onto the estate the night I had arrived. Jethro had drugged me—bastard. And I could still feel Daniel's probing nasty fingers on my core.

Jethro growled, "Enough." Leaving his family, he grabbed my wrist and stomped toward the closest horse truck. "Time to go."

I couldn't stop goosebumps scattering over my arms at the horrible reminder of Daniel's groping.

Silently, Jethro guided me to the side of the truck and opened a small door camouflaged by decals of his family crest. The entire transport was rich and gleaming with money.

As I stepped into the musky warmth of horse and hay, I said, "The night you stole me. Why did you drug me?"

Jethro froze, blotting out the light from the small door and instantly making the large vehicle claustrophobic. "I did it to make it easier."

"On who? You?"

He slammed the door closed, leaving us in gloomy light. "On you. I made it so you wouldn't fight and cause yourself harm."

I crossed my arms, a horrible suspicion filling me. "Wrong. I think you did it for you. So you wouldn't have to face my tears or put up with my panic."

Jethro shoved me out of the way, moving down the gangway between the two stalls. I spun around, following him. Two horses' rumps faced us with food bales secured within grazing distance and hay on the floor.

"Who exactly are you, Jethro Hawk?"

Jethro ran his hand along the horse's ebony side. My stomach fluttered to witness the sudden softness in him and it turned my heart to mush to see the animal's reaction to his master.

Its ears swivelled in welcome while its flank twitched for more. A gentle huffing sound came from velvet nostrils—a sigh of contentment.

"I'm the man who does what he needs to, but you already know that." Giving me a backward glance, he didn't stop until he passed the two horses and entered the small space at the front of the stalls. In the spacious compartment, there were two seats bolted to the floor facing the horses. Saddles, blankets, and bridles hung from hooks. Every wall and space had been utilised to house horsey paraphernalia.

Windows let natural light in from above, along with a skylight, but they were too high to see.

"Let it go, Ms. Weaver." Sitting down, he pointed at the identical seat. "Sit down before you fall down. Can never be too careful with that damn vertigo of yours."

I sneered at him. "Bet it makes you feel stronger knowing I have an ailment that can strike me down at any time."

He sniffed. "You're right. It does." His eyes narrowed. "Now. Sit."

The truck suddenly rumbled and coughed as the engine turned over. The horses behind me nickered. One stomped its metal hoof on the floor.

I turned around and sat quickly, just before the lumbering vehicle shot into gear.

Fumbling with my seatbelt—hoping it would be strong enough to keep me upright if I happened to suffer a bad spell—I yelped when a long grey nose nudged my leg.

Jethro chuckled. "For someone who says she's in-tune with the law of right and wrong, you don't seem to have experience around animals."

He smiled as the black beast in front of him arched its neck, trying to get at his master.

I had no reply and sat very still as the animal in front of me nudged my leg again. In one demanding move, the horse shoved its way into my heart and I slid straight into love with the beautiful dapple grey. Its huge glossy eyes spoke of ancient worlds and kindness, and I had a vivid recall of my love of unicorns when I was younger.

I'd always wanted a pony—as most girls did. But living in central London and being daughter to a man focused only on textiles meant my dreams were directed into more practical things.

My memory of meeting Jethro with my nanny as chaperone came back.

I reached out to stroke the nose of my newfound love. "Unicorns *do* exist."

My heart swelled as the horse snuffled my knee, its forelock flopping over one eye and catching in its thick eyelashes.

Jethro stiffened. "What did you just say?"

I glanced over, never taking my hand from my warm companion. I waited to see if recognition would flare in his eyes. Did he remember that brief meeting, too?

When I didn't answer, he snapped, "Well?"

I shook my head. "Doesn't matter." Bringing the conversation back to a subject he obviously adored, I asked, "What's his name?" I scratched the horse between its eyes, straining against my seatbelt to get closer.

Jethro never took his eyes off me. Something happened…something I couldn't explain. The harshness, the frost in his mannerisms…they seemed to thaw a little. His head tilted, looking less tense and arctic than normal.

Butterflies spawned in my belly to see yet another side of him. Being around these beasts did something. It did more than relax him—it gave him a place to hide. He seemed to feed off the simplistic animal gentleness.

He took his time answering, but when he did, his voice was soft, beguiling. "Not him, her. Her name is Warriors Don't Cry. But her nickname is Moth."

Moth.

Soft-winged and subtly stunning. It was perfect. I wanted to keep her.

"And the other one?"

Jethro sat still, drinking in the black beast before him. "This is Fly Like The Wind. But he's my wings, as I cannot fly, so I call him that."

So, that's Wings.

The one who carried Jethro away when he'd reached all

that he could bear. A wash of gratefulness filled me to think that he had something that didn't judge—didn't try to control him with family tradition.

Perhaps, I should learn from Wings. Perhaps, I should look past the hatred and despair and look deeper. There was something redeemable inside Jethro.

I know it.

"When will you let me see?"

Jethro's nostrils flared. "Pardon?"

Silent courage filled me from touching Moth, and for the first time, I laid it out plainly with no anger or resentment. "When will you tell me what the debts mean to your family? What is the point of all of this? How have you gotten away with it for so long—because the Debt Inheritance wouldn't hold up in any court of law. How did your family go from serving my ancestors to owning..." I waved my arm at the horses, encompassing the world outside the truck and Hawksridge.

I should've stopped there, but I had one last question. A burning question that I would give anything to know. "Why can't I hate you for what you are? Why can't I stop myself from wanting you? And why am I still here? Playing these games and believing that in the end, it won't be my head in a basket and you holding an axe, but something entirely different?"

Thick silence fell between us. Only the snuffles of Wings and Moth broke the tension clouding thicker with every breath.

Finally, Jethro murmured, "If I do the job I'm supposed to, you won't earn a single answer to your questions, nor learn anything about me."

"You're not doing a good job then," I whispered. "Because I already know more about you than you think."

He rolled his shoulders. "I have no doubt that in time you'll learn everything you want to know."

"Including your secrets?" I whispered again, filling my voice with feeling. "Will you trust me enough to show me the truth?"

He looked away, tugging the forelock of his horse. "That,

Ms. Weaver, is like blindly believing in unicorns. You can't be mad at me, when in the end, you find out they never existed."

I gasped.

He *did* remember.

He murmured beneath his breath, "I suggest you focus on reality and stop looking for magic in a world that only wants to destroy you."

Silence fell like a heavy curtain, slicing between us and putting an end to all connection.

We stayed quiet the remainder of the journey.

POLO WAS THE only contact sport I enjoyed.

Hunting was a solo pastime—something that was both a hobby and a curse. But riding and being around horses had been my one saving grace as a kid.

Still was.

I permitted myself a brief second where I leaned against Wings and breathed in his musky scent. My heart rate hadn't equalized ever since we'd arrived an hour ago.

What the hell had happened in the carrier coming here? Why had Nila chosen that exact moment to bombard me with questions that had every power to skin me alive?

Jasmine had been wrong to say I had to make Nila fall in love with me. I'd tried—I'd spun some concoction in the shower about her fabricating a web and capturing a Hawk. It'd sounded ridiculous and so unlike me that Nila's eyes had widened, noticing my slip.

There would be no seducing her with deception. No winning her with tricks. If I wanted her to fall in love with me—to grant me another way of fixing myself and being able to survive the next ten months until my inheritance took place—I would have to let her inside me.

Allow her free reign to my complications and disease. I would have to let her *see* me. All of me.

And I didn't have the power to do that. Regardless of what Jasmine thought.

Sighing heavily, I looked out over the large grassy field. Polo players were dotted about, tending to their horses beside a mismatch of caravans, floats, and cars. Tyre tracks had squelched through sodden grass, turning green to mud.

A little distance away, the polo arena was pristine and untouched, just waiting for galloping horses to tear it into a brown mess. And just beyond was a movable grandstand taking centre stage—looming over the field, offering fabulous viewpoints of the soon-to-start match.

Men and women milled about, finding their seats in the tiered chairs or making their way to the tents below which housed gourmet snacks and exclusive wines. There were no hotdog stands or cheap beer in plastic cups. These events were for the elite of England—families with a bank balance in excess of ten million pounds. Caviar, foie gras, and salmon mousse were on the finger-menu along with some of Hawksridge's wine and vintage beer.

Nothing inferior was allowed.

I peered harder, trying to spot Nila in her black dress amongst the teaming mass of spectators.

Nothing.

What do you expect?

Kes would've taken her to the reserved tent on the outskirts of the food and grandstand area. We had our own private gazebo where guests were encouraged to socialise. We also offered uncut diamonds at rock bottom prices to all those we trusted.

Not only was polo beneficial for my mind-set, but it was also a brilliant day for our bank account.

When we'd arrived, I'd deliberated on how best to avoid Nila while taking her to where she needed to be. All my worrying was for nothing as Kes had appeared the moment I'd backed Wings down the ramp and hobbled him to the tethering post.

Moth was his horse, but he summoned a stable boy to attend to her while he offered to take Nila to the viewing area.

With a weighty look at me, Nila had nodded and disappeared with my brother. I hated that she went with him so easily, but at the same time, I was happy to see her go. It gave me time to get my head on straight before the match started.

Hopefully, once I'd had a day on the field with the sound of racing hooves in my ears and power in my veins, I would be better.

I would be stronger.

Moth nudged my spine. I twisted to pat the dapple grey. Nila's reaction to the horse hadn't escaped me. She'd melted the moment Moth had demanded attention.

I doubted she'd ever had pets growing up—her father seemed too consumed with his empire, and I wouldn't be surprised if he put his children to work the moment they understood how to wield a pair of scissors.

The Weavers had always been the same—treating their offspring like slave-labour—getting wealthy off the toils of family who were denied a childhood.

My heart suddenly warmed. *Maybe I can give Nila what she's been missing?*

Kes had no affinity with Moth. She was a good horse, came from a prestigious breeder, and the most tolerant of mares. But she was just a tool to Kes.

What would Nila do if I gave her Moth?

Would she open her heart more readily? Would she see I only meant to do what was required of me while trying to protect her from everything in my power?

Standing between the two horses, I scratched each behind their ears.

Moth was soft and kind and reliable. But she was no match for Wings. Where Moth was eager to please and fast to react, Wings had a heart similar to mine—an imposter's heart where obedience was required but breaking the rules was the only way to survive.

Rubbing Wings down, I quickly saddled him and held his head while I fed the bit into his mouth. He stomped, pawing at the ground.

I could've had the stable hands tend to him.

But I wanted to do it.

It relaxed me, and with Nila in my life, I needed all the relaxation I could get.

The sun was out and today could be a good day. If only there was one other person here, it could've been perfect.

Pulling out my phone, I called my sister.

It rang a few times too long and the familiar panic where her safety was concerned came over me.

"Jethro? Why are you calling me—isn't the match about to start?" Her soft voice came down the phone, sliding straight into my ear.

"You really should've come with us, Jaz. The sun is out and the sky is crystal clear."

"Maybe next time."

Maybe next time.

Her favourite expression.

Only thing was there was never a next time because she would refuse to go on that outing, too.

I sighed, running a hand through my hair. "Okay, well I better go. Just wanted to check on you and let you know I'll win again and give you the crystal vase or whatever shit they give us."

Jaz giggled. "Okay. Be safe. And remember what I said. Try to figure out a way to face what you are. No more 'fixing'. Get that woman to love you then you can hide again."

I didn't want to tell her that it'd gotten to the point where I could no longer hide—even from myself.

"Sure, easy done." My tone dripped with sarcasm. Before she could respond, I added, "See you when we get back tonight."

Hanging up, I looked at the screen.

I spotted Kestrel striding back alone across the field. I

knew he would've stopped to place a wager on our team in the betting gazebo.

My stomach tensed.

Nila would be on her own. Cut and Daniel would never leave the gambling tent, so I just had to hope to God that whoever was mingling in our private space would leave her alone. She'd be surrounded by Black Diamond brothers peddling illegal stones. She would be untouchable under their protection. Not to mention imprisoned if she had a lunatic idea of running.

Escaping us was never that easy. There was a reason why her ancestors never fled.

My fingers drummed against my phone. Going against all better judgement, I opened a new message and typed:

Kite007: *I'm assuming you haven't replied because of what happened the other day. But perhaps now you're ready to talk. You have questions. Lots of questions. What if I told you it would be easier for me to answer this way than any other?*

My heart rate spiked, hovering my finger over the send button.

What am I doing?

Not only was it a disaster waiting to happen to write things down for anyone to read, but I had no intention of answering any of the questions she'd asked in the truck.

I always knew Nila would eventually find out that I was Kite. Hell, I wasn't exactly subtle—but I'd always planned to let the ruse die a death when she did. It wasn't needed anymore. I'd had enough enlightenment of her thoughts. And having the ability of talking this way only made the connection between us harder to ignore.

It was too dangerous. Secrets were too easily shared when hidden behind closed doors. Things I never intended to say suddenly had the audacity to find their way into a faceless message.

My fingers hovered, tingling with the urge to press send.

Do it.

I did.

"Ready to kit up?" Kes asked, shrugging out of his over-shirt and revealing the team colours below.

My temper flared to think Nila had feelings for him.

Feelings for my damn brother.

Feelings that I'd made happen by letting her chase the wrong path.

"Yes. I'm ready." Depositing my phone into the saddlebag, I unfolded my matching colours and slipped them on.

Another reason I'd wanted to kill off Kite was to give Nila no choice but to be honest to my face. I didn't want her running to Kes. I didn't want him anywhere near her.

She's mine, goddammit.

With a shaky hand, I tied my cravat and shoved Nila Weaver unsuccessfully from my thoughts.

Game time.

It's time to win.

There were very few places where I could be completely free.

In fact, I could count three in total.

One, when I went to see Jasmine.

Two, when I took Wings for a gallop away from cameras and family and obligations of being someone I wasn't.

And three, when I let down every guard on the polo field.

I fed off people's energy. I drank the players' nervousness, revelled in their tingling excitement, and for once, I was grateful for the disease I lived with.

We took our positions.

In my hand, I held my reins and a short braided whip. My cream jodhpurs, polished black knee-high boots, and gold velvet waistcoat over the billowing old-world sleeves of my white shirt made me feel like a knight about to joust for some fair maiden's affection.

Kes grinned, sitting atop Moth and her nineteen hands of

elegant muscle. Wings was only eighteen hands high, but he had something Moth didn't. He had ferocity that rippled around him. Other horses felt it. Their nostrils flared, their eyes tracking him wherever he went.

He was an anomaly.

Just like his owner.

The Hawks were well known for hosting polo matches and commandeering the rules of any game we were invited to. Common rules that we broke were: no horses to be higher than sixteen hands, and multiple mounts per player.

I flatly refused to play on any other horse but Wings. Therefore, the rest of the players were forced to follow my lead.

Another rule we tweaked was to have a longer half-time. Instead of the stupid length of ten-minutes, we stipulated an hour—the horses needed it, seeing as we didn't change mounts.

And an hour would be perfect for what I had planned.

I had every intention of seeking out Nila and finishing what she started this morning. What I wanted to do to her would be a fuck-load better than any showerhead.

The umpire cantered onto the pitch. The game we were about to play would be fast, brutal, and mentally draining. Men were known to break legs from an incorrectly wielded hook or concussion from falling mid-flight.

The umpire spun his speech while everyone nodded but didn't listen. We all focused on the hard white ball in his hand.

The moment the ball hit the turf, it would be on.

The horses jostled and pawed, tasting imminent war.

After the umpire had finished his spiel, the other two members of our team came forward. In a close circle, we slapped mallets in a final hurrah before kick-off.

"I got your back," Kes said, his eyes glowing beneath the shadow of his helmet. His matching waistcoat held the number four. His role was to protect the leader, stop others from scoring, and had no restrictions on where he could go on the field.

I nodded, tugging at my cuffs and curling my gloved fingers firmly around my mallet. "First play is offensive. Steal the ball on the throw-in and slam this chukker so we can crush their hopes."

I wore the number three on our team. My role was tactical leader and the best player—it wasn't ego, just simple fact.

My teammates nodded and touched their visors in acknowledgement.

Excitement bubbled in my chest. It was such a foreign elusive emotion that I quickly became drunk on it.

Trotting to our places, I smiled at Kes, "Ready, brother?" Out here there were no his or mine. No firstborn bullshit. No diamond smuggling or family legacy.

Just speed and accuracy.

Kes smirked. "Ready to whoop your ass."

"We're on the same team, moron."

He laughed. "On here we are, but we both know we can still lose even when on the same side."

Wasn't that the God-awful truth?

We were flesh and blood. By right, we should have each other's back—yet we'd been bred to compete against one another. If I were suddenly to 'disappear or have an accident', Kes would take my place and rule.

Not because he wanted it—he already knew I would give him more than our father ever did—but because he was the substitute.

Born as a plan B.

At least there had been some planning in his conception. Daniel, however, was the accident. Not required and definitely not wanted.

Kes held up his mallet. I did the same and we swatted a salute. "Let the best man win."

I nodded. "Best man."

Two minutes later the bugle sounded, the ball flew, and the world ceased to exist as I threw myself into the match.

Nila

I'D LIVED A life of privileged upbringing.

I'd been pampered and spoiled; lavished with praise when I followed my father's wishes and began sewing at barely ten-years-old.

Vaughn and I lived a life of decadence and culture.

Theatre productions, pottery classes, language and disposition tutors—even fencing lessons.

Thanks to my upbringing, I had talents I would never use, and a brain cluttered with useless education.

I'd always felt as if I'd been born into the elite. Despite working twelve-hour days and toiling in workshops, I didn't begrudge our family's business from absorbing my life and turning me into yet another cog in the Weaver Empire.

I was rewarded handsomely, earned pleasure from seeing something grow, and never wanted a different life.

However, there were a few times when I our wealth made me self-conscious. I found it hard to make genuine friends at school. Stipulations came with any connection, and I became the girl invited to a sleep-over or party, only because I came with a credit card that brought unlimited pizza and drinks.

It was yet another reason why I'd gravitated toward my twin. V had the same problem. He'd been crushed when he fell for a girl, only for her to break it off the moment he bought her the necklace she'd been begging for.

We were both hurt by others and became sheltered because of it. Money was supposed to make life easy but it was more of a curse than a blessing. And I'd never felt it so acutely as I stood on the side-lines of the polo match and watched the man who owned me galloping up and down.

Jethro looked...*free.*

For the first time since I'd met him, he looked...*happy.*

His face was blank of all responsibility.

His body liquid and graceful.

His eyes warm and golden as he leant over the withers of his horse and whacked the ball so hard it skidded like a comet down the field.

Out there he escaped everything he lived with and the hatred I felt toward him—the disgust and despair at finding my family buried on the moor—softened.

I couldn't hate someone who lived in the same cage as I did. I couldn't hate someone for being a simple tool for his father. And I definitely couldn't hate someone who spent his whole life looking for a way out.

Before, when we'd arrived, and sunlight had streamed in as the ramp of the truck opened, I'd suffered a relentless need to run. People and open spaces and cars all waited to help me flee from the Hawks. It would be so easy—wouldn't it? To somehow escape the attention of my guards and dart to a bystander with tales of ludicrous debts and inhumane treatment.

I could be saved.

I could go home.

But I'd paused and asked questions that I doubted I would ever find answers to. Why did my mother, grandmother, and great-grandmother stay? Surely, they would've found opportunities such as this and escaped?

I knew the reasons for my procrastination: I wanted to be the last Weaver taken. But my ancestors...what was their reasoning? Did they perhaps share the same goal I did—did they believe they could change their fate or murder the Hawks instead?

Did they fail?

Am I destined to fail?

The *smack* of the ball resonated like thunder as Kes hooked his stick around an opposing player, giving Jethro time to swoop in and shoot the ball toward the goal.

My heart raced as Jethro's firm legs wrapped around his galloping steed. His gloved hands wielded his stick like a dangerous weapon, while his concentration level sent a flush of wetness between my legs. I wanted to become so precious to him that he looked at me with the same unbarred happiness.

My wonderings of boosting a car and fleeing faded with every heartbeat. Watching Jethro be free gave me the truth I'd been looking for.

I was an idiot to stay. To not take the fateful opportunity.

But I'd come to the conclusion: I would rather be an idiot and win, than a coward and run.

I didn't think I would like polo. I couldn't have been more wrong. I'd never witnessed something so intense, so visceral.

The rumbling earthquakes formed by eight horses thundering past would forever live inside my soul. My dreams would always conjure Jethro how he looked right now—capable, joyous, completely perfect in every way.

Another strike and the ball shot past, followed by a mass of muscle and men. The clatter of sticks colliding and grunts of players fully in the throes of sport sent my tummy frothing with bubbles.

I'd been told to stay in the gazebo under the watchful eye of Flaw. But I grew bored and resentful as Flaw orchestrated a magical event of disappearing diamonds followed by huge sums of cash changing hands.

The moment the bugle had sounded, I'd rushed out to witness the game. And now, watching the sea of sweat-glistening men, I'd found heaven.

Jethro suddenly looked directly at me. His arm jerked,

pulling the reins tight and causing Wings to toss his head mid-gallop. My entire body tingled as Jethro just stared. We held eye contact far longer than was safe, and the moment he was too far away, I felt bereaved—as if he'd stolen my heart and taken it flying up the field with him.

I wanted to chase after him. I wanted to steal Moth from Kes and fight *beside* Jethro, rather than against him. I wanted the rush, the fear, the intoxicating knowledge of invincibility. But most of all, I wanted what Jethro had

. . .

freedom.

I wanted to be as happy as him. To be at peace like him.

I wanted to stare into his eyes while he was truly himself—no games, no lies, no debts.

Kes suddenly stood up in his stirrups, high fiving Jethro for effortlessly scoring another goal.

Jethro smiled. He positively glowed. He was resplendent.

Then the bugle trumpeted and the game began anew.

His happiness turned sharp with aggression. He and Wings moved as one—gliding so smoothly it looked almost telepathic—pirouetting mid-gallop to intercept the ball and steal it. Jethro…or should I say Kite…dominated the entire game.

He truly is one of a kind.

Tears came to my eyes as I finally acknowledged what lived beneath my hate.

My lust was slowly evolving, slowly growing. And I wished I had the power to stop it.

But I had as much power as stopping my heart from tripping into love as I did from tearing myself from the match. I fell into disgrace.

By the end of the first half, my knickers were damp and my heart ached. Every muscle hummed as if I'd been beaten, and I couldn't stop the small voice repeating over and over:

You're falling for him.

You're falling for him.

You're falling for him.
I wasn't.
I couldn't.
I'm not!

But no matter how hard I tried, the words enemy, tormentor, and adversary ceased to have meaning.

Other words came instead: ally, accomplice…friend.

When the bugle blared, signalling half-time, I sagged in relief. I needed to find a cool dark place and glue myself back together. I couldn't let anyone—especially Jethro—see me in such broken pieces.

Out of the corner of my eye, I noticed Wings cantering toward me. Jethro sat proud and regal atop him, his golden eyes blazing with passion and need.

My stomach somersaulted.

He wants you.

I shook my head. He couldn't touch me. Not when I was so…delicate. There would be no way I could halt the mess inside and find my way back to sanity if he touched me.

Run.

It's the only way.

Leaving the border of the arena, I darted through the crowds and away from my feelings and the man I couldn't face.

Ladies giggled as the gates were opened to carry on the time-old tradition of stomping on the divots caused by the horse's hooves. Music floated across the sun-drenched field from large speakers.

I left it all behind.

Walking briskly past the Hawk's private gazebo, I caught the eye of Flaw. He crooked his finger, motioning me to go inside. I shook my head and pointed to the perimeter of the grandstand, indicating I needed some space.

He frowned then weaved through customers, who'd no doubt bought a smuggled diamond or two, and made his way toward me.

No, I need time alone.

I broke into a jog.

My ballerina shoes coasted over the thick grass whereas ladies in heels struggled, their pretty shoes sinking into the mud.

Before the match had started, I'd been in my element—drinking in the designs of their gowns and improving on styles that intrigued me. All around, women clustered in beautiful fabrics, laughing beneath hats that dripped with organza and hand-stitched lace flowers.

Now those same fashions were in my way as I wriggled through the dispersing crowd and ducked down the side of the grandstand.

No one disturbed me as I kept my eyes trained on the ground and didn't stop jogging until I rounded the back of the tiered seating and disappeared into the hushed world of scaffolding and churned earth.

The second the shadows claimed me, I breathed a sigh of relief.

Thank God.

There was no one here apart from stacked chairs and boxes of polo equipment.

I could let go of my iron control and indulge in a moment of self-pity. I was screwed up, and I had to find some way of fixing myself.

You're not falling for him.

You're not.

I found a place to recline and hung my head in my hands. "You can't be, Nila. Think of your family. Think about why you're here. About your promise."

My voice fell around me like the tears I wanted to shed.

You know how wrong all of this is.

You know what he means to do.

I groaned, digging my fingers into my hair and tugging. A single tear rolled down my nose. It hovered on the tip like a jewel, before splashing to the dirt below.

At least I was hidden. Jethro wouldn't find me, and by the

time we returned to Hawksridge, I would've torn out my heart and destroyed all notions of having feelings for him.

I would do what was necessary. What was right.

I just hope I have the strength to do it over and over again.

Taking a deep breath, I drifted further into the gloom. I liked my hiding spot. I never wanted to leave.

You can hide from him, but you can't hide from your feelings.

"Shut up," I scolded myself. "Don't think about him. Not anymore."

"If it's me you're thinking about—I command you to ignore your advice."

My heart flew into my mouth. I spun around.

Big mistake.

Jethro stood behind me. Scuffs stained his tan jodhpurs and mud splattered his polished high boots. He'd rolled up the cuffs of his billowy sleeve shirt and removed the velvet waistcoat revealing the shadows of his stomach beneath the translucent fabric. His five o'clock shadow was rough and ragged while the bones of his face spoke of stark desire and even starker emotion.

My entire body stiffened. My lungs refused to operate, suffocating me inch by inch.

His eyes met mine and everything we'd been avoiding crackled with uncontrolled potency. The unseen force was tangible, powerful—almost visible with ribbons of lust that pebbled my nipples and sent a clench of furious desire through my core.

His breathing escalated as we stood locked in place, bound together by the swirling cloud of need. We didn't speak—we *couldn't* speak.

His tongue licked his bottom lip.

Our eyes refused to unlock. The more we stared, the deeper our connection became.

I couldn't look away.

His smell of musk and leather shoved me from my dangerous precipice, and I slid down and down into scandal.

I'm not falling for him.
I've already fallen.

Jethro sucked in a breath, his fingers opening and closing by his sides.

I couldn't go on like this. Feeling this way. Hating and loving this way.

I couldn't *lie* anymore.

My heartbeat drummed in my ears, behind my eyes, in my every fingertip. My tattoo blazed, the diamond collar tightened, and I knew out of everything that had happened, after everything the Hawks had done, this was the moment where I lost.

Right here.

Right now.

This was why I couldn't run.

This desire.

This fate.

I fell in love.

I turned my back on everyone but myself.

I gave up any notion of ever leaving.

I moaned low in my chest.

Such a simple, subtle whisper.

But it was the starting gun to the explosion that was imminent between us.

The air went up in flames, gusts of heat erupted as passion singed my very soul.

Jethro moved.

He propelled himself into me, his large hands capturing my cheeks and holding me prisoner as he walked me backward until I stumbled against the scaffolding.

His touch was a bonfire. His hold was freedom and a cage all at once.

His forehead crashed against mine, his nose kissing my nose, his breath replacing my breath.

In that simple fusion of flavour and souls, we gave up. We gave in. We answered the same pounding conclusion—the same unmentionable dilemma.

We can't do this anymore.

His head tilted and I trembled in his hold as his fingers dug painfully into my cheekbones. I panted for his kiss. I moaned for it. Almost cried for it.

But he paused for an eternity, breathing hard and fast as if he couldn't believe the preciousness of what was occurring.

This was a gift. A charm. A wish come true.

I'd become enraptured by my capturer. My tormentor. My would-be murderer. I only had eyes for him. My heart only beat for him.

Where does that leave me?

What does this mean?

Jethro groaned, his touch trembling as if he'd heard my silent questions.

I should've had more self-control. I should've found a way to stop this.

But I shoved away my fears and willingly slid the final slope into madness.

I arched my chin, grazing my lips against his.

He froze.

Then, he melted.

His fingers slinked from my cheeks to the back of my skull. I cried out as his tongue tore into my mouth and his hands fisted in my hair. With fingers full of my black strands, he tugged my head back, forcing me to open wider, kiss deeper—give him everything.

I'd like to say I retained some resemblance of myself. I'd like to admit that, while I'd fallen, I still knew who I was.

But that would've been a lie.

There was no me without him.

No Nila without Jethro.

No Threads without Kite.

I knew that now.

And it butchered me in ways no threats or torture ever could.

Tears leaked from my eyes as our lips danced and tongues tangoed.

Our murmurs and moans intertwined until the serenade of our desire overshadowed the music from outside and our racing heartbeats. Every sweep of his taste left a glowing fire around my heart, my skin, my soul.

He demanded everything but gave more in return.

In my arms, I held the *real* Jethro. The one I'd seen but never believed was true. He was strong and brilliant and kind.

And he cared for me. So much.

Never untangling our lips, Jethro bent a little and gathered the material of my dress. Shoving it upward, he groaned as I wriggled and helped, forcing the fabric to bunch around my waist.

He froze as he found the lace garter and wickedly sharp dirk. His eyebrow raised; very slowly, he slid the blade from against my flesh and held it in his fingertips.

I tensed, daring him to berate me for such precautions.

His mouth opened to speak then his eyes darkened with approval. "Use this wisely—if you need to." Throwing the blade to jab upright in the dirt, he murmured, "But I'll never give you a reason to use it on me."

We fell together again. Our lips melded into one slippery seal. I conquered his body—running my fingers over every inch of him. His nipples peaked as I stroked them beneath his shirt and his back bowed as I reached down and cupped his hot erection.

Sweat slicked our skin as our finesse perished, turning into fumbling urgency.

With swift hands, Jethro shoved my knickers to my ankles and waited as I kicked them away.

His eyes incinerated me as he grabbed my arse and hoisted me, pinning me in his arms against the scaffolding.

His lips claimed mine again, eating my every moan. I pressed my fingers into his rock hard biceps, relishing in his strength. Then I lowered my touch to undo the button and zipper of his jodhpurs.

His forehead furrowed as my fingers slid inside the dark heat of his boxer-briefs and captured his scalding cock.

"I'm going to fill you," he murmured, thrusting into my hand. "I'm going to give you what I've been told all my life I couldn't give."

I bit my lip as I fumbled with pushing the tight material over his hips. I didn't need to ask what he couldn't give me.

It was obvious.

It wasn't physical or even emotional.

It was more than that.

The catalyst of what made us human.

The ability to adore.

"I want to spill inside you, Nila."

My eyes snapped shut. My body sung with dark music, twisting me, moulding me into some wanton creature. I opened my eyes and kissed him. "What are you waiting for?"

He positioned me so he could hold me with one arm. With his free hand, Jethro cupped my cheek, running a calloused finger across my lips. "Nothing...not anymore."

My blood turned into a river of molten hunger.

With fumbling hands, I freed his cock, running my thumb over his slippery crown.

Jethro threw his head back, rocking into my palm.

My mouth watered to lick at the glistening sweat at the base of his throat.

I stroked him, harder and faster as pleasure hijacked my body.

Jethro shook his head, his eyes squeezed closed. "Stop. I'm too close...too fucking close." His hands clutched at my arse again, spreading me shamelessly, presenting my wet pussy that was so close to his cock.

"Guide me inside you." His eyes flashed. "Please, Nila. Let me fuck you."

Unashamedly, I opened my legs wider.

Jethro breathed in my ear. "Today, you're all mine."

I bit his lobe, clamping my teeth harder than I intended. He flinched as I whispered, "Not just for today."

His body shuddered. His movements became jilted and eager.

Without a sound, I positioned his cock between my legs and lowered a fraction, angling him inside.

Oh, God.

My eyes rolled back as Jethro growled, "Fuck, you feel so right."

The words wrenched me from my stupor, granting me another clue.

I didn't feel good or wet or warm—or any manner of things a man might say to a woman as he entered her.

I felt *right*.

Right to him.

Home to him.

Sucking in a breath, he thrust, sliding inside me.

The friction of the scaffold behind me bruised my spine as Jethro held me firmer in his arms. Instinct made me wrap my legs around his hips as he buried himself deeper and deeper.

He groaned as I rocked on him. My desire stole the pain of his size, twisting it into a heady aphrodisiac that made me cry out with longing.

Every inch of him invaded me—stretching me, claiming me.

Jethro bit my neck, trailing teeth down oversensitive skin. "I belong in you."

I shuddered as his hips pulsed. I couldn't agree more.

His arms tightened as he secured me in his grip; his legs spread further to balance. I knew he was preparing himself for an unrelenting pace, and my unrequited orgasm bloomed into being, eager, aching.

He thrust particularly hard, his muscled stomach kissing mine with every stroke.

My heart twisted deliciously. I hooked my arms around his neck, holding on and presenting myself completely to this man who held my soul.

Then everything else faded.

Hawks, Weavers, and all things twisted between us.

It was just me and Jethro. Heat and need.

He drove into me with powerful strokes, pressing me relentlessly against the scaffolding. My shoulder blades screamed for mercy, but my pussy begged for more.

I wanted punishment for falling for him.

I needed chastising for going against everything I'd believed.

Jethro seemed to understand. Our eyes locked and we drove each other on. Riding each other's body, hard and brutal.

I lost myself in the rhythm, sinking my fingers into his thick hair.

Tugging his mouth to mine, I kissed him deep.

Our breaths became one; the ache inside my womb increased until I flamed with urgency to shatter. The pain of riding on the knife-edge of an orgasm layered the pleasure, turning it into a sharp almost unbearable delight.

Jethro dug his fingers into my arse, driving harder. His voice betrayed where his thoughts were. "Only once." He grunted as he increased his rhythm. "Only once can I be this free."

I couldn't think straight. I was entranced, mesmerised. *What does he mean?*

A loud groan wrenched from Jethro's chest as his cock thickened inside me. His shoulders bunched as he bounced me faster in his arms.

My muscles tightened as bands of bliss prepared to release.

Jethro growled, capturing my mouth. His tongue pulsed savagely in time with his hips. He stole my thoughts. I lavished in the rushing hotness of my blood. Gushing, pushing into my core.

My heart bucked in my chest; I couldn't get enough oxygen. I moaned, tearing myself from his lips to bite his shoulder. His arms trembled holding my weight. He sucked in a breath. "Fuck, Nila. I can't—I'm gonna…"

I knew where he was. He was in the dark abyss—the depth of pain where he normally lived. Only in the darkness existed stars and comets and lightning bolts just waiting to shatter and shower us with light.

"Give me everything…" My legs curled around his hips, driving him up the final cliff. I impaled myself as hard and as deep as I could.

"Christ." His face tensed. He gave up.

I followed him.

Our rhythm turned frenzied, fucking and rutting and taking everything we could.

"I'm with you," I murmured just as my orgasm stole my voice and hurled me into the cacophony of explosions.

Jethro's eyes opened; we drowned in each other. His golden irises glimmered with everything he couldn't say. The truth was a blazing thing, sharpening the bands of release, twisting my orgasm into something catastrophic.

I screamed.

It was the only thing I could do to expel the pleasure inside.

I was swept away on a galaxy of popping stars. Starburst after starburst, comet after comet. I shattered utterly and completely.

Jethro cried out, pressing his forehead against mine as hotness spilled inside. His body quaked as wave after wave of cum filled me. The tender ache in my womb both calmed and strengthened, welcoming him into my body.

He'd come inside me.

For the first time.

On some basic level, I owned him. He'd mixed himself with me. He could never take that back.

He was mine as much as I was his.

Now and for always.

Something else could be yours for being so stupid.

I could get pregnant.

My heart thudded with panic, but it was overshadowed by lingering waves of pleasure. I would have to deal with that— but not yet.

Not now.

It seemed as if our release went on forever, but it was only a few moments. A few scrumptious moments that healed and broke us.

After the ebbs of orgasm faded, I uncramped my toes and sighed.

Jethro unlocked his arms and withdrew. Wetness slid down my inner thigh as I puddled down his heated body. I could barely stand.

Jethro shivered, tucking his glistening cock back into his boxer-briefs and zipping up his trousers. He was pulling away already. There was no chance I would let him. He couldn't give me what he did and then shut down.

Straightening my dress and scooping my knickers and dirk from the floor, I said, "You know, don't you?"

He stilled. "Know what?"

"What I was thinking about as you found me."

I wasn't prepared for the way his face softened or how his eyes turned into a warm sunrise of caring. "Yes. I know."

My heart pitter-pattered with fear. Would he use it as a tool to hurt me further or would he honour that my feelings were sacred and not to be toyed with?

He ran a hand through his hair before cupping my cheek and smiling sadly. "Thank you, Nila. Thank you for what you've just given me."

With a single kiss and a heavy sigh, he disappeared.

Jethro

THAT NIGHT I had no urge to see Jasmine.

No urge to fix myself or try to find my ice.

I had no desire to change or hide or do any manner of things I'd done all my life to exist within my household.

I was grateful.

Beyond thankful.

She cares for me.

I'd felt it.

I'd lived it.

She'd poured the truth down my throat and taken all the wrongness inside away.

I'd never been so happy than when I'd slid inside her. Never been so completely content holding her in my arms.

I lay in bed and smiled, just for the beauty of smiling.

I was at peace…for the first time.

The only time.

I was just…*me.*

Jasmine was right.

Nila had the power to cure me.

She held something that after today I doubted I could ever live without.

To be cared for so deeply.

To be wanted so fiercely.

Despite all my faults and downfalls, she welcomed me.

She gave me a sanctuary deep enough and pure enough to hide in.

My eyes burned with thanks. I wanted to shower her with gifts and promises. I relived the intoxicating joy of finding something so treasured.

You came inside her.

My heart skipped at the thought. It was stupid of me to be so reckless, but in that moment, I couldn't care less.

It was perfect. I had to come inside her. I wouldn't change a thing.

Being with Nila today had allowed me to demolish my walls—be strong enough to drop my guard and take her with nothing bared.

I gave her the *truth*.

The truth of who I was.

And in return, she gave me the strength to believe there might be a way after all.

I might not have to continue hiding.

I might finally be free.

Nila

MY OLD HEART was broken.

It'd been replaced with something not of flesh and blood but diamond and immortality.

I'd fallen for a smuggler, a biker—a fiend.

I'd fallen for a boy from my past, a man from my future—a friend.

For four days after the polo match, I didn't see Jethro. I didn't try to find him or turn on my phone to message him. We had things to talk about, but I liked the newly blossomed connection too much to overthink it.

I missed him but understood him.

Understood what he'd be going through.

For four days, I spent most of my time sewing and cutting out patterns for a sequence of gowns that would be the headline pieces of my new design. On a daily basis, my mind hurled profanities at me; reminding me that I lived on borrowed time. That the Hawks were not to be trusted. That I should run and never look back.

But my heart argued just as loudly. Encouraging me to believe in what I'd found with Jethro. To trust that I had the power to change our fate. To give us a bit more time.

I didn't know how yet, but there could be a happy ending.

There has to be.

Hawksridge Hall was quiet—more so than normal. Most of the Black Diamond brothers, including the Hawks, were busy with a large shipment that I'd heard held a pink diamond weighing in excess of eighteen carats.

I'd lingered in the dining room long enough to know that such a stone was almost priceless and would fetch untold millions on the black market.

At night, I slept in my luxurious bed and pondered all things Jethro. I became self-absorbed—completely wrapped up in my feelings for him.

A small part of me hated the woman I'd become. The old Nila would never have removed herself so completely from her family—especially Vaughn.

But at the same time—they removed me.

And Jethro had taken me in.

However, there was no denying that my soul was torn and bruised.

Jethro had given me everything beneath the grandstand that day, and by doing so, he robbed me of my hate and the power of injustice that kept me fighting every day.

It wasn't fair.

It wasn't right.

But there was no changing the will of a Weaver's heart.

I was alone now. More so than when I'd first arrived.

I would never be welcomed back with my family, never be able to return home.

Jethro had successfully torn me from my past, stripped me of my mind, and abducted my heart.

I wasn't okay with that.

I couldn't be.

And that was why I had to do the same to him.

I stroked the diamonds around my neck. I'd come here believing I would never be strong enough to fight. But unbeknownst to Cut, he'd brought a disease into his home. Day-by-day, I undermined his foundations, stealing what was his from beneath him.

I had the tools to continue to wreak havoc…*all but one, that is.*

I needed one last thing to make my arsenal complete.

It was time to know where Jethro disappeared to.

It's time to find out what exists behind the door on the second floor.

I looked at the clock above the fish tank in my room. Just past midnight.

I'd heard the men rumble off in a smog of motorcycle smoke an hour ago. If there were any night to investigate—tonight was it.

The corridors would be empty, and Daniel would be far away from delivering his threats of harm.

Resolution filled my veins. I sat up in bed and swung my legs over the side.

It took me two minutes to pull on a pair of yoga pants and slip into an old hoody before collecting my ruby-encrusted dirk and shoving it down my waistband.

With my heart thundering, I slipped out the door and padded down the corridor.

My ears strained for night prowlers. I tiptoed to every corner and dashed quickly past cameras blinking above the large tapestries.

Hawksridge Hall breathed deep and dreamless—vacant of its usual inhabitations, letting me slink beneath the moonlight undisturbed.

I found the spiral staircase where Jethro had dragged me up and scurried to the top as fast as I could. If I stood at the bottom and deliberated, my bravery might desert me.

My fingertip itched, almost as if it knew this was the floor where Jethro had etched his initials into my skin.

I peered above the paintings, locking onto the flashing red lights of yet more cameras. There seemed to be more on this level…protecting something. Protecting what?

I did my best to walk beneath them, to try to stay out of range, but I didn't know the first thing about dodging a security feed.

Jethro would know where I'd been.

He'd be able to watch my every recorded movement. And even though I feared the retribution I might face, it didn't stop me from sneaking to the door he'd knocked on.

The moment I stood outside, my heart switched from pounding to frantic.

What the hell are you doing?

What did I think I would do? Knock and ask politely why Jethro came up here when he ran from me? Did I perhaps think I could turn invisible and snoop around a room while the woman I'd heard slumbered?

You're an idiot.

I stood there dumbstruck. I should never have come.

My lungs stuck together as something rustled on the other side of the door. A soft light seeped through the crack below, bathing the carpet in a warm glow.

I swallowed my yelp as a shadow interrupted the light, pausing the same way I had.

I took a step back. *Stupid. So stupid, Nila.*

No one in this house was safe to go visiting on my own late at night. I wanted to slap myself for being so stupid. I'd put myself in moronic danger.

My fingers reached for my pilfered knife.

I turned to leave, fear dousing my blood with ice.

The sooner I was back in my quarters, the safer I would be.

"You can come in, you know," a quiet feminine voice said. I froze.

No one spoke, waiting for the other.

A never-ending minute ticked past before the voice came again. "I won't tell and I won't hurt you. I can see you lurking outside my door. I have a camera mounted outside, so unless you want to run and pretend this never happened, I suggest you come in before my brothers or father find you up here."

My stomach rolled; a sickening wave of vertigo crippled me. I stumbled forward, grasping at the wall.

I sucked in large breaths, repeating Vaughn's poem for me.

145

Find an anchor, hold on tight.
Do that and you'll be alright.

The spell disappeared as quickly as it had arrived. It pissed me off. I thought I'd learned to control them better. Turned out my body was toying with me. Making me believe I had one less problem to worry about, when in reality, it was just biding its time.

"You don't look well. Come in. Please. Let's talk." The soft voice encouraged and seduced and I craved somewhere to sit for a moment.

Gritting my teeth, I pressed down on the door handle and entered the room where Jethro visited.

My eyes darted around the large space. Lemons and greys and colourful carpets. Sweeping fleur-de-lis silver curtains framed a huge wraparound window with a comfy seat big enough for a whole family of bookworms to curl up on and read.

"You must be the new Weaver."

I bit my lip, spinning on the spot. I missed her in the first sweep. She'd been so still, so well hidden in the welcoming décor.

I found her sitting beside her bed in a large chair covered by a coral blanket. "You needn't fear. I'll delete the recording. No one will know you came here."

I should've relaxed in gratitude. Instead, I stiffened.

I stared at the female equivalent of Jethro. Out of all of Jethro's siblings, his sister looked the most like him. Jethro was the diamond—sharp, faceted, and so pristinely perfect he shot rainbows from every angle. This woman was the mirror image. Her dark hair was sliced with precision, hanging like a silk curtain just past her jaw. Her eyes were more bronze than gold while her round cheeks and full lips were the direct contradiction of sweet but sultry.

I drifted forward, stumbling a little as my vertigo played with the outskirts of my vision.

The woman didn't move, just waited for me to go to her.

Her fingers locked together in her lap, her entire lower half covered by the plush blanket.

When I stood awkwardly in front of her, she motioned toward her bed. The covers hadn't been turned down and it didn't look slept in. The crisp yellow of her linen looked like a lemon meringue pie and just as delicious.

"Sit, please."

I sat. Not because of her order, but because my wobbly legs refused to stand any longer. Who was this woman, and why did she look at me as if she knew everything about me?

I blushed.

Everything?

God, I hoped not. How could I face Jethro's sister if she knew how much I wanted him? How could I look her in the eye knowing I'd had her brother inside me, and despite my conflicted emotions, wanted him every second of every damn day?

"Do you talk or did you make a vow of silence before entering my room?" The woman cocked her head, her hair cascading perfectly in glossy heaviness.

Shaking my head, I swallowed. "No. No, vow."

We stared at each other. Her assessing me and me assessing her. Two women of similar age, with a man in the centre polluting our right to be strangers. We'd only just met, but whatever we said would be weighed and found wanting, knowing we weren't on equal footing.

The thought depressed me.

She held a permanent place in Jethro's life. He openly adored her—I could tell just by looking at her.

I was jealous.

I was sad and happy at the same time.

I hadn't come here looking to make a friend, but I hadn't come here expecting to find her, either.

"Should we start simple or would you rather get to the heart of the matter?"

I shifted higher on her bed. "I think starting with the truth would be more beneficial. Don't you?"

A ghost of a smile tilted her lips. "Ah, now I get it."

"Get what?"

She narrowed her eyes. "Why my brother is struggling."

My heart flip-flopped. "Jethro?"

She nodded.

"How is he struggling?" I didn't dare hope for an answer. Could it truly be that easy?

The woman laughed quietly. "You truly do go for the heart."

What does that mean?

Was it a simple turn of phrase playing on her last words or had Jethro said I'd captured his heart? I'd tried to ensnare him with my games of seduction and beguile. But perhaps by giving him my love…I'd stolen his in return?

Could that be true?

Forcing myself to stay present, I asked, "Who are you?"

The woman leaned forward, extending her hand. "I'm Jasmine."

Mirroring her, I looped my fingers around hers, and we shook slowly, still sizing each other up like an untrusted opponent.

"You're his sister," I whispered, breaking our touch and placing my hands in my lap.

"I'm many men's sister."

"You know who I mean."

She leaned back, sighing a little. "Yes, lucky for you, I do know who you mean. Let's get the introductions out of the way, shall we?" Running French-tipped fingernails through her hair, she recited, "I'm second born to Bryan and Rose Hawk. I chased my older brother into the world as soon as possible, and that fact alone makes us closer than my other two siblings. I love him more than I love myself, and I know what he lives with every day with being the firstborn of a family so steeped in tradition and persecution that it's become an unhealthy combination. I know what you've done to him, and as much as

I want to hate you for smashing apart his world and making him struggle more than I've ever seen, I can't."

I couldn't breathe properly. Like a dying person only interested in air, I was only interested in what Jasmine had to say about her brother. "What does he struggle with? And how did my arrival have anything to do with what's happened to him?"

Her forehead furrowed as her hands fisted in her lap. "Don't play coy in my domain, Nila Weaver. Don't come in here and fish for information on my beloved brother in the hope to twist it into a weapon. I don't hate you, but it doesn't mean I won't if you continue to torture him."

Wow, what?

I held up my hands in surrender. "I don't want to hurt him."

Liar.

I wanted to hurt him by manipulating him to go against his family—to choose me above all others. Even his sister.

Did that make me a hateful person? To want to be the one person he loved more than anyone?

"I...I—" *I have feelings for him.*

The truth danced on my tongue, but I couldn't admit it. I'd barely admitted it to myself, let alone a woman who looked at me with curiosity and disdain.

Jasmine waved away my fumble. "Regardless, you've already hurt him. And as much as I would like to stop you, it's your burden now, as much as mine."

"Burden?"

My mind raced, wishing I knew just what we were discussing.

"You're the one who's forced him to face an alternative to the way he's been living. Thanks to you, the other method of coping is no longer working. It's up to you to give him another."

Anger took over my confusion. How dare she layer me with responsibility when I was nothing more than a captive in her home? "I think you're forgetting one important fact. I'm a prisoner of your father's. I'm a toy for your brother. I have no future thanks to your insane family and have no wish to help one of you."

Lying again, Nila.

I just hoped she swallowed my fibs better than her brother did.

Jasmine leaned forward. It was only subtle, a gentle inclining bringing us closer together, yet I felt her encroachment in every cell. This woman rippled with indignation and righteousness when it came to Jethro. Her unwavering devotion was both humbling and terrifying. "Too late. You're the one who coaxed him into your bed. He fought you. But, from woman to woman, he wasn't strong enough for you. And that excites and upsets me."

My shoulders slouched; her riddles made my head hurt. "What exactly is wrong with him? Why does he think he can only live if he surrounds himself in ice and removes himself from any emotion whatsoever?"

Jasmine sniffed. "That's his secret to tell, and I will not break his trust. And you don't understand—there is nothing wrong with him. He's perfect. Just...not perfect for this family."

"You're of the same blood and seem very close. Are you saying you aren't fit for this family, either?"

Jasmine smiled. "Smart. I suppose you could say that. Jethro and I are a different breed. Born and bred to the same parents but we inherited a different kind of madness than the rest of my relations."

I didn't want to hurt her, but I needed to know. In over a month that I'd been a ward of the Hawks, Jasmine was the first woman I'd come across, not counting the maids. Why was that?

"Does your mother live here, too?"

Jasmine pursed her lips. "My mother is of no consequence. Besides, I'm the protégé of Bonnie Hawk. I have more than enough maternal guidance."

That was the second time I'd heard of Bonnie Hawk. Kes had told me she was in charge of the family's expenses—his grandmother.

As much as I wanted to meet this elusive woman who held an entire family of men under her thumb, I wanted to stay under her notice for as long as possible.

We sat in silence for a time, before Jasmine said, "You should go. And don't tell Jethro you came to see me. He wouldn't handle that well."

"Why?"

She stared for a long moment, as if deciding what to divulge. Finally, she said, "Because in his mind, we are both his. Both under his protection and both in our own little pockets of reality where he can cope. If he knew we'd met and discussed him, the pressure of keeping us protected would increase."

I felt like a parrot as I asked again, "Why?"

"Because, Nila Weaver, he's been raised having no one to protect him and living in a world where just the hint of being who he truly was meant he could be gone tomorrow. Ever since he could understand the differences between him and our father, he's lived with the shadow of his own mortality. Cut wouldn't hesitate, you see…"

She swallowed, a sudden flare of pain filling her gaze. "He's lived twenty-nine years hiding, because if he didn't, one day he'd be gone and he'd leave me all alone. Knowing that we had met would only give him something else to fear."

My heart pounded with every word she spoke. "Fear?"

Jasmine hunched, her voice drifting to a fateful whisper. "Fear what we spoke about. Fear how much of his nature came to light. Fear just how much you knew, because ultimately, it's not him who has the power to destroy you—but you who has the power to destroy him."

By the time I crawled into my bed, my head hadn't stopped spinning.

Jasmine was prickly and wise—an enigma who adored her brother and would do anything to protect him.

Her words were an invitation but also a threat to stay away.

Would she soften if she knew I'd fallen for him?

Would she help me understand him—grant me the help I needed to claim Jethro for my own?

She was as confusing as her brother.

And I knew our conversation hadn't ended. I would return. Again and again.

Until I learned the truth.

But I also had other questions—many, many questions.

It hadn't escaped my notice that she sewed. There'd been an in-progress cross-stitch on her bed, along with a paper chart folded haphazardly. Was she like me and enjoyed the simple creation…or…was it more sinister?

Could she be more Weaver than Hawk?

And if she was…what did that mean?

I tossed and turned, unable to shut off the voices inside my head forming outlandish conclusions.

Just as the dawn stole the stars, sleep finally crept over me.

But it wasn't restful.

Yet more questions chased me into dreamland.

Why did Jasmine never come down from her room?

And who truly wielded the power of the Hawks?

Jethro

THE WEEK AFTER the polo match passed uneventfully.

Tuesday, I went for a hunt on Wings.

Wednesday, I saw Nila at breakfast before leaving to hide in my office until sundown.

Thursday, I was out late dealing with a special shipment of pink diamonds already purchased and due for delivery to a private yacht docked for one night in Southhampton.

Friday, I tried one last time to 'fix' myself, but Jasmine was right. The ice no longer worked, no matter what I did.

But I had a better option—a new regimen that Nila had selflessly given me.

Saturday, I spent the afternoon with Kes and the Diamond brothers playing poker in the billiards room of the Hall—deliberately giving my heart time to adjust to the life-shattering change of what'd happened between Nila and me.

I was ready to admit to myself that my world had changed.

It was time to face what I'd been running from all my life.

However, the next day smashed my hopes and dreams and hurled me right back into the darkness where I belonged.

The last day of the week…the day that belonged to love and togetherness, only brought pain and sadness.

Sunday, I received the worst news of all.

"Jethro, come with me, please." Cut popped his head into my bachelor wing.

I jumped as if I'd been caught red-handed, just like I'd done most of my life whenever he'd appeared out of nowhere. Sliding a pillow over the tiny sharp knife I used to open the old cuts on my soles, I glowered at my unwanted visitor. "Come where?"

Nila had given me hope that soon I could stop hurting myself in such a way, but until I could be sure what she felt for me was irreversible, I had to use something to keep me in check.

Ice wasn't working—pain would have to do.

Cut's gaze fell to my scarred feet. "Do you need a session?"

The concern in his eyes was the key ingredient to how he'd been controlling me for so many years. He made me believe that he was there for me. That he wanted to help me. That I was the chosen one and deserved to inherit all that he had to give.

Of course, it was all bullshit.

Neither of us could erase what had happened between us that night. The night where we used Jasmine so terribly in a fixing session that we'd stepped over an uncrossable line. I'd refused. Over and over and over again.

He'd pushed and pushed and pushed.

I'd snapped.

I'd almost killed him.

And he'd said the words that were a noose around my neck and shackles around my feet for the rest of my days.

"Do you think your life is a gift? Do you think I can't take it away? I've been so fucking close to killing you, boy. A fraction away from ending the embarrassment of knowing what you are. I only hesitate because I believe you can change. You carry my blood. You cannot be such a disgrace. I won't let you be such a disgrace."

I was only alive because he hoped he'd finally cure me.

Every year that passed, he hovered over the birthday cake made especially for his firstborn and contemplated killing me with cyanide.

Or a hunting accident.

Or a shipment gone wrong.

So many ways to dispatch me. I lived in constant awareness of traps and mercenaries ready to steal my God-given right to breathe.

All because I didn't conform.

He also told me what would happen if he *did* kill me. What he would do to not just Jasmine but Kestrel, Daniel, and anyone else I held dear—not that there were many. He couldn't care less if it meant he would be left with no heir. He believed he was invincible and lacked the fundamental trait of a father: love.

He didn't love his children. Shit, he didn't even like us.

Therefore, we were disposable if we displeased him.

That sort of panic...that sort of fear...continued to have a hold on me. No matter my age or strength—I'd lived beneath the shadow of death for so long, I didn't know any other way.

I was a fucking idiot.

Placing my feet into a pair of moccasins, I shook my head. "Thank you for your concern. But I'm fine."

Cut cocked his head. "You're a terrible liar."

Gritting my teeth, I stood up and smoothed down my black t-shirt. I wore no colour today—only black. I should've known that the colour would bring only darkness.

"I'm still following your orders. I'm still loyal."

Cut smiled coldly. "For now." He ran his fingers around his mouth, eyeing me up and down. "However, we shall see if you pass the next test."

My heart lurched. Tests weren't new. I'd been made to complete many of them as I grew—to prove that a son like me could become a man like him.

"What did you have in mind?"

Skinning an animal while it's still alive?

Hurting another one of the club whores?

Cut's smile sent shivers down my back. "You'll see."

I hated when he did this. I never knew if he was walking me out like a horse to be shot or if he genuinely wanted to prove to himself and to me that I was getting better.

For a few years, I'd been good. I'd found how to hide myself in blizzards and snow and be everything he wanted me to be.

That was before he informed me that Nila was my twenty-ninth birthday present. There'd been no cake that year—no threat of cyanide.

Only the detonation of my soul in the form of a woman I couldn't deny.

Forcing a smile, I asked, "What about some father and son time? Forget the test. Let's go for a ride. Talk business."

Over the years, he'd schooled me on the running of the empire. Those sessions were the only time he relaxed and enjoyed interacting with me. Although, he wasn't ready to give up his power—I could tell. Regardless that our customs stated it would be mine soon, I knew it wouldn't be a simple matter of handing over the throne.

"No. I have a much better idea." Cut opened the door wider. "Come on. Let's go."

My knees locked. Something inside told me to refuse. This test would be worse than everything I'd been subjected to.

"Perhaps another time. I have to—"

Go find Nila and indulge in what she feels for me.

What would Jasmine say if she knew I'd achieved the impossible? Nila Weaver liked me...possibly even loved me.

My stomach tangled with my heart. I'd managed to stay away for six days, but I'd reached my limit. I needed to feel her fight, her goodness, her wet hot heat. I needed to forget about my fucked-up existence and live in hers, if only for a moment.

Cut waved his hand. "No. This supersedes whatever you were about to do." Snapping his fingers—a trait I'd adopted—he growled, "Come along. It won't take long."

Hiding my nervousness behind the glacial façade I still managed to invoke around my father, I followed him from my wing.

Wordlessly, we moved through the house. Every step flared the pain in my feet, giving me something to focus on rather than my whirling imagination of what was to come.

The nights were getting longer, encroaching on the sunlight day by day—only seven p.m., yet it was already dusk.

I swallowed my questions as Cut moved purposely out the back door and toward the maintenance barn at the rear of the estate. Most people had a shack that housed a broken lawnmower and a few empty flowerpots.

Not us.

Our shack was the size of a three-bedroom house, resting like a black beetle on the immaculate lawn.

The air temperature bit into my exposed arms as we stalked over the short expanse of grass and disappeared into the musty metallic world of saw-dust shavings and ancient tools.

Along with servants to ensure our daily needs were met, we also had carpenters, electricians, roofers, gardeners, and gamekeepers. Running an estate such as Hawksridge took millions of pounds per year.

The minute we entered, two carpenters who were lathing a chair leg turned off the machine and subtly left the room. Dusk on a Sunday and still the staff worked—our insistence for perfection ran a brutal timeline.

"Good evening, Mr. Hawk," one worker mumbled on his way out. His eyes remained downcast with respect, his shoulders hunched.

Cut wielded a power that made lesser men—including myself—want to run and hide.

When I was in charge, I would change that. I would change many things.

Cut moved deeper into the workshop, peering into the other rooms where paintings waited for restoration. Only once he was sure we were alone did he turn to me to follow.

With unease building in my gut, I did as ordered and moved into the back room where knick-knacks and miscellaneous childhood toys had been dumped.

"What is it that you wanted to discuss?" I asked, standing still in the centre of chaos. Deliberately, I pushed my heel harder against the ground, activating a deeper throb from the new cut. It wasn't that I liked pain. In fact, I hated the stigma and weakness of cutting myself. I didn't get pleasure from it—but I did get relief from my disease by being single-minded and focused.

Cut shrugged out of his leather jacket, placing the embroidered Black Diamond apparel on Jasmine's old nursery cot. His hair was unruly and grey, his jawline sharp and unforgiving.

"Show, not discuss." With a secretive smile, he moved to the large termite-riddled cupboard at the back of the room. He removed an old brass key from his pocket and inserted it into the lock.

As I moved closer, my heart stopped beating.

It couldn't be.

Yet it was.

Cut grabbed the handles of the cupboard and swung the doors wide, revealing what he'd shown me the night of my sixteenth birthday. That same night, he'd made me watch what he did to Emma Weaver. He made me witness video after video of what he'd done to Nila's mother, all while beating me if I ever dared look away.

Sickness rolled in my gut.

My hands balled.

Palms sweated.

Shit. Shit. *Shit.*

Once again, my father had reminded me of my place and how fragile my wants, dreams, and very existence were.

My eyes burned as I drank in the age-old equipment passed down through generations. Shelf after shelf of torturous items used in extracting debts from the Weavers.

Cut's face darkened, motioning me forward when I stayed locked to the floor. "I think it's time you and I had a little chat, Jet." Taking one particular item from the cupboard, I knew what he would make me do.

And I knew whatever love Nila felt for me would vanish like it never existed.

I couldn't move, but it didn't stop Cut from prowling toward me and placing the hated item into my shaking hands. Curling my fingers around the salt shaker, I hated that something so simple could deliver something so unforgivable.

My father murmured, "You have one last chance, Jethro. Use it well."

Ice howled.

Snow fell.

Blizzards blew like fury.

I hung my head and gave in.

Motherfucking shit.

That was yesterday.

A Sunday I would never forget.

Today was Monday.

A Monday that I wished I could erase.

Last Monday had been full of freedom, kisses, and passion; polo and sex and blistering new beginnings.

This Monday was full of mourning and pain. Today was the day I became the true heir to Hawksridge because if I didn't, I doubted I would wake in the morning.

Cut hadn't said as much. But it was what he *didn't* say that made the biggest impression.

Do this or I'll kill you.

Obey me or this is the end.

Cut had seen what I knew he would. He took great pleasure in informing me that he knew I'd fucked Nila. He knew I'd chased after her during half-time at polo, and he knew my allegiances were changing.

It'd been a long fucking night.

After our talk, he'd forced me to go deep, deep inside. He tore away any progress Nila had made with me and filled me with snow once again.

In an odd way, I was grateful.

Grateful because without him tampering with my psyche, there was no way in flying fuck I would've got through today.

I thought I'd had months.

I thought I'd been the one in control of when the next payment would happen, but as always…I was wrong.

Cut had seen my ultimate plan before I'd even finalised the details.

He'd understood my tentative scheming of dragging out the debts until I was thirty. By then, I would've been in charge. By then, I might've found a way to spare Nila's life without losing mine.

I had the Sacramental Pledge over the Debt Inheritance.

I'd put things in place to end this—once and for all.

But none of my forward thinking mattered anymore.

Today was the day Nila paid the Second Debt.

THE MOMENT JETHRO walked into my quarters, I knew.

We'd slept together three times, spent only weeks in each other's company, yet I knew his soul almost as well as I knew my own.

Mystery still shrouded him, still hid so much, but I'd learned to read his body language.

I'd learned how to listen to his heart.

"No," I whispered, clutching the tulle I'd been working on to my chest.

Jethro looked away, his face blank and unfeeling. "Yes."

I didn't need words to tell me what had happened. The truth was far too vivid to ignore.

His father.

His father had shoved him back into the blizzard and slammed the door in his face. He'd done something to him that wedged a canyon between us and left us with only one thing.

The debts.

Our emotions were on hold.

Our connection severed.

My heart sank.

I let the lilac tulle slip through my fingers, destroying the carefully pinned pattern of a ball gown that would be my centre piece of my Rainbow Diamond Collection.

Last night, I'd formulated a few goals. If I intended to stay at Hawksridge, to finish whatever had begun between Jethro and me, I had to give the outside world an explanation.

I had to put an end to the suspicion about what'd happened to me.

People were talking. This morning, I'd turned on my phone and browsed a few websites for what they thought happened to me. Scarily, there were a few very close to the truth—it seemed strange that something so incomprehensible could be guessed at so closely.

Almost as if someone had been telling secrets that they shouldn't.

Vaughn perhaps?

Could he be behind the leaked knowledge? I wanted to ask him but he hadn't replied to my messages. He'd gone completely silent.

Regardless, it didn't matter. I was stuck here, and I had to find some way to deal with what was out there. It was time to announce a new fashion line, and at the same time, put those rumours to rest.

Along with the hunches on my disappearance, I'd also read Jethro's message that he sent the morning of the polo match. His words were sincere but also full of regret. Would his offer to answer my questions via text still stand—even when he looked at me as if he were dead inside?

Pulling extra pins from my cuffs, I shook my head. "Jethro…it's too soon."

I thought I'd have weeks yet…months even. *You didn't think—you hoped.*

If I had known this would happen, I would've gone to him sooner. I would've forced him to face the truth and discuss once and for all what'd happened between us last Monday. Instead, I'd done nothing but work. I didn't wander the premises or go for a run. The constant fear of where Daniel lurked had kept me trapped better than any bars or cage.

Trembles took over my chilled muscles. "Surely there must be a way to stop—"

"Quiet, Ms. Weaver. I have no patience for your begs." Stalking toward me, he growled, "You know what is expected of you."

I searched his gaze for the warmth and golden glow of before.

There was nothing.

Closing the distance, I wrapped my arms around his frigid body. Once again, his extremities were cold. No heat. No liveliness.

"Jethro...please..." Nuzzling into his chest, I willed him to feel my panic, to comprehend how terrified I was of paying another debt.

He balled his hands. "Let me go."

I snuggled closer. "No. Not until you admit that you don't want to do this."

His fingers landed on my shoulders, prying me away from him. "Don't presume to know what I want."

"But it's too soon! The lash marks have barely healed on my back. I need more time."

Time to mentally prepare.

Time to steal you away.

"How do you know the timeline for what will take place?" Leaning forward, he snatched my wrist and dragged me forward. "You don't know a thing about anything, Ms. Weaver. There is no script—no right and wrong when another debt can be taken. It's time."

The cold finality in his voice siphoned into my blood, delivering a vicious vertigo attack. I fell forward as the room flipped upside down.

I cried out as I stumbled, swaying to the side only for Jethro to jerk me upright.

I hated the weakness inside me. I hated that there was no cure.

I would be afflicted all my life.

Is Jethro the same?

Could whatever he suffer be the same as my vertigo? Incurable, unfixable—something accepted as broken and forever unchangeable?

While I swam in sickness, Jethro dragged me over to the ancient armoire where I'd placed my clothes and shoved aside the hangers to reveal the back panel. Pressing hard on the wood, the walnut veneer sprang open, revealing a secret compartment with hanging white calico shifts.

I moaned, trying my damnedest to shove aside the lingering after effects of the attack, and struggled weakly as Jethro turned his attention to my grey blouse.

Without a word, he undid the pearl buttons, quickly and methodically with no hint of sexual interest or burning desire.

My limbs were endlessly heavy. I lamented the unjust fate of my last name as he pushed my stretchy black leggings to the floor.

Leaving me dressed only in a white lace bra and knickers, Jethro snagged a calico shift and dumped it over my head.

I blinked nauseously as he tugged my arms through the holes as if I were a child.

What was going on? Where was the man who'd held me while he came inside me? Where was the softness…the gentleness?

The minute I was dressed, he demanded, "Take off your shoes."

I stared into his gaze, looking for a smidgen of hope. I wanted to reach inside and make him care again.

He stood taller, a flicker of life lighting up his features. "Don't. Just…it's better this way." He sighed heavily. "Please."

I tensed to fight. To argue. But his plea stopped me.

Ironically, I was the one about to be hurt—made to pay a debt I had no notion of—yet he was the one most in pain.

He needed to stay in his shell to remain strong.

Despite my misgivings and terror bubbling faster and faster in my blood, I couldn't take that away from him.

I'd fallen for him. What sort of person would I be if I willingly stripped him bare when he wasn't coping? Even if he'd been tasked to hurt me?

Only a stupid, love-struck one.

Do something, Nila. It's you or him.

Wrong.

Grabbing his hand, I pressed our tattooed indexes together and summoned all my courage. "We're in this together. You told me so yourself."

He tensed; his face twisted with unmentionable emotion. Hanging his head, he nodded. "Together."

"In that case, do what you need to do."

We stood awkwardly, both wanting to say things that would break the fragile bravery of the moment, but neither strong enough.

Finally, he nodded, and pointed at my shoes.

I didn't argue or reply.

Kicking off my jewelled flip-flops, Jethro led me silently out the door and through the Hall.

Every footfall sent my heart higher and higher until every terrified beat clawed at the back of my throat. I'd been scared in my life. I'd bawled my eyes out when Vaughn had almost drowned at the beach. I'd become almost comatose with terror when I knew I'd never see my mother again.

But this...this marching toward the Second Debt turned my blood into tar. I moved as if I were underwater, suffering a terrible dream I couldn't wake from.

I wanted my twin. I wanted him to make it better.

Leaving the Hall behind, Jethro continued to march me over the freshly mowed lawn, past the stables and kennels where Squirrel and a few foxhounds lounged in the autumn sun, and over the hill.

His footsteps were interspersed with an occasional limp— barely noticeable. Was he hurt?

The shift I wore protected me from nothing. The breeze disappeared up the sleeves and howled around my midriff, creating a mini cyclone within my dress.

My trembles ratcheted higher as goosebumps kissed my flesh.

"What—what will happen?" I asked, forcing myself to stay strong and stoic.

Jethro didn't reply, only increased his pace until we crested the small incline. The moment we stood on the ridge, I had the answer to my question.

Before us was the lake where Cut and his sons had fished for trout on his birthday. It was a large manmade creation in the shape of a kidney. Willow trees and rushes graced its banks, weeping their fronds into the murky depths.

It would've been peaceful—a perfect place for a picnic or a lazy afternoon with a book.

But not today.

Today, its shoreline didn't welcome ducks and geese, but an audience all dressed in black.

Cut, Kes, and Daniel waited with unreadable stares as Jethro propelled me down the grassy mound and closer to my fate.

Cut seemed happier than I'd seen him since I'd arrived, and Daniel sucked on a beer as if we were at his favourite ballgame. Kes had the decency to hide his true feelings behind his mysterious secrecy. His face drawn and blank.

Then my eyes fell on the woman before them.

Bonnie Hawk.

The name came to me as surely as if she wore a name tag. This was the elusive grandmother—the ruler of Hawksridge Hall.

Her lips pursed as if my presence offended her. Her papery hands with vivid blue veins remained clutched in her lap. Her white hair glowed as she sat regally, poised better than any young debutant, not an elderly croon. The chair she sat in matched her bearing, looking like a morbid throne with black velvet and twilled claw-foot legs.

A staff member stood beside her with a parasol, drenching

the dame in shade from the noonday sunshine.

It hurt to think the sun beamed upon such a place. It didn't pick favourites when casting its golden rays—whether it be innocent or guilty—it shone regardless.

I looked up into the ball of burning gas, singeing my retinas and begging the sun to erase all memory of today.

Bonnie sniffed, raising her chin.

Cut stepped forward, clasping his hands in glee. "Hello, Ms. Weaver. So kind of you to join us."

"I didn't exactly have a choice." I shuddered, no longer able to fight the terror lurking on the outskirts of my mind. Claws of horror sank deep inside me, dragging me further into panic.

Cut grinned, noticing my ashen skin and quaking knees. "No, you didn't. And you have no idea how happy that makes me."

Turning his attention to his son, he said, "Let's begin. Shall we?"

Jethro

I NODDED.

What else could I do?

If I refused, Kes would step in. If I refused, I would be killed.

My eyes fell on my grandmother. She hoisted her nose higher in the air, waiting for me to start. Cut had deliberately brought Bonnie to watch—to be there if I failed.

I have no intention of failing.

I'd managed to stay cold the moment I stepped into Nila's quarters. Even when she'd looked into my eyes and snuggled into my chest, I hadn't warmed. I intended to remain aloof and removed until it was over.

It was the only way.

Cut stepped back, squeezing his mother's shoulder.

Bonnie Hawk looked up at him, smiling thinly. He was her favourite. But just like her son, she couldn't stand her grandchildren.

Jasmine. She stands Jasmine.

That was true. If there was anyone who'd excelled in this family and played perfectly in the role she'd been given, it was Jaz.

Cut said, "Begin, Jet. Pretend we aren't here if it will make you feel any better."

I held back my snort. I never wanted to forget that they were here. If I did, I'd lose any hope of being icy and slip. I'd find a way to take it easy on Nila and avoid certain parts of this debt—just like I'd done with the First Debt and not freezing her the way I should have.

Today, there would be no leniency. Today, Nila must be strong enough to face the full brunt of what my family would do to her.

Stop avoiding the truth.

What you will do to her. You alone.

In that instant, I wanted to hand the power over to Kes. Make him do it—so Nila would hate him instead of me.

Nila stood quivering beside me. The air was chilly but not cold enough to warrant the chattering of her teeth or blueness of her fingers.

She's petrified.

And for good reason.

"Jethro, I suggest you begin. I'm not getting any younger, boy," Bonnie muttered.

Daniel snickered, gulping down another mouthful of beer. "Snap, snap, old chap."

Kes crossed his arms, locking away his thoughts completely.

I looked to the piece of equipment that had been secured to the pond's banks. It remained covered by a black cape—for now.

Soon, Nila would see what it was, and she would understand what would happen.

But first, I had to be eloquent and deliver the speech I'd been taught to memorize since I'd been told of my role.

Grabbing Nila's arm, I positioned her on the patch of earth that'd been decorated with a thick pouring of salt. I'd done the design. The sunrise had witnessed my artistry as I followed an ancient custom.

Nila's eyes dropped to her feet as I pressed her hard, telling her with actions alone not to move.

"Oh, my God," she murmured, slapping a hand over her mouth.

My wintry ice saved me from feeling anymore of her panic; I locked my muscles as I prepared to recite.

The pentagram she stood in gave a giant hint as to the debt she would be paying.

Her black eyes met mine, her hair whipping around her face, just like it had when she'd found the graves of her ancestors.

It was almost serendipitous that she would pay this debt now—especially after I'd thought that she'd looked like a witch casting a curse on the Hawks.

"As you can see, Ms. Weaver. You stand in a pentacle star. It's well known that the five-pointed star represents the five wounds of Christ. It's been used in the Church for millennia. Yet a reversed pentagram is the symbol of dark magic—a tool wielded by Wiccans and practiced regularly in witchcraft."

My family stared enraptured, even though they knew the tale by heart.

Nila seemed to shrink, her eyes never leaving the thick rivers of salt penning her in a motif of wickedness.

"Your ancestor was found practicing the dark arts, for which she escaped severe punishment. In the 1400's, it was common for poor folk to seek help from those who promised quick riches. They'd be lured into believing a weed would cure boils or a toad would turn them into a prince. Those who had luck with their spell or incantation did more than just seek men or women who practiced magic—they wanted the power for themselves. They became immersed in Wicca and turned their backs on religion.

"Needless to say, they were caught. Their whereabouts would be noted, their stores of dried herbs confiscated, and the sentence no one survived decreed. They were a traitor to their faith, but they would be given a choice—prove their innocence by drowning, or admit to their sins by burning at the stake and returning to the devil they worshiped."

Nila's pasty cheeks shimmered with cascading tears. Her nose went red from cold and she wrapped her arms around herself, partly to ward off the chill but mostly to keep herself from running.

No ropes bound her. She could leave. She could run.

But she also knew we'd catch her and I'd have to add another punishment for her disobedience.

All that I knew. All of it I understood with one look into her glassy eyes.

I even knew she wasn't aware she was crying—completely enthralled and mortified with where my tale would go.

Taking a deep breath, I continued, "All of what I said is true. However, it came with rules—like most things."

Cut nodded as if he'd personally been there and watched the pyres burning.

"Destitute people were caught while those wealthy enough weren't. It didn't mean that women who dined on cakes and tea and employed servants to wash away their crimes didn't dally in potions—far from it. They were the most proficient. They sold their concoctions to other well-to-do housewives and bribed any official who dared to ask questions about their faith."

I made the mistake of looking at Nila again. Her lips parted and a silent word escaped.

Please.

Tearing my gaze away, I forced myself to continue, "Your ancestor was no different, Ms. Weaver. She blatantly did what she wanted. She brewed so-called elixirs and cast so-called curses. And she did it all from the drawing room of the Weaver household—the same household the Hawks cleaned and maintained for her.

"A few years passed where she went undetected, but of course, she made a mistake. She suffered the misfortune of creating a potion for an aristocratic friend's offspring. It didn't work. Her remedy didn't heal the friend's child—it poisoned him."

Nila buried her face in her hands.

"Word got out, and the mayor came knocking. He'd turned a blind eye up until now, but he could no longer ignore her wrongdoings and buckled under the pressure of whispering folk.

"When he arrived to arrest her, Mrs. Weaver announced she'd been doing it under duress. She was a kind, simple woman with no more power in her blood than the next.

"Needless to say, the mayor did not believe her—he'd seen with his own eyes what happened to the boy who'd died from one of her vials. But he was on the Weaver's payroll. If he sent the richest man in town's wife to the stake, he would kiss his extra salary goodbye. But if he didn't bow to the wishes of his parish, he could face the noose in return."

I swallowed, hating the next part. When Bonnie had told me what'd happened, I'd been almost sick with rage. To think that the Weavers got away with such things.

My lips twisted at the ironic truth. Now it was us who got away with murder—right beneath the noses of the law.

"Mrs. Weaver came up with a solution. She promised it would benefit everyone. Everyone but the Hawks, that is."

Nila bowed her head, hunching into herself.

Bonnie snapped, "Listen, girl. Listen to the disgusting actions from the bloodline who birthed you."

Nila's head came up; her shoulders straightened. Her jaw set and she latched her gaze on mine, just waiting for me to continue.

Shoving my fists into my jeans pockets, I said, "She told the mayor a secret…a lie. She said it wasn't *her* practicing, but the hired help's fourteen-year-old daughter. She said she'd caught her red-handed selling potions from the kitchens. She fabricated untruths of how my ancestor's daughter had been swindling and tarnishing the Weavers name for years.

"The mayor was happy with such a tale. He would have someone to answer to the angry mob and at the same time keep his salary. The Weavers gave him a bonus for his loyalty and the poor Hawk daughter was carted away to be thrown into jail to await trial."

Daniel laughed. "Get it, Nila. Do you see where this is going?"

I glowered at him.

Cut snarled, "Shut up, Dan. This is Jet's production. Let him finish."

Daniel sulked, tossing his empty beer bottle into the reeds by his feet.

I sighed; it was almost over.

No, it's not.

I still had to extract the debt.

I hardened my heart, blocking out everything but the next ten minutes. If I sliced up my day and focused on bite-sized pieces, I could get through this.

I *would* get through this.

"For a week, she rotted in the cells with barely food or water. By the time the trial came to pass, she was delirious with hunger and disease. The Hawk daughter pleaded her innocence. She stood before a court of twelve and begged them to see reason. She tore apart every conviction against her and argued her case that any right-minded human would've seen was all Mrs. Weaver's doing. But the truth does not set you free."

Nila twitched as I said it, her eyes flaring with knowledge from our past discussion on the matter.

Looking away, I said, "She was sentenced to burn at the stake at sunrise."

Nila moaned, shaking her head in horror.

Bonnie Hawk muttered, "Now do you see why we hate you so?"

Rushing ahead, I finished, "One saving grace was she was granted a choice. The daughter was told she could prove her innocence or admit her guilt." Moving toward Nila, I wound my fingers in her hair, cursing my heart for tripping as the black strands rippled around my knuckles. "What do you think she chose, Ms. Weaver?" I brushed my nose against her throat, doing my utmost to tame my cock from reacting to her delectable smell. "Fire or water...what would you choose?"

Nila shook harder, her eyes like black orbs of dread. She tried to speak, but a croak came out instead. Licking her lips, she tried again. "Innocence. I would take innocence."

"So, you would prefer to drown by water than be purged by fire?"

Another tear trickled down her cheek. "Yes."

"Yes, what?"

Bracing herself, Nila said loudly, "I would choose water."

I nodded. "Exactly.

"And that's what my ancestor chose as well."

Nila

I WAS ABOUT to be drowned.

I was to repent for heinous lies, to prove my innocence from witchcraft that I didn't practice, and perish the way so many innocent girls had done in the past.

In the 1400's, the law system was run by the Church. And the Church had ultimate control. It didn't matter that they sentenced a young girl to death. It didn't matter that she was innocent. Even if she chose trial by water, she would still end up dead.

The proverb from those days came back to haunt me.

Ye innocent will float upon their demise while ye guilty will sink just like their dirty souls.

Both scenarios ended in death.

There was no justice—only a deranged mob looking for entertainment by heckling and ripping a young girl's life apart.

Shaking my head, I tried to rid the images inside my brain.

Jethro vibrated before me, his back to his family, his eyes only for me.

Beneath the golden ice lurked a need for me to understand. To forgive him for what he was about to do.

How could he ask me that when I didn't know if I would survive?

If you do go to your grave today, don't condemn him any more than what he is.

Somehow, I'd gone from martyrdom to just being a martyr—still unable to hurt him—even while he hurt me.

I nodded—or I tried to nod—I was so stiff my body barely moved.

Jethro's nostrils flared. He saw my acknowledgement, my permission to proceed.

You're insane.

Maybe you are a witch.

You seem to believe you're immortal and can't be killed.

That might be true. In that moment, I wished it were true.

With his back straight and legs spread, Jethro asked the question I'd been waiting for. "Do you repent, Ms. Weaver? Do you take ownership of your family's sins and agree to pay the debt?"

I almost collapsed I shook so hard. It was the exact same question Jethro made me answer before extracting the First Debt.

Before I replied, I had a question of my own. Looking directly at Bonnie Hawk, I asked, "When I first arrived, I was told I would be used callously and with no thought. I was told the firstborn son dictated my life and that there would be no rules on what he did with me." My voice wobbled, but I forced myself to go on. "Yet, everything you do follows strict repetition. Re-creating the past over and over again. You're bound by what happened as much as us. Surely you're powerful enough to tear up such guidelines and find it in your hearts to let go."

My hands balled as anger shot fierce and hot. "Let this madness end!"

Bonnie's mouth parted half in amazement, half in joy.

Her hazel eyes twinkled as she leaned forward, pointing a knobbly finger in my direction. "Let's get something straight, young lady. My grandson is bound, as you say, by records kept for hundreds of years. He has to follow each one perfectly. But the rest—anything outside of paying the debts—that is purely at his discretion."

She cocked her chin, looking at Jethro.

He stood frozen.

"*He* is the one who decides if you're to be kept apart or shared. *He* is the one who decides if you deserve leniency for obedience or punishment for insubordination."

Her dry lips pulled back over cavity-riddled teeth. "There is something you don't know, Nila Weaver. And normally I wouldn't tell a guttersnipe like you what conversations go on within my family, but it should make you grateful to know. Do you *want* to know, child?"

The wind stole my hair, snapping it around me like black lightning. Standing in the pentacle seemed to summon powers I didn't have—transferring ancient magic that should remain dead and buried. The back of my scalp prickled; I inched closer to the edge of the salt, needing to leave. "Yes. I want to know."

Shooting a look at Jethro, I tried to imagine the conversations he had with the people he held most dear. Was there anyone he let himself be free with? *Just his sister.* I knew that from the way Jasmine spoke of him. He lived with a large family yet remained so alone.

Bonnie Weaver took a shallow breath. "Jethro came to me a few days after your arrival with a request to keep you to himself."

"Grandmamma—" Jethro began.

Bonnie glared at him. "No. I can tell her. Perhaps she'll obey you better and we can move on before the moon rises."

Jethro's nostrils flared as he nodded, looking over his grandmother's shoulder, removing himself from the conversation.

Bonnie waggled her finger at me once more. "Your arrival was meant to be celebrated. You were a gift for my son and grandsons. You were meant to be shared." Her lips spread broadly. "Do you understand what I'm saying to you, child?"

Sickness rolled in my gut.

Yes, I knew what she referred to. Jethro had said as much

when he made me crawl like a dog to the kennels. He'd said I was to be passed around. But it never happened.

My eyes flew to him.

Even then...even when he was so awful, he was protecting me from worse.

The sickness disappeared, replaced with an intolerable ache inside my heart.

"Yes, I understand what you're saying."

Bonnie Hawk sat back, dropping her bony hand. "Good. You'd be wise to remember that. Remember that we have rules but freedom, guidelines but exceptions, but most of all, immunity against whatever we please to do."

Cut cleared his throat, moving forward and stealing the limelight. "Enough." Snapping his fingers at his son, he ordered, "Jethro. Ask the girl the question again."

My back tensed. The breeze died, untangling itself from my hair and letting it drape like a death shroud over my shoulders.

Oh, God.

My feet tingled to be free from the pentagram, but at the same time, I didn't want to move. Perhaps I was safe inside this five-pointed salt etching. Perhaps whatever pathway was conjured could steal me away and protect me from the Second Debt.

She was only fourteen.

The Hawk girl had died to protect my ancestor. She would've been petrified and so betrayed. Why was I any better than her? Why did I deserve to be freed when she was killed for a lie?

I swallowed as Jethro faced me completely. His hands were fisted by his sides, his face blank and cold. "Do you repent, Ms. Weaver? Do you take ownership of your family's sins and agree to pay the debt?"

His voice echoed in my ears. I wished he were asking me anything but that. I fantasised about a different question. So many different questions.

Do you want to run away with me?

Can you forgive my family for what they've done?
Have you fallen for me, like I've fallen for you?

Infinitely better questions. But ones I would never hear.

I'd delayed as much as possible.

I had nothing left to do but get it over with.

Bracing myself, I locked eyes first with Jethro then with each member of his deluded family. He didn't need to ask me twice—regardless of my stalling. I knew my role—my part in these theatrics.

If there was any power at all in the pentacle, I summoned it now. I summoned age-old wizardry and asked for one thing:

Let me endure, so I may pay the sins of my past. But let me survive, so I may put an end to those who hurt me.

The wind howled, fluttering the hem of my shift...almost in answer.

Balling my hands, I said, "Yes." My voice carried loud and clear with a touch of defiance. "Yes, I accept the debt."

Cut's forehead furrowed as if he were pissed with my strength and ownership of something so terrible. He looked robbed. He looked furious.

Jethro, on the other hand, looked stricken. His face went white and he nodded. "In that case, let's begin."

I closed my eyes, taking one last moment to fortify my soul.

You can get through this, Nila.
You can.
They won't kill you. Not yet.

Another bout of shivers overtook me. It could be entirely possible that after this, I would wish they would. I might want them to kill me and put me out of my misery.

Jethro gritted his jaw and moved toward the ominous looking contraption that remained hidden beneath a black cloth. Every time the breeze caught the edge, I tried to see what it was. The brief glimpses of wood and leather gave me no hint.

Wrapping his fist in the fabric, Jethro tore it off with a flourish.

My heart instantly suffocated.

I stepped back, scuffing the salt line and breaking the pentacle boundary. Thunder boomed on the horizon; heavy clouds inched closer.

I'd seen one of those things—a long time ago—in a book called *Fifty Ingenious Ways of Torture*. Vaughn had checked it out from the local library. I'd hated the book so much. He'd chased me around the house with it, flicking pages of blood and gore and absolute pain.

I didn't need water to drown me. My fear did that spectacularly well on its own.

It was a seesaw.

A terrified giggle bubbled in my chest. I liked seesaws. V had double-bounced me more than once as we played on them as children.

But this wasn't just any seesaw.

This one destroyed all happy memories of ever being on one. I would never *ever* go on another.

Not after today.

Not after this.

Jethro didn't look at me, stroking the end closest to him—what looked like a simple tree-trunk. It'd been carved into a smooth post with leather handholds hammered into the wood.

There were four straps in total.

My eyes followed the length of the seesaw, taking in the fulcrum before gritting my teeth and forcing myself to stare at the other end.

That was where I would go.

That end wasn't smooth or basic. It'd been modified. It was…*it's a chair.*

A simple wooden chair with cuffs for wrists and ankles. There were no cushions, no luxury—a prison cell suspended over the deep lake. It faced toward the pond, barring me from seeing what would happen on shore.

It was worse than any whipping post or dungeon.

Jethro leaned on the wooden joist, tilting the pendulum to

sway the chair from the glistening water. It moved as if it was possessed, floating effortlessly, swinging toward me as if it knew I was the one destined to sit.

I moved back, tripping over my feet in my rush.

I bumped into something solid and warm. Jumping, I swallowed my squeal as Kes's strong fingers came around my shoulders, rubbing me with his thumbs. "Trust us. We won't let you drown. We know you're innocent of witchcraft and don't need to prove that by taking your life." His voice lowered, barely registering in my ears. "Hold your breath and let your mind wander. Don't fight. Don't struggle."

His circling thumbs made me want to vomit. His kind-heartedness only made this worse. Jerking out of his hold, I stood shivering in my shift. "Don't touch me."

His eyes tightened with hurt, and for some inexplicable reason, I felt as if I owed him an explanation.

I'm so cold.

Fear had stolen everything.

I'd never quivered so badly—never been so terrified. My teeth chattered harder and I bit my tongue. Pain flared, a trickle of blood tainting my mouth.

Jethro came up beside me. He held out his hand. "Ready, Ms. Weaver?"

No.

I'll never be ready for this.

I paused, swallowing blood and every urge to beg.

If we were alone, I would've toppled to my knees and wrapped my arms around his waist. I would've had no decorum or self-control. I would've promised anything, given him everything, if only he put a stop to this.

Please, don't do this.

His eyes narrowed, glinting with anger. His family watched our every move.

That was it, then. There was no way out. He was resigned to this. And so must I.

Dropping my head, letting a curtain of ebony hair block me

from this world, I nodded.

"You need to say it," he muttered. "Say it out loud. Admit that you deserve this."

Closing my eyes, I died a little inside. Forcing myself to raise my hand, I presented myself to him.

Jethro stole my wrist; his cold touch seeped like permafrost into my already freezing body.

With a tug, he stole me from the pentagram and dragged me toward the chair. "You still haven't said it, Ms. Weaver."

My panic had become physical, slapping a gag over my mouth. I struggled with the word. One simple little word.

Stepping toward the chair, I whispered, "Yes. Yes, I admit I deserve this."

Jethro made a mangled noise in his chest.

I closed my eyes.

It was done.

Jethro

TYING HER DOWN was one of the hardest fucking things I've done.

Not because my family were watching and I had no way of fucking up the debt.

And not because my heart dripped with icicles and frost.

And not even because I was so fucking close to snapping and showing everything that I was.

But because I'd promised myself the next time I restrained her, I would be granting her pleasure not pain.

I'd wanted her to writhe beneath my tongue while she was bound. I wanted to taste her as she came apart while suspended. And I wanted her delicious moans to fill my ears while she was trapped.

I wanted her to give in to me. To *trust* me. To give me every single pleasure she could feel.

When I'd fucked her in her quarters that second time, I'd made a vow to take her completely. To take her my way...all the way.

That meant getting inside her head, her heart, her mind. I wasn't satisfied with owning her body. It didn't give me what I craved. Only her complete submission and immeasurable love could do that.

I would've taken days. Days to extract everything she had

to give me. The word 'torture' came from the origins *to twist*. I would've twisted Nila's emotions so she'd carry me forever in her heart. I would've made a home inside her so I could be finally fucking free.

She could give me a cure no one else could grant. She could switch every pain I had into something…*more*.

I wanted more.

I wanted everything.

And now, I would have nothing.

Now, she would forever associate being tied up as something to be avoided, especially by me.

Her rapid breath fluttered over my face as I bent over her and pressed her forearm against the armrest.

The white shift didn't hide the ghost of her lingerie, nor the peaking of her nipples. Her skin was cold, her lips growing bluer by the minute.

She hadn't even been in the lake and already she looked hypothermic.

She's as cold as me.

The leather slipped a few times from my grip as I fumbled to feed the buckle. Luckily, my back blocked my motions from my father—otherwise he would see my frost was thawing. He would see the haunting in my eyes of being so close to this woman while she hated me.

Nila was the culprit—my undoing.

She melted me.

She was the fucking sun. And I was about to splash out her heat.

Once her wrists were shackled, I ducked to attend to her ankles. Her legs jostled as her shaking grew worse. Her teeth chittered and chattered, her hair sticking to the cold sweat dotting her brow.

I hesitated a moment too long. Reaching out, I wrapped my fingers around her leg, preparing to fasten the cuff.

She gasped, dragging my eyes to her.

Fuck.

It was a terrible mistake to look at her.

She looked so small. So easily broken. Her eyes were too wide for her face; her skin stretched over bones that might shatter if she became any colder.

I tried to look away.

I tried.

But I couldn't.

Our gazes locked; I groaned under my breath as the connection between us only strengthened. The diamond collar around her neck sparkled even as the clouds above us blotted out the sunshine and gathered dark grey.

Nila stopped shivering, almost as if she found sanctuary in my gaze.

I stopped fighting, almost as if she tamed the insanity inside me.

What was this...this tether? How had she captured me so completely, and how the fuck did I sever it?

The deeper I fell into her, the worst it got.

Her panic siphoned into my soul, twisting my gut until I wanted to vomit. Her flesh turned white as the moon and just as ethereal.

In the starkness of what was about to happen, she'd never been so beautiful, so bewitching, so intense.

My knees wobbled, itching to kneel before her and place my head in her lap. To just rest...and pretend none of this existed. To have her comfort me.

Cut growled under his breath, smashing through our moment, rendering it dead.

Nila sniffed, tears glossing her eyes.

The link between us had been so bright, but now it was back to darkness.

You're running out of time.

Gritting my teeth, I forced myself to work faster. My fingers moved swiftly, securing the buckle around her left ankle.

I looked up one last time. Needing her to know that I'd

come to her full of nothing, but now she'd filled me with everything.

She looked into my eyes, then glanced away.

I wanted to tell her I was sorry. I wanted her to see in my gaze what I could never say aloud.

Forgive me.

With a soft moan, she closed her eyes, cutting me off completely.

Her dismissal butchered my heart, dug it out with a dirty blade, and sent it splashing into the pond. The hole left behind filled with algae, water, and bracken. I was a fucking bastard. I should stop this.

But I won't.

I wanted what I'd inherit on my thirtieth birthday. I was selfish, greedy, and vain. I wanted Nila, too. I believed I could have both.

If only I had more time.

You don't have more time. Not today.

Securing her other ankle, I stood.

I waited for her to look at me—to give me some sign she understood that we were in this together. That despite what I did, the tattoos overrode my loyalty to my family and bound me to her.

My Weaver.

Her Hawk.

I waited another second, and another.

But she never opened her eyes. Her forehead furrowed harder, her fists curled tighter, and she withdrew from me until there was no emotion left—just a tiny dying star that once had shone so bright.

Leaving me heartless and bleeding, she gave me nothing else to do.

I slipped into my role as torturer and began.

PLEASE, GRANT ME strength.
Please, grant me power.
Please don't let me scream.

Fettered to the chair, I kept my eyes squeezed as tight as possible—so tight—no light entered, no swirling colours from behind my eyelids. Just pitch black darkness.

When Jethro looked at me with agony in his gaze, I'd pitied him. He held so many secrets in his golden depths. So many rights. So many wrongs.

I could have a lifetime with him and never understand.

But in that moment, I *did* understand, and I both despised and bled for him. He was supposed to give me strength by making me hate him. I wanted to rue him as much as I did the day I found my ancestor's graves. Hate would've kept me warm and alive.

But he'd stolen that by looking destroyed, crippled with conflicting loyalties.

It made me fall harder.

It made me slam to the bottom of my feelings for him.

I wanted to praise him for letting me into his heart. I wanted to tell him I had the capacity to love him in return.

But I didn't.

I couldn't.

He didn't deserve it.

And then, I found my hate again.

I hated him for being too weak and not going against his family.

I cursed him for not having the courage to choose.

Why should he choose me?

He barely even knew me.

But souls were wise things. They always knew before the brain or the heart. There was no discriminating—if you saw your perfect other…you knew—instantly.

There was something there from the beginning.

Just like there had been for us.

And it would remain there until Jethro successfully tore it out and killed it.

Because even though we were linked by this fragile, fluttering thing, it wouldn't take much to ruin. It was already on the brink.

He's sentenced me to pay the Second Debt.

How many more would he carry out?

Did I trust him to be strong enough to end this before my life was stolen?

Looking over my shoulder, his family glowered at me as if I'd killed their loved ones with a barely spoken curse. They watched with trepidation—as if they believed I'd descended from the witch they hated and would turn them to toads at any second.

Superstition perfumed the breeze. Hate bloomed from the roses. And impatience spiced the water lilies.

I missed the intimacy of the First Debt. I missed the throbbing chemistry between Jethro and me even while he did something so wrong. It had just been the two of us. Together.

Now, it was just me against them.

"Do you know what this is, Ms. Weaver?" Jethro asked, stealing my attention.

I pressed my lips together. My neck hurt from straining to look over my shoulder.

When I didn't answer, Jethro recited, his voice silted and cool. "You're sitting in a ducking stool. It was used traditionally as a torture method for women. Its free-moving arm swings over the river to extract truth and confessions by ducking into the freezing cold water."

He looked away from me, pacing between the reeds. "The length of immersion was decided by the operator and the crime of which the woman was accused. It could last for just a few seconds, but in some circumstances, the process was continuously repeated over the course of a day."

He faced me. "Do you know the crimes the ducking stool was used for?"

I didn't answer. I refused.

I made an oath not to scream. I refused to entertain them with my cries.

Kes came forward, answering on behalf of Jethro. "Most common crimes were prostitution and witchcraft. Scolds were also punished by this method." His lips tilted. "Know what a scold is, Nila?"

I couldn't stop my head from shaking.

Shit, I didn't mean to react.

Jethro's eyes narrowed, his chest rising sharply.

"A scold was a gossiper, shrew, or bad tempered woman," Kes said.

Jethro glared at his brother. "Even though I have experience with your temper, Ms. Weaver, I cannot say you are a scold." Running a hand through his hair, he finished, "Regardless, this is to show you how death by water can be one of the most frightening things of all. This is how my ancestor died. This is how you will pay."

Snapping his fingers, Jethro ordered, "Turn your head. Look away."

Another avalanche of fear tumbled through me. I couldn't do this!

"Turn around, girl!" Cut snapped.

I don't know how I did it, but I slowly resettled on the

hard wooden seat, and tore my eyes from Jethro. The pond before me twinkled like cold jewels—blue and green and black.

My heart grew bigger and bigger in my chest until it filled every inch. I couldn't breathe. I couldn't think. I couldn't blink.

Noise came from behind me; I had to fight every instinct to look.

Trust in Kes. He said they wouldn't drown me.

Suddenly, the chair swooped upward. It went from being glued in the mud to flying high over the earth. I gasped, smashing my lips together to contain my scream.

No. No, no, no.

My fingers had nothing to hold onto. My wrists kissed the wood, held in place by tight leather. My legs couldn't move. I was well and truly caught.

The ducking stool wobbled as whatever force held me up readjusted to my weight. The breeze was stronger up here, whistling over the water like tiny mournful flutes.

The view would've been idyllic with the weeping willows and ducks preening on the banks. But I was caught in my worst nightmare.

I didn't want to see anymore.

Squeezing my eyes, I wished I'd been blindfolded. I didn't want to witness what was to come.

Don't open your eyes. Don't open them.

Someone's hands brushed against my ankles. A mechanism was locked then another swoop higher and higher sent my stomach splattering to my toes.

I'd been in theme parks before—I'd ridden a rollercoaster once in my life. Once was more than enough, even though V adored the loop de loop. I didn't understand his joy of making himself dizzy when I lived that way every day.

I'd found no thrill in being bound to an uncomfortable ride, listening to the *clack-clack* of the rollercoaster wheels as we clawed our way higher up a mountain of track. Every clatter of the rails sent equal measures of panic and excitement…until we reached the top…and just hovered there.

We'd hovered like a bird, basking in being on top of the world.

That was where I hung now.

Gravity defying—a girl in a white dress suspended above a dark green pond. A girl who would've done anything to have been born a Smith or a Jones or a Kim.

And then the rollercoaster slipped from weightless to bullet, freefalling over the mountain and hurling me into terror.

I promised myself I wouldn't scream.

It was a hard promise to keep.

The chair lost its support, leaving my belly above me as I fell and fell and fell.

Forever I fell, before splashing into frigid wetness.

The moment the water lapped around my ankles, I gave up trying to be brave.

The water slurped and sucked, devouring my legs in an instant.

The human part of me—the girl inside—was shoved aside by instinct and horror.

I squirmed, gasping louder and louder as the ice welcomed me, faster and faster. The wooden chair surrendered to the water, letting it lap its way almost seductively up my legs, over my waist, my breasts, my throat…my…

…mouth.

I arched my neck as best I could. I fought against the pond's embrace.

I managed one last gulp of life.

Then, I disappeared.

I became a prisoner of the lake.

I promised myself I wouldn't scream.

I lied.

The instant the water crashed over my head, I lost it.

Well and truly lost it.

My eyes flew open in the murky gloom and I screamed.

I screamed as if I would die. I screamed as if my body was being torn in two and eaten alive. I screamed as if this was the end.

Bubbles cascaded from my mouth, gifting all my oxygen to a passing trout in a riot of glistening froth.

I promised myself I would stay calm. That I would listen to Kes's advice and get through this with complete trust, knowing that eventually I would be hoisted back up.

That was another lie.

I had no understanding of time.

Seconds were minutes and minutes were years.

I bobbed in a substance that would kill me with no way free.

It was enough to send me into insanity.

I didn't care I could break an arm or leg fighting against the securely buckled straps. I didn't care I could snap my neck by thrashing hopelessly in the chair. And I definitely didn't care I could break my mind by letting the horror of being drowned consume me.

I couldn't stand it.

I'm dying.

I can't fucking stand it!

And then, just like any rollercoaster, another incline halted the fatal swoop and hurled me back into the heavens once again.

The weight of the water pressed down on my skull and shoulders. My eyes burned from rushing water. The pressure. The unrelenting grip the lake had on me. It fought the pull. It didn't want to let me go.

The sodden material of my gown sucked to my skin as my chair was raised and raised until...

Pop.

The water relented, letting me break the skin of the pond and leave a watery death behind.

Thank God—I can breathe!

Up and up I swooped, spluttering and dripping rain from above. I breathed and coughed and choked and sobbed.

I sucked in air as if I only had one purpose in life: to revive myself and regain my sanity.

My heartbeat was frantic—palpating, double beating—far too fast and petrified.

My long hair plastered to my face. Every mouthful of oxygen I sucked, strands smothered my mouth. More panic screeched through my veins. The claustrophobia was more than I could bear.

Through the forest of my hair, I had to see behind me. I had to look at Jethro and let him see how much I'd unravelled. I wouldn't be able to stand another dunk.

I won't.

Quaking, I looked over my shoulder. My hair tugged, plaiting wetly around my throat as I focused on the banks.

Through drips of water, I vaguely noticed the four Hawk men. All four had their elbows locked, pushing down on the pendulum and gripping hard to the leather handholds.

The strength it took to raise and plummet me into the pond exceeded that of one man.

This debt.

This atrocity had become a family affair.

Jethro, Kestrel, Daniel, and Cut.

Together they played roulette with my life, and in a perfect harmony, they shifted as one and began the rollercoaster all over again.

Their side of the seesaw rose; I dropped.

"No!" I screamed, thrashing in the chair.

But they ignored me.

Faster and faster they dropped me until they disappeared; once again, my aquatic grave welcomed me.

The water's kiss devoured my feet, my thighs, my breasts…my head.

I sank quicker.

Like I belonged.

The second time was no better.

If anything, it was worse.

My lungs burned.

They felt as if they bled with my submerged screams.

My heartbeat sent ripples of horror through the water cradling me. Sonic sound waves alerted fish that I would soon be easy prey…that I was moments from slipping from this world and into another.

One that hopefully treated me better.

I struggled harder, bruised deeper, and drove myself quicker into madness.

I screamed again, unable to hold in oxygen. Something scaly swam beneath me, tickling my toes. Fronds of water grasses and quick flashes of movement from frogs all sent my mind twirling into darkness.

Images of Loch Ness monsters and sea creatures with wicked sharp teeth stole the remainders of my rationality.

I want to breathe.

I want to live.

I strained for the lighter green of the surface. Crying and pleading and drinking gallons of pond scum in my struggle to stay alive.

Time played a horrible joke on me. It never ended.

There was no reprieve…no air.

The emerald depth of the water crowded me, closing in tighter and tighter—crushing me like a tin can beneath its gentle waves.

This ducking lasted longer, or maybe I was destroyed already. Perhaps it was shorter, but I'd run out of reserves to hold on.

I wanted to stop fighting.

I wanted to succumb.

How weak I was.

How fragile.

How broken.

My fighting gave way to twitches. My muscles fought on their own, demanding oxygen I didn't have to give.

My hair hovered around me like it was alive, swaying like seaweed, promising an easy existence if I just followed its gentle dance and give in.

Just…give in.

Give in to the gentle lullaby of sleep.

If I died, I won.

The Hawks would lose as I would be free…

My struggling ceased and I hung there as if I was no longer bones and breath, but weightless freedom. My shift billowed like wings around me, sending me deeper into the abyss.

It was quiet down here. Quiet and calm and…drifting.

I drifted…

I faded…

Then the weight began again, folding my chin against my collar, tugging me from the deep. Pounding, pounding pressure as I was wrenched from my emerald tomb and hurled into the clouds again.

Gravity was now my foe, making everything so eternally heavy. My chest was an elephant. My head a bowling ball.

And I was weak.

So weak.

Air trickled down my throat, mixing with water I'd drank, making me retch. As each mouthful registered, my brain awoke, kicking me into survival. I moaned and begged and devoured every drop of oxygen I could.

I couldn't look up. I couldn't look behind me.

All I saw was blackness. But something granted me inhuman strength to twist in my bindings and look, just once, behind.

The clouds were dark and threatening, shadowing the Hawks in sombre gloom.

Jethro's golden eyes burned me from the banks, superseding all distance, glowing like amber or sunlight—or paradise.

Paradise…

I would like to go to paradise.

But then I looked at Cut, Kes, and Daniel.

Their eyes were the same damn colour.

All of them.

Four men. Four wishes and wills—but one pair of identical eyes.

Evil eyes.

Horrendous eyes.

Eyes I never wanted to see again.

Daniel asked, "Have you given up your power, you wicked witch? Are you cured of the infection of magic?"

Jethro shoved him, cursing him beneath his breath.

Then, I fell again.

The men released their hold, shooing me from dryness and gifting me to a wet crypt.

As the water crashed over my head the third time, I gave up.

There was no point in fighting.

I was done.

I lost all track of time.

Up, down, up, down. Wet to dry and back again.

Every ducking I grew weaker…faded faster.

How many times did they raise me, only to drop me a few moments later? I believed Jethro when they said some torture sessions went on all day.

It felt as if this lasted forever.

I couldn't move. I had no energy remaining.

Underwater again, my heartbeat raced until it splintered my ribs, cleaving me open, letting water pour down my throat and slosh into my lungs.

Delusions were no longer something to fear, but to be *embraced*. Delusions brought fantasies to life, soothing me, eradicating monsters from my world.

Down here, unicorns existed. Up there, only beasts.

I opened my mouth wider, slack-jawed and spaced.

Perhaps I had a gift I didn't know of.

Perhaps I was a mermaid and could breathe water better than air.

Perhaps I could transform and swim far, far away from

here.

I would try.

Anything was better than this.

The icy ache in my chest as the water filled me like a balloon was foreign and frightening.

But then it grew warmer.

And warmer.

It comforted me.

The pain left.

The panic receded.

I said goodbye to life.

Death slid over me with the sweetest kiss.

I smiled and sighed and gave into the deep.

SHE WAS DEAD.

I knew it.

I couldn't explain how I knew.

But I did.

I'd done it.

I'd killed her.

She'd left me.

IT WAS OVER.

I existed in a fog of warm, comforting blackness. I didn't have a conscience or stress or worries.

I was *content.*

This nether world had no stipulations or rules on how to be. I just was. With no thoughts corrupting me.

I liked it here.

I preferred it here.

I sank deeper and deeper into the billowing softness.

I belong here.

Then something tugged on my mind.

I swatted it away, curling into a ball, becoming invisible.

The blackness grew darker, wanting to keep me just as much as I wanted to keep it.

But the tug came again, harder, stronger.

I fought it.

But it was so persistent. It scrabbled at my mind, breaking my happy bond and dragging me unwillingly from the deep.

It wrecked my contentedness.

It broke my happiness.

No!

I turned feral.

You can't take me.

I belong here. Not there.

Here I had a sense of infinity. I wasn't just human, I was so much more.

I didn't want to go.

I like it here.

Here where I don't care or want or fear.

But whatever it was wouldn't listen. It pulled me faster and faster from my sanctuary.

Blackness faded, becoming brighter and brighter.

I had no choice but to hurtle toward the light, breaking in two with sadness.

Then everything disintegrated.

The darkness. The comfort. The gentle kind of warmth.

It all vanished.

I froze, completely lost and vulnerable.

Where am I?

Something brilliant and bright shone into my eyes. I blinked in pain, seeing an echo of the deep yellow sun.

The clouds are gone.

I blinked again. Bringing the world I once knew into focus. It made me wish I was blind.

With my eyesight came an unfurling of senses as my soul slipped back into a body I no longer wanted, breathing life into limbs that'd turned into a corpse.

There was something I was supposed to do in this world. Something extremely important.

The knowledge slammed into me with wet panic.

Breathe!

I couldn't breathe.

A shadow crossed the blistering sun, pressing soft lips against mine. My nose was pinched then a huge gust of air whistled down my throat, bringing sweet, sweet oxygen.

My chest expanded then deflated.

Not enough.

More. Give me more.

The life-giver understood, once again filling me with breath along with forgiveness, sorrow, and regret.

I retched.

Strong hands flipped me onto my side, patting my back with solid thumps as I vomited up bucket loads of lake.

It hurt.

God, it hurt.

My lungs turned inside out with agony as the overstretched organ gave up trying to survive on water, holding out eager hands for air instead.

With air came life, and with life came the knowledge that I'd died.

Tears sprang to my eyes.

I'd died.

And I preferred it.

I sank into despair.

How had I given up so easily?

Then realization slammed into me of who I was and where.

I was Nila.

This was the Second Debt.

All around me stood Hawks.

Bastard, traitorous Hawks.

Then it didn't matter anymore.

Pain enveloped me in a heavy cloak, squeezing me from all angles. Agony I'd never felt before battered me like a storm. Agony lived in my head, my heart, my bones, my blood.

Everything hurt.

Everything had died.

Coming alive was sheer torture, welcomed by a ring of devils.

"Come back to me, Nila." Jethro breathed into my ear, barely registering above the bone-crippling agony I lived. "I won't let you fucking leave me." He licked a tear leaking from my eye. "Not yet. I won't let you leave, not yet."

I couldn't look at him.

I couldn't listen to him.

So, I focused on the spot on top of the hill—on a black

speck spotlighted by the waning sun.

No, not a speck.

A woman.

Dark hair, feminine grace.

Jasmine.

Seeing her stole my tension. I relaxed. My screaming muscles stopped twitching, melting into the mud upon which I lay.

I didn't need to fight anymore.

Jasmine was regal with honour and resplendent with pride—exactly as expected from any Hawk descendant.

I had the strange urge to wave—to have her grant me mercy.

How was it possible someone could wield so much power even while she was as broken as me?

I'd drowned and come back to life.

I'd been fixed.

However, Jasmine never would.

My eyes drifted from her beautiful face to her legs.

I sighed in sympathy for such a plight.

Wheels replaced legs. Footholds instead of shoes.

Jasmine Hawk was paralysed.

Wheelchair bound and reclusive.

It all suddenly made a lot more sense. About Jethro. His father. His sister.

And then it all became too much.

I drifted off into fluffy clouds.

I said goodbye for the second time.

I CARRIED HER unconscious form back to hell.

I turned my back on my father, grandmother, and siblings.

I let them whisper about my downfall and plot my death.

I did all of those things because the moment I'd felt Nila give up, nothing else fucking mattered.

Money, Hawksridge, diamonds—none of it.

It was all bullshit.

And I didn't fucking care.

All I cared about was making sure Nila healed.

I couldn't let her die.

She couldn't leave me alone.

Not now.

Stalking up the hill, across the grounds, and into the Hall, I ignored the Diamond brothers who'd been watching the spectacle with an array of binoculars and telescopes, and stormed to the back of the house.

In the parlour loomed a huge swinging door, disguised as a bookcase.

Years ago, the door had hidden a bunker. A secret entrance into the catacombs below the house. They were there to save my ancestors from war and mutiny.

Now, that bunker had been converted and served a different kind of function, along with an addition found ninety years after the first brick had been laid.

Nila's body was icy and soaking. Her clothing dripped down my front, leaving a trail of droplets wherever we went. Her long wet hair trailed over my arm like kelp. Not for the first time, I fantasised I'd plucked a kelpie from the pond and taken her hostage. My very own water nymph to keep for good luck.

She would make me right.

She had to.

Pulling on a certain book, the mechanism unlocked, swinging the door open.

Nila didn't stir.

She'd stopped shivering, but her lips were a deep indigo that terrified me more than her unconscious whimpers. She teetered on death's door—even now—even though I'd resuscitated her with mouth to mouth and given my soul as well as my air, she still haemorrhaged life.

It was as if she *wanted* to die.

Wanted to leave me.

Her brittle body made me focus on things I wasn't strong enough to face.

I'd grown up.

I'd begun to see.

I'd begun to believe she was it for me. The only one who could save me from myself.

Slinking through the door, I was careful not to bump her head. Her body lay strewn like a fallen angel in my arms—as if I'd caught her mid-plummet to earth. Her lips were parted; her arms dangled by her sides.

I had to get her warm and fast. I knew exactly how to do it.

Locking the door behind me, I descended the spiral staircase. I had no way of clapping to turn on the sound activated lights, so stomped my foot on the stone step, grateful when balls of light lit up one after the other, leading the way in the dark.

Electricity had replaced gas, which in turn had replaced

naked flames that used to flicker in the medieval lanterns on the wall.

Moving forward, each bulb guided me further beneath the house, until I travelled beneath my own quarters and the bachelor wing above.

The bunker had been extended far past its original footprint. The crude concrete walls had been meticulously updated with large travertine tiles and top-of-the-line facilities.

Countless contraptions existed that I could use to warm Nila.

We had a steam room, sauna, and spa.

We had everything money could buy.

But none would be good enough.

I needed something bigger, grander...hotter.

I needed something money couldn't buy: the power of nature.

The scent of sulphur enveloped us as I continued down the corridor and into the humid world beneath Hawksridge. The cave had been discovered after the first part of the Hall had been erected. A workman died falling through the hole when setting new foundations—the cave had been stumbled upon by pure fluke.

Natural springs were a fairly common phenomenon in England—closely guarded by those who had them and a public luxury in places like Bath. Ours had remained a family secret for generations.

The sapphire water never dropped below forty degrees centigrade. Ever. It was consistent and somewhere I used to come a lot—somewhere that Jasmine visited almost daily with her maid to ease her atrophied muscles.

Moisture dripped from the earthen walls, plopping quietly back into the pool where it'd come from. A perpetual circle of death and rebirth.

I didn't stop to strip.

I didn't waste a moment.

Holding Nila tight against my chest, I walked down the

carved steps and into the shoulder-deep spring. Every wade made my skin tingle and burn. I couldn't handle such warm waters all at once—I had to ease into it, allow the ice inside my soul to melt little by little.

But now all I cared about was raising Nila's body temperature.

I didn't care about my shoes or clothes.

Shit, I didn't even care I had my cell-phone and wallet in my pocket.

Everything was inconsequential; the urge to heal her before it was too late far too strong.

Not only had I scarred her back, but now I'd scarred her with death.

I have to fix this. Quickly.

As the warm liquid lapped around my waist, it stole Nila's weight, almost tugging her from my arms. Unwillingly, I unlocked my grip, letting her float away from me, bobbing buoyantly on the surface.

Her eyes didn't open. She didn't show any awareness that she felt the warmth after being so cold.

With cupped fingers, I poured hot water over her head, trading the iciness of the lake for the welcoming embrace of the spring.

Waterfall after waterfall I poured on her scalp, careful not to let the droplets slide over her nose or mouth.

It took too long.

The only noise was the gentle splash of water as it rained through my fingers.

Every second waiting for her to wake up ruined my every heartbeat.

I lost track of time. My eyes never left her blue, blue lips, and it was only when the deep colour began to fade that I finally relaxed a little.

Her fingertips weren't ice cubes any longer, thawing thanks to the warmth of the water.

When she finally did start to rouse, she began to shiver.

Violently.

Her teeth chattered and her hair tangled on the surface, jerking with every tremble.

Gathering her close, I held her as ripples arched from the epicentre of her body, fanning out to lap against the three metre wide pool.

Every twitch from her resonated in me—I didn't think I'd ever be stable again.

I continued to pour water over her head, cascading it over her frozen ears, willing her cheeks to turn pink.

Her soft moan was the second sign of her being alive. However, if she was aware of what I did, she didn't show it— she refused to open her eyes.

I couldn't blame her.

I wouldn't want to look at the man who'd done this either.

Sighing, I pressed my forehead against hers. No words could convey everything I felt. So I let silence do it for me.

I filled the space with so much fucking regret. Regret for today, for yesterday, for tomorrow. For everything I was and could never be.

I didn't know how long we hovered in the cave beneath my ancestral home, but slowly the silence filled with more than just sorrow and apology. It filled with a need so fierce and cruel, I struggled to breathe.

Pulling back, my eyes met Nila's black ones.

I froze as she slowly stood upright, dropping her legs beneath the water. Her hands moved. Slowly and weakly, she cupped my face.

I stiffened within her hold.

A hitched sigh fell from my lips.

I would permit her to slap me. I would let her take out her rage. After all, I deserved it.

I knew she was angry. The colour in her cheeks and glitter in her eyes hinted at her rage. I felt her temper building as surely as I felt the small eddies of natural thermals in the water.

I nodded, bracing for punishment.

But she didn't move.

We just stared and breathed and tried to understand each other's betrayal.

My lips tingled for hers. My cock wept for her body. And my heart...shit my heart begged to unlock and let her own it.

"I forgive you," she finally whispered, a single tear rolling down her cheek.

That one phrase cleaved me in two, and for the first time in my life, I broke. I wanted to fucking cry over a lifetime of misuse. Over a childhood I'd never been able to enjoy and an adulthood I'd never been able to embrace.

I wanted to fucking kill for what I still had to do and for what I had become.

I should slip beneath the water and take my own life. I was done fighting. Done pretending.

If I could've saved her by ending my struggles, I would have.

I would've sacrificed all I fucking knew to save her.

Licking my bottom lip, my eyes fell to her mouth.

There was just too much to say. Too many hurts to uncover and I didn't have the strength.

Not yet.

Nila floated before me, her breath hitching as I gently captured her hips and dragged her weightless body against mine.

Her eyes flared; her body bowstring tight.

Her fingers dug into my cheeks, holding me at a distance but not struggling to swim away.

My hands burned where I held her. I was grateful she let me touch her at all. But it wasn't enough. I wanted more.

Lowering my head, I tore past her anger and searched for the emotion from the polo match.

I needed to see I hadn't destroyed what I'd witnessed that day. Slowly, it appeared—floating to the surface of her eyes, blazing true.

She still cared for me.

After all that I'd done.

Fuck, I'm a monster.

Guilt crushed my chest, spinning rapidly with body-melting desire.

"Kiss me, Nila," I whispered. "Let me bring you back to life."

The water waked as she jolted. Her hands landed on my chest, tensing to push me away.

I shuddered as her fingertips scrunched my shirt.

Then, instead of pushing me, she pulled me.

Her hand slinked up around my neck, tugging my mouth to hers.

I sucked in a breath.

And she obeyed.

Nila

EVERY INCH OF me hurt.

My lungs were battered and bruised; my throat raw and raspy. My head pounded and throbbed. Every time I breathed, it seemed as if my ribcage had one purpose in life: to stab my heart to death.

I was alive...and paying the price.

Drowning wasn't fun.

Being drowned multiple times, even less so.

I never wanted to go near water again.

Yet you're in a pool with Jethro.

You're in a pool kissing *Jethro.*

My mind hurt trying to understand how he'd destroyed me in water, yet healed me in the same substance.

Cruel then comforting.

Murderous then reviving.

Two sides to everything—not evil or good or even aware of its perception. Just a single entity being used in different ways.

Water could be an enemy, but also a lover.

Could the same be true for Jethro?

His lips slid against mine. Wet and warm and gentle.

He didn't force me. He didn't try to control the kiss I'd given him.

And for that I was grateful.

I took my time. Tasting him—tasting his regret.

I did my utmost to swim deep into his soul where the truth just waited to be found. I needed to know what he suffered from. I had to find out if I wanted to remain living.

His head twisted, changing the direction of the kiss so our bodies danced closer. The tip of his tongue licked my bottom lip, shooting a ripple of lust into my belly.

I had to trust in him. Trust in *this*. Had to believe. Had to hope.

Opening my mouth, I welcomed his tongue inside. Licking him, encouraging him, giving into the dark and dangerous undercurrent flowing between us.

He groaned, gathering me closer. Pulling back, he clasped my cheeks with his large hands. "I want you to know."

My damaged heart fluttered. I didn't speak, but I knew my question glowed in my eyes.

Know what?

He sighed. His chiselled cheekbones and dark brows made him look guilty and sorrowful all at once. His thick eyelashes shadowed stunning eyes and his lips—they promised to be the perfect drug to make me forget about my pain.

In the hazy steamy world, I saw how tightly reined he was. His soul didn't just have shadows—it had holes. Holes that might never be stitched together again.

He was heir to an empire worth untold millions. He was smart, capable, and strong. In hindsight, it was inevitable that I would fall for him. How could I not? It was almost a relief to admit that I stood no chance against his spell.

But if he'd ensnared me, then I'd ensnared him.

He suffered the same conflict.

Jethro brushed a thumb over my lips, his touch trembling softly. "You make me better even while making me worse."

My throat tightened, triggering the soreness from previous screaming. The tattoo on my fingertip burned as if recognising he was my other half—whether I wanted it or not.

In so many ways, Jethro was old beyond his years, yet so young at the same time.

"You need to tell me," I murmured. "Let me understand."

"Can't you understand that I've been fucked up ever since I first texted you? I'm insane, but you're the only cure for my insanity."

My heart thundered. The first verbal admission that he was Kite.

It was more than he'd given me before, but it wasn't enough.

"I'm listening and not judging." I couldn't stop myself from adding, "And you made me the same way. I'm mad over you, Jethro. You have to give in."

With a blended noise of frustration and grief, he kissed me again, twisting my thoughts with an eager tongue. I wasn't strong enough to stay firm while he was determined to sweep me away. The kiss distracted me from what he'd said, what I wanted him to say. Despite myself, I mirrored him, massaging his tongue with mine, strengthening our desire.

Don't let him hide.

My restraint barely existed, but I couldn't permit him to change the subject—no matter if I preferred the new topic.

Breaking free, I pushed my fingers into his hair, holding him firm. "Tell me, Jethro. Tell me everything."

He breathed hard, his eyes never leaving my mouth. "Isn't it enough to know you've got me by the heart?" He suddenly grabbed my hand, splaying my fingers over his chest. "Can you feel that?"

My lungs stuck together as my heartbeat kicked into a flurry.

Jethro breathed, "It's become so bad, I can barely breathe. For years I've struggled—my whole fucking life."

I tried to take my hand back. I couldn't stomach feeling the irregular thump of his heart beneath my fingertips. Its rhythm was screwed up, confused…lost.

His face held such yearning, such turmoil. Staring at me

that way gave me too much power. Too much authority over his soul.

But it also soothed me—proved that having control in my future was right here—in my grasp. I only had to be brave enough to take it.

Curling my fingers on his chest, as if I could carve his heart out and hold it in my hand, I stared into his light coloured eyes. "Tell me."

"I'll tell you what I can…but later."

"No, you won't. Tell me now."

"What more do you want from me, Nila?" he suddenly snarled. "Don't you see? Do you really need to hear it?"

His fear thickened the air.

Yes, I could see something was wrong. I could almost understand it.

But I needed him to admit it.

"You can't hide. Not this time. Not with me."

Silence webbed around us.

Then finally, his head bowed in defeat, but there was relief in his gaze. "I'll tell you. All of it. What I am. What it means. I promise. I'll tell you."

WHAT I AM. What it means.
WHAT I AM. What it means.
The promise echoed in my head.
Why had I promised such a thing?
Why did I think I could?
Because she needs to see the truth. She needed to know so she could forgive me.

I kissed her again—trying to stop her from seeing my fear at being open and true.

Holding her jaw, I pressed my lips harder against hers, signalling that I would keep my promise, but not right now.

Right now, I needed to be inside her.

Right now, I didn't have the strength.

It was selfish of me to take more from her when she'd only just recovered, but something inside me howled for what she could give.

I needed it before I had the capacity to talk about what I was.

Only then would I find the courage.

I'm selfish.

I'm a bastard.

She paused for a second, as if deciding whether to let me drag her from words to actions. Then her tongue met mine, returning my kiss with a greed that sent my cock on fire.

Her arms wrapped around my waist, holding me reverently.

It was more, so much more than I deserved. My breathing hitched.

Slowly, the kiss evolved into an admittance of feelings and longing. Our breathing accelerated, echoing in the cave.

Needing nothing between us, I pushed Nila away and grabbed the hem of my t-shirt. The water sucked the fabric against my stomach, gluing it in place.

With a tug that sent a wash of droplets raining over Nila, I tore it off and threw it to the side.

Nila stood there, her gaze drifting down my exposed torso. Her dark beauty stole my fucking breath. Her hair hung like wet silk. The shapeless white shift moulded to her curves, thanks to the Velcro-like ability of water.

Wading toward her, I ducked a little and captured her hem below the water's surface. Without a word, I pulled it up over her thighs and hips then hid her face as I pulled it over her head.

Her arms fell to her sides, lethargic and weak from what I'd done.

Leaning forward, I reached behind her and unhooked her bra. I bit my lip as the fabric fell away, exposing what I'd been dying to see for days.

Her nipples were pink and hard, pinpointed with the same desire that existed in my cock.

Never looking away, I captured the lace on her hips and pulled her knickers down her legs. She trembled but didn't stop me. I shouldn't do this. She needed to rest.

But I had no choice.

I had to take her.

It was the only way.

Her touch landed on my shoulder for balance as I removed her underwear. Her gaze darkened before a slight mask slid into place, hiding depths that I needed to see.

I'd done that. I'd made her build walls. I'd made her hide—

same as me.

I couldn't permit that.

Throwing away her underwear, she stood before me naked and completely trusting. Giving me everything I demanded so damn selflessly.

"I'll never be able to thank you," I whispered.

"Thank me for what?"

"For caring more about my own welfare than your own." Capturing her face, I breathed, "I can feel you. I know that doesn't make sense, but the moment you give in to me; the moment you let yourself submit…it saves me. I can't explain it, but you heal me, Nila."

Her eyes glistened. A soft smile graced her lips as she pressed her cheek into my palm. "Don't be afraid of me, Jethro. Don't be afraid of what's growing between us."

I kissed her. Her mouth opened, her tongue dancing with mine.

Breaking apart, I said, "I won't. I'm not letting you go. You're mine, do you understand?"

She nodded, shyness pinking her cheeks. "I belong to you."

I shivered with relief, with gratefulness, with every fucking comfort I'd never had.

With fumbling hands, I undid my belt and pushed my jeans and boxer-briefs down my legs. Kicking off my shoes, I stripped. The water made it a trial to discard the unwanted clothing.

Urgency echoed in my limbs, making me rush. She'd admitted she was mine. I had to confirm it.

The hot water flowed around my erection, lapping at my balls—more arousing than air.

I ached to fill her again.

Gathering her close, I pressed my forehead against hers and wrapped my arms around her tiny waist. "I want to make you come. I want to erase what happened today and give you a better memory."

She lifted her face to the natural cave formation above us.

"Here?"

I nodded.

I wouldn't be able to walk with the pounding flesh between my legs. I was a fucking saint taking it slow. One touch from her and I'd explode.

Brushing her hair from her neck, I whispered, "I'm going to fuck you...here." Trailing my lips along her jawline, I murmured, "I'm going to make you moan...here." Baring my teeth, I bit her throat, filled with the primal need to mark. "I'm going to make you scream...here."

She shivered, letting her head fall back, surrendering to me.

I bit her again—I couldn't help myself. I nudged her diamond collar higher up her throat and bit hard. I couldn't ignore the instincts demanding me to claim.

I wanted to give her a gift. A gift where I gave her more than just my body but my heart. There would be no pain, debts, or degradation. Only us.

"I want to care for you, Nila. I want to show you how much I value what you've given me."

The driving urge to climb inside her grew with every heartbeat. The anticipation made it all the more sweeter, but I'd reached the end of my self-control.

Dropping my gaze, I followed my hand as I cupped her breast and squeezed. Her back curved, forcing more of her flesh into my fingers. I pinched her nipple then ducked and covered her other breast with my mouth.

She groaned, hugging my head to her, demanding that I lick harder. The erotic sound of her pleasure sent shock-waves through me.

Thank fuck she didn't like sweet and gentle. I'd tried to be soft—for her sake. I'd tried to control myself. I wasn't such a monster to add more injuries, not when she'd been through so much, but I silently thanked her that she needed what I did.

That she wanted me fierce and true. Nothing bared.

My fingertips flexed around her nipple, dragging another soft moan.

I couldn't stand it any longer.

Standing to my full height, I captured her mouth in another kiss. Her beautiful lips met mine, her tongue licking with passion and hunger. As our kiss deepened, I banded an arm around her, pressing her flat stomach against my cock.

She arched into my caress, her fingers flying into the water to wrap around my length.

"Fuck," I groaned as her tight hold sent my mind exploding with lust.

My hips rocked, forcing myself deeper into her palm. The joy of having her touch me—of me touching her—wasn't enough. I needed more.

I need fucking everything.

Picking her up, I waded to the side and spun her around. The moment she faced away from me, I couldn't stop myself from grinding my cock against the crack of her arse.

Her fingers clawed at the earthen side, her head flopping forward as I cupped her breasts from behind and squeezed to the point of pain.

Dropping one hand, I trailed it down her belly, not stopping until I found her slippery cunt. I sucked in air as I found a different kind of moisture.

Her arousal was thicker, silkier than the water around us.

I bit the back of her shoulder, pressing a finger deep inside her. The way she gave in to me made me soar. The guilt, the hate—it all faded.

She bucked, her mouth falling open. "Ah…"

Her gentle sound of bliss unravelled me faster.

This was what I needed. *Her.* Where had she been all my life? Why had I fumbled for so long without her in my arms?

Never again.

Never fucking again would I be so alone.

Her torso twisted in my arms, her hand cupping my bristle-covered jaw. "I can feel you."

Fuck, she was too perceptive.

I couldn't speak.

Nila's lips tilted into a sensual smile. "I can feel so much when you let go. When you let me in."

I kissed her.

I had no choice.

Her body wriggled against mine as I slipped another finger inside her pussy, rubbing her clit with my thumb.

"You're so fucking gorgeous...so strong." Words spilled from my mouth, disappearing into her hair, down her back, dripping into the water. "I'm so damn hard, I'm in agony. All my life, something was missing. And now I've found it." I rocked my dick against her, making my need so much worse. "I found you. I stole you. I took you from others who didn't appreciate the gift of what you are, and now I'm never letting you go."

She moaned, her eyes blazing with lust.

I thrust again, welcoming the heat and bliss of being naked with this woman. "See what you do to me? See how much I need to crawl inside you and never fucking leave?" I rolled my hips, panting at the delicious friction.

Nila gasped, her spine bowing in invitation. "God, don't stop. Tell me everything. Don't be afraid. If you want me to beg, I'll beg. If you want me to scream, I'll scream. Just..." Her legs spread in the water as she bent over the side, looking at me over her shoulder. "Just never stop being honest with me. This...what you're giving me, Jethro, it makes everything worthwhile. It makes everything I believed *real*."

Her cheeks glistened as she smiled through her tears. "Nothing could've prepared me for this. Nothing could've taught me to feel this way. I'm ready to forget everything. I'm ready to be selfish and steal you like you stole me."

She cried out as I thrust my fingers deeper inside her, tearing my name from her lips.

"I—I only want you," she groaned. "Only you. Promise me that I can keep you. Promise me."

My heart...shit, my heart.

It unlocked.

The padlock fell free.

Her words were a key. Her forgiveness and love and strength and everything that made her pure stole me from my life of pain.

She changed me.

Right there.

Right then.

I became hers.

Irreversibly.

"I promise," I swore. I needed to climb into her soul and cement everything we'd just confessed. "I'm so messed up over you. I—" I couldn't talk anymore. I was too fucking fragile. Too overwhelmed.

I grabbed her chin, twisting her neck to kiss me. I took her mouth savage and strong. I drove my tongue past her lips and admitted once and for all that I might be a Hawk; I might be a son destined for tragedy, but none of that mattered as long as I had her.

She trembled in my hold as I kissed her deeper, harder. My thumb swirled on her clit, matching the rhythm of my fingers driving in and out of her pussy.

Her hips moved, using me to drive herself to ecstasy.

"Promise me that you'll never cut me out. Promise me that you'll never walk away—no matter how badly I fuck up." I wanted to bind her in this moment—an ironclad agreement that she would never leave—no matter how bad things got.

Because I would fuck it up. She would end up hating me.

I had debts to extract, her brother to dispatch, and an empire to steal.

I wasn't perfect. Her love didn't make me a better man—it just gave me the strength to continue fighting.

Her inner walls fluttered around my touch. My mouth watered to taste her.

"I—I promise." Another cry escaped as her hips rocked harder on my hand. I wrapped my arm tighter around her.

"Oh, God…yes…Jethro…*please*…" Her face flushed,

every muscle hummed with the need to release.

She gave me complete control over her body and soul.

I lost it.

"Christ, I want to be inside you." I grabbed my cock, riding my palm. "So much. So fucking much." I jacked off with brutal violence, trying to tame the lust in my blood all while making it worse.

I'd never needed anyone as much as I needed her.

I'd never had the need to draw pain or bite or devour. But now I did. I wanted to *ruin* her. I was out of my mind with fucking desire.

Nila reached behind, steadying my hand. Her breathing was as ragged as mine. "I need it, too." Biting her lip, she guided my pounding erection between her legs and pushed against the side. "Don't hold back. Never again. I can handle what you have to give."

I shivered. "Fuck, Nila."

She wanted everything.

She wanted me. All of me. The twisted parts. The dark parts.

Me.

She was…peace. She was…sanity. She was…*home.*

She wants me.

I clenched my jaw. Her heat beckoned me. I was no longer human but an animal who needed to claim his mate.

Fisting the base of my cock, I bent my knees and thrust.

We both groaned.

It felt so fucking *good.*

Her slipperiness coated me, but it wasn't enough. She was too tight.

A tameless growl echoed in my chest as she pushed back, forcing me to fill her faster.

"Shit," I grunted as she pushed again.

"More. I need more," she begged.

I almost came from the exquisite tightness of her body. Every ripple of her muscles was like a fist around my girth. My balls twitched, preparing to spurt inside this woman—my fucking woman—now that I was rightfully home.

"I have to work you. You're not relaxed enough."

She shook her head, her face twisting with need. "No. Give it to me. Goddammit, Jethro, please…fuck me. I can't…" Her core contracted as I thrust again.

My lips pulled back as I drank in her piercing lust. "You need me inside you?"

"Yes. God, yes."

I drove harder. "You need me to fuck you?"

Her head flew back as I forced my size past her body's limits. "Yes. I need you. All of you."

I was only half-way in. My dick was too much for her. As much as she wanted me, as enticing as her moans were, I refused to hurt her more tonight. Tonight was about pleasure.

"I'm going to fill you."

"Please."

"I'm going to fuck you so hard, you'll stay wet for days just thinking of me taking you in this pool."

Nila bit her lip. "Do it, Jethro. Punish me. Teach me that I belong to you."

Fuck.

I'd never been a talker in sex. Never saw the allure of dirty whispers. But now all I could think about was talking filthy and wrong.

Reaching between her legs, I rubbed her clit—faster and faster with one goal in mind.

"You're going to come for me, little Weaver. You're going to drench my dick and let me inside you." I breathed harder, rocking faster, forcing her higher.

"No, I want—"

"You don't get what you want. This is what *I* want. I want you to know who's fucking you. I want you to know whose cock is taking you. I need you to scream for me, Nila."

I didn't give her any reprieve. I forced her to feel everything. I wanted her orgasm. She owed me her pleasure.

Nila stiffened; her elbows gave out as she flattened against the side. "Stop—wait…"

"No." I thrust with each swirl of my thumb, gradually spreading her—crawling inside. "I'm the one taking you. I'm the one riding you. I'm the one you want. Admit it!"

Her mouth opened as she silently screamed. Her entire focus turned inward.

I thrust harder. "Say it. Admit that you want me. Admit that you like what I'm doing to you."

Her eyes wrenched open, connecting with mine.

My heart fell down a rabbit hole, completely under her spell.

"Yes, I admit it. I feel you. I want you so much! Fuck me. Please…fuck me."

I couldn't deny her.

My hips rocked, my thumb swirled.

"Come. Come on my cock."

Her body rebelled, clamping around me. I struggled to breathe. I groaned as her pussy flexed tighter and tighter. I saw fucking stars.

"Jethro—" Her breathing turned to breathless pants. The muscles along her spine contorted with pressure. She wiggled, trying to dislodge my hold on her clit. "It's too intense—"

I didn't let her move. "You don't know the meaning of intense. I'll show you intense. I'll show you what it's like to live in a world full of fucking intensity." Bowing over her, I bit her ear. "Come, Nila. Come for me. Let me give you pleasure after the pain I've caused."

Her legs gave way; a long moan crawled from her throat. Then, she detonated.

I caught her as an orgasm ripped through her core, sucking and melting around my cock. "Yes…Oh, my God…"

I clamped a hand over her mouth as she screamed in delirium. My forehead furrowed as incredible waves of pressure milked my cock as her pussy contracted.

I wanted to come. Shit, I wanted to come.

With each wave, her body tried to reject my size, but then…on the final crest of her orgasm, wetness gushed. She welcomed me with perfect rapture.

I groaned.

"I'm taking you now, Ms. Weaver. You're all mine."

Bending over her, I let myself loose.

In one vicious rock, I claimed her. I slid deep, deep inside.

There was no resistance. Nothing barring me from filling her completely. The head of my cock banged against the top of her, tearing a guttural grunt from my chest.

"Christ!" I thrust again, loving how deep I could go. Her liquid heat slicked over me, turning friction into sheer-minded lust.

I could've come right there.

I could've come a hundred fucking times.

But yet again, I needed more. So much *more*.

Nila's hands slapped on the side, her fingers struggling for purchase as I stopped thinking, stopped feeling, and gave into what I needed.

I rode her.

So. Damn. Hard.

I claimed her.

So. Damn. Hard.

I grabbed her hips and punished both of us for finding what we never thought we'd find. I broke myself by shattering my walls and admitting without her…I was nothing.

Nothing.

I fucked her. I loved her.

I gave everything to her.

My teeth sank into the spot between her shoulder and neck as sweat ran down my back. I wanted to puncture her skin. I never wanted to let go.

The diamonds in her collar reflected the sapphire of the water, blinding me.

Her whimpers echoed in my ears as she tilted her head, giving me more authority, more control with my primitive hold.

Unable to stop myself, I bit harder, licking her salty skin, relishing in her flinch.

My teeth sank deeper, and only once I tasted the faintest tang of blood did I stand up and fuck her harder. My fingers gripped her hipbones, conveying greed and possession. My entire mind-set became feral, needing to conquer this woman.

My woman.

Nila turned her head, pressing her cheek to the side. A wince knitted her brows, her lips bowed in pain, but I couldn't stop.

Wouldn't stop.

"Yes. More, Jethro. More."

My chest rose and fell with laboured breaths, my muscles spasmed as I sent my body hurtling into euphoria.

Her eyes opened and I lost myself in the dark chasm of mesmerizing love.

She loved me.

She fucking loves me.

The unmistakable vulnerability of such an emotion tore open my heart.

The cuts on my feet bellowed as I dug my toes into the silty bottom and rode her harder, giving her my entire length thrust after thrust after *thrust*.

"Nila—fuck—"

I jerked. My orgasm shot unrestrained from my balls. It exploded up my cock with such intensity, I folded over her back. "Goddammit," I groaned, sucking in her hair as savage streams of cum erupted from my tip.

Her inner muscles demanded more, conjuring every last drop of semen I had to give. The release kept going and going, threatening to burst my heart as my body continued to devour hers. Ecstasy sparkled in every cell as I hit the top of her, spurting one last time as deep as I could go.

"Feel that?" I asked, grunting as a final wave stole my ability to breathe. Sweat ran down my temples, drenching my hair. "You're inside me, Nila Weaver—as surely as I'm inside you."

"You're it for me, Jethro. You've destroyed me." Her voice was soft, dreamy.

I bent to kiss her—the sweetest, gentlest kiss. "You're wrong. You're the one who's destroyed me."

Ending the kiss, Nila just watched me. No words. No questions.

She accepted everything I gave her. She hadn't looked away while I lost myself in her—she'd given me something I'd never had before. She gave me everything—let me witness how true and steadfast it was.

Trust.

Connection.

No lies.

She fucking loved me.

She'd given me a new beginning.

Nila

"WHEN WILL YOU tell me?"

Jethro's step faltered, his eyes shooting to mine.

His naked torso was damp and flushed with heat from the cave-springs, a white towel riding low on his hips.

He'd offered to carry me, but I'd chosen to walk—even though I was just as naked with only a towel hiding my modesty.

I was *alive*.

The sooner my body remembered how to move, the better.

Even though hate had killed me, love had revived me.

Jethro had salvaged me and brought me back.

He'd done more than bring me back.

He'd given me a new home—inside him.

I'm alive because of him.

The Second Debt had taken everything from me.

But Jethro had given it back a hundred fold.

We ghosted to a stop outside my bedroom door. Jethro was the perfect suitor, walking me home after the strangest day of all. His hand came up to cup my cheek, a sigh escaping his lips. "I will tell you, but it's not a simple matter of blurting it out."

I turned my head and kissed his palm, never breaking eye contact. "Whatever it is, I'll understand."

He smiled sadly. "That's the thing; you probably won't. To tell you what I am means I'll have to tell you everything. About the debts, the reasoning, my role." He hung his head. "It's a lot."

I shuffled closer, wrapping my arms around his warm body. "Tomorrow. Meet me after breakfast and take me somewhere far from here. Tell me then."

His nostrils flared. "You want to go off the grounds? Away from Hawksridge?"

The thought excited me. I didn't want to go back to London or seek out my old life—not anymore, but it would be nice to go somewhere just the two of us.

A date.

"You can trust me, Jethro. You know that. I wouldn't run if you took me somewhere public."

A painful shadow crossed his face. "I know you wouldn't. And that's what fucking kills me."

My heart stuttered. "Why?"

He slouched, pushing me against my door so my back kissed the wood and his lips kissed mine. The kiss was fleeting and soft, but the emotion behind it squeezed my chest with an agonising weight.

I didn't know what the weight was. But the pressure built and built with words dying to leap free.

I.

Love.

You.

After what had just happened between us, it was all I could think about. I wanted to scream them. Blare them. Let him know that my caring for him wasn't conditional or cruel.

I loved him. For *him*. For his soul.

His lips skated over mine again—the sweetest connection. "Jethro," I breathed. "I—I lo—"

He froze, slamming his fingers over my mouth. "Don't say it." Dropping his touch, he shook his head. "Don't say it. Please, Nila."

"But why shouldn't I…when it's the truth." The weight on my heart grew deeper, stronger. I had no choice but to tell him. The words physically suffocated me, needing to be said. "You mean everything to me." Placing my hand over his heart, I whispered. "Kite…I'm in love with you. It doesn't come with conditions or commands. I can't hate you for what you did today or what you might do in the future. I'm scared and lost and absolutely terrified that I'm doing the wrong thing by choosing you over my own life—but…I have no choice."

He sucked in the sharpest breath. "You called me Kite."

My heart bottomed out.

His name bulldozed through the partition I'd managed to keep in place. My feelings toward Kite plaited with my feelings for Jethro.

I slammed deeper into love.

He's mine.

His eyes squeezed closed, pressing his forehead on mine. "Nila…you—you don't know what you're doing to me." He trembled in my arms, his hands bracing himself on the door. "Take it back. I—I can't take so much from you."

"I can't take back something that already belongs to you."

Tears.

I wanted to cry.

I wanted free my terror at falling in love. I wanted to beg him to be strong enough to choose me after stealing everything that I was.

I couldn't compete with what he did to me in the spring. He'd reached inside me and ripped my heart from my chest. I didn't fight it. In fact, I'd carved it out for him.

My hands were bloody from presenting it to him with open arms.

I.

Love.

Him.

Before, I was in a cage.

I wasn't any more.

I could see. I was free. I *believed*.

"Tomorrow." He exhaled shakily. He clasped my jaw, running his thumbs over my cheeks. "You're mine. You deserve to know the man you've chosen—the man you've saved."

A shooting star sliced through my soul. "I saved you?"

A soft smile tugged his lips. "You have no idea, do you?" He kissed my forehead, filling it with overwhelming feeling. "No idea what you've done to me."

His delectable smell wisped around us. I wanted to fall into him and never let go.

He whispered, "Tomorrow, everything that I am becomes yours."

I shivered at the truth in his eyes, the echoing affection. "Tomorrow."

With a barely-there kiss, he transmitted every emotion he couldn't say and backed into the shadows of the corridor. "Tomorrow, I'm taking you away from here. I'll give you what you've selflessly given me. I'll tell you…everything."

Overnight, I'd turned from a supple young woman to arthritic hag.

I didn't sleep. I doubted I'd ever be able to sleep again with the excitement of what today would bring.

Jethro will tell me.

Finally, I would know.

Last night, I'd thought about reading the Weaver Journal to see how my mother and grandmother felt paying the Second Debt. Had they made note of it? Or were they like me and saw what the Journal was—a way to monitor our hearts and minds? I wanted to see if they'd done what I did: fall for their tormentors.

But despite my bouncing mind and infectious energy, my body grew stiffer by the moment.

It ached, it screamed, it needed to rest.

I'd returned from the dead.

Relearning to live again wasn't easy.

I would have days of recovering ahead and it became painfully obvious when I went to stand. My shoulders cried from the simple motion of shoving my sheets away. My legs promptly went on strike as they touched the thick carpet.

I remained vertical for a brief moment, before face planting instead.

I didn't walk anymore, I hobbled.

I didn't talk, I croaked.

I wore bracelets of bruising around my wrists and ankles, and my skin retained its ghostly white, as if I hadn't quite shed death's grip.

No matter how alive I'd been with Jethro last night...today, I was paying for it.

I hadn't wanted him to leave—not when he was blistering open and profound. I would've preferred to fall asleep in his embrace. But I knew that, regardless of our alliance to one another, his family was still in charge. Things had to go on as if nothing had changed—even though everything had.

My stomach rumbled, adding another discomfort on top of all the rest.

I couldn't remember the last time I'd eaten.

After a slow shower and an even slower time of getting dressed, I headed to the door, hissing between my teeth with every step.

I wouldn't permit my body to steal my plans for today. Jethro was taking me away. He would talk. Nothing would destroy that.

Perhaps it could *wait until tomorrow.*

The thought of returning to the softness of my mattress almost made me turn around.

No!

I was just stiff—that was all. As long as I got on with life, I would heal faster.

Gritting my teeth, I forced my aching muscles to slowly

propel me toward the dining room.

As I pushed open the double doors and entered the cavernous space with its dripping blood-red walls and excessively big portraits of past Hawks, my attention swooped to the armoury and the empty place that had held my dirk.

That same dirk was now tucked into the waistband of my yoga pants.

The scents of freshly brewed coffee and intoxicating aroma of buttery pastries turned my hunger into a sharp pang.

Cut looked up from his newspaper, a large grin splitting his face. "Ah, Nila! You're awake from the dead." He laughed at his tasteless joke. Folding the paper, he waved to a few free chairs.

The dining room was a busy place this morning. Black Diamond brothers were scattered around the twenty seated table, eating an array of full English breakfasts.

Tugging on the cuffs of my long sleeve baby-blue jumper, I drifted forward, cursing the creak in my joints.

I second-guessed my need for breakfast and hovered by a chair. If I didn't sit down soon, I'd fall, but I didn't think I could tolerate eating with my archenemies.

Where is he?

I needed to make sure Jethro hadn't had second thoughts. That we were still together—still true.

"I see Jet revived you."

Daniel's voice made my head snap up. He sat between two bikers, gnawing on a sausage.

Crap, I hadn't seen him. If I'd known he was here, I would've forgone an entire day of food.

Daniel sneered. "He's such a soft-hearted prick. If it were me, I would've just let you drown."

My fingers curled around the back of a chair. "Lucky for me, you're not firstborn."

Daniel lost his smirk. His face grew black. "Not lucky for you, though, little Weaver."

What did he mean by that?

Then the doors swung wide and Jethro appeared.

The man who'd drugged me, kidnapped me, and stolen my heart strode quickly to my side and took my elbow.

Every atom wanted to sway into his support. Every cell demanded I turn and kiss him.

But I couldn't.

I couldn't let Cut see what'd happened.

It was one thing to be blatant in my hate for Jethro at the beginning, but now it proved a hard task to pretend. I had to openly despise him, all while suffocating my heart from showing the truth.

It took all my willpower, but I sidestepped out of Jethro's hold. "Don't you think you did enough yesterday? Don't touch me."

Jethro sucked in a harsh breath.

Daniel chuckled, smacking his lips. "Seems you're as hated as us now, brother. Congratulations."

Jethro's eyebrows knitted together, his gaze flaring with hurt.

I willed him to understand.

The tightness suddenly faded around his mouth, his forehead smoothing into a perfect mask.

He knows.

His gaze met mine. With a barely noticeable nod, he agreed to our deception. A second later, a cold shield slammed over his face as effortlessly as breathing. He glittered with ice, so pure, so sharp.

If I didn't bear the marks of his teeth and fingertips from loving me so roughly last night, I would've doubted what was real.

I swallowed hard.

It's only a trick.

It's what needs to happen.

It was us against them now. This was the biggest secret of all.

My attention dropped to what he held in his left hand.

The Tally Box.

The room had been fairly silent since I entered, but now hushed anticipation filled the space.

"Glad to see you remembered," Cut said, taking a sip of his coffee.

Jethro nodded at his father, pulling out a chair for me. "Sit, Ms. Weaver. There's something we need to do."

Unable to hide my flinch from bending sore joints, I settled into the offered chair.

Only once I sat did Jethro take the seat beside me.

Folding his long legs beneath the table, he shuffled closer. His aftershave and natural scent of woods and leather trickled into my lungs, causing my heart to squeeze.

My mouth popped open as something pressed against my knee.

Jethro refused to meet my eyes, but I knew it was him, touching me…comforting me, granting me strength.

I sucked in a breath as he nudged me harder. The pressure sent combustible lust fizzing through my blood.

The heavy weight from last night settled on my chest. Words I wanted to spill gathered thickly, drowning me. I wanted to talk to him. I wanted to ask questions and hear his answers.

I want to know him.

Every inch.

Jethro continued to lean his leg against mine. He did it so calmly, all the while pretending nothing was different.

"Get on with it, Jet," Cut ordered, his attention locked on us.

Jethro nodded curtly. "Of course. Don't rush me. I think I've proven I'm more than capable of doing what needs to be done."

Cut smashed his lips together.

Jethro's eyes narrowed as he opened the Tally Box.

My heartbeat sped up as he lifted out the apparatus he would need. Keeping my attention on the needle and ink, I rubbed my foot against his ankle.

He tensed, but continued on as if everything was fine.

Last night, he'd given me power over him in the form of his life.

I knew things no one else did.

And after today, I would know everything.

Jethro was mine, and I would help save him, just like he said. We could change our fates from the plague of his family.

"Hold out your hand," Jethro murmured, ignoring the table of onlookers.

My heart raced as he held up the tattoo gun.

Pressing my knuckles against the wood of the table, I bit my lip as he turned on the gun.

His hair had grown longer and it fell over his forehead. My fingers itched to brush it away, to press below his chin and bring his mouth to mine.

The air shimmered between us, growing thicker with lust.

My pussy ached from him taking me so roughly last night, but I wanted more. I wanted it harder, deeper, faster. I doubted I'd ever have enough.

Jethro bristled, fighting against the building heat humming where we touched. When it came to touching in public, we had no armor against the truth.

My gaze shot to Cut. My feelings were far too obvious—he'd see…he'd know. However, his attention zeroed in on his son, his hands steepled before him.

I gasped as the sharp needle bit into my skin. I endured the tiny teeth as they stained me with ink. The burn this time was faintly familiar, filling with memories—becoming part of the design as much as his initials.

It only took a moment.

Jethro reclined, eyeing up his penmanship. There, on the pad of my middle finger, he'd completed another *JKH* .

A debt for a debt.

A tally for a tally.

The residual pain couldn't compete with my other aches

and bruises. It was rather refreshing to have a wound that was sharp, rather than bone-deep and throbbing.

Jethro turned off the gun and handed it to me.

Wordlessly, he splayed his beautiful long fingers and never stopped looking at me as I inked my ownership on his mirroring finger.

My lines were straighter this time, more confident. I embraced the marks because now it only bound us tighter together, rather than recorded a new debt.

When I'd finished, he had two branded fingers.

Like for like.

Same for same.

Jethro nudged my foot again, keeping his face blank and almost cruel. I pressed back, never looking up as I turned off the gun and placed it back in its box.

Awareness scattered over my forearms. I couldn't stop a gentle sigh as Jethro deliberately brushed my pinky with his, tucking away the discarded vial and locking the lid.

Cut muttered, "Good to see you learned from your past mistake and things are following accordingly." Waving at the sideboard groaning with food, he added, "Eat, both of you. You have a large schedule."

My throat closed at the thought of what that could mean.

Cut narrowed his eyes. "Jethro, you're in charge of the Carlyle shipment. The stones arrive in a few hours. You know what to do." Turning his cold glare on me, he smiled. "And, Nila, you've been summoned by my mother, Bonnie, for tea in her boudoir."

My heart raced.

Jethro threw me a look.

What about our plans?

He glared at his father. "Ms. Weaver was subjected to enough yesterday." His voice lowered as he spoke through clenched teeth. "Give her a few days, for fuck's sake."

Knives and forks screeched across crockery as the Diamond men turned to see Cut's reaction.

Cut fisted his hands on the table. "Don't you—"

"Um, sir?"

All heads turned to the youngest member of the Black Diamonds, a twenty-year-old man named Facet. His floppy blond hair and kind eyes were a direct contradiction to the leader he now addressed.

Cut's forehead furrowed. Black anger covered his face. "What? What is so fucking important you interrupt me mid-sentence?"

Facet shifted awkwardly. "Sorry, sir. Won't happen again. But, eh…we have company." His eyes flew around the room, looking for someone to help bear the brunt of his leader.

No one moved.

The guy sucked in a breath, reluctantly delivering his news. "I tried to stop them from entering the grounds. We did what you said. But they ignored us." Sweat gleamed on his upper lip. "Even the gatekeeper at the lock house couldn't stop them."

"What the hell are you talking about, boy?!" Cut exploded.

Facet jumped. "They have a warrant, sir. They—they barged past, regardless of our warnings. We reminded them that we own their department—that our brotherhood is beyond their reach." He hung his head. "It didn't do any good."

The entire table sucked in a breath.

Warrant?

Could it be?

Jethro went deathly still beside me. Every connection we shared froze, no longer a two-way street of togetherness and affection. A road block slammed into place, masking his every thought.

I glanced at him from the corner of my eye. My heart squeezed as he stared fiercely at the opposite wall, refusing to look at me.

"Jethro—" I breathed.

His jaw locked; snowflakes flurried around him as he pulled more and more away from me. Goosebumps dotted my flesh.

Cut roared, "Tell those fucking pigs to get off my land. Their warrant means jack-shit."

"Sir, I've told them. But they won't listen. They say—they say they're here for—"

Jethro burst out laughing—a cold, cynical chuckle. "That low life piece of shit. He did this. They're here for her." He looked at the ceiling, his face twisting into nightmares. "Of course, they fucking are."

A warrant could mean many things. It might not have anything to do with me. Yet a screeching, tearing noise echoed in my ears. *It's my soul.* The awful ripping sound was my soul splintering in two. If they had come for me…that meant…

I'm saved.

I'd wished for this very thing to happen.

I'd prayed for this. I'd begged for this.

Escape.

So, why—if it was true—did I wish to run to my quarters and hide?

I don't want to leave him.

I can't *leave him.*

Not after last night.

Jethro balled his hands, his eyes sharp and deadly. He snarled at Facet, "Tell them they can't fucking have her."

My heart squeezed. Pain blazed through me with more agony than I thought possible. He wouldn't give me up. He *couldn't* give me up.

We were one now. It'd been written in the stars and on our very skin.

Escape.

The word slithered through my brain, bringing forth thoughts of London and home. I shook my head, trying to dislodge the steadily building allure.

You could go home.

No, my home is here now.

But you'd be safe again…

My steadfast promise to stay and steal Jethro from his heritage faded…I became *confused*…

I swallowed, lubricating my throat. "Jethro—please…"

I needed him to fight for me. To prove that this was my place, my destiny.

Jethro clenched his jaw, shoving his chair back and standing. "Quiet!" Pointing a finger at Facet, he growled. "Do they, or do they not, have a fucking warrant for what's mine?"

Facet swallowed. "Yes."

"How?" I blurted, causing every man to look in my direction. "How do they have a warrant?"

Facet's mouth fell open, looking to Cut to see if he should reply.

Cut glowered at me as if I'd brought the apocalypse to his door.

No one spoke.

What did my father do?

How did V find a way to free me?

My heart winged thinking of my twin. He'd promised he would never give up. I should've trusted him.

I should be more grateful.

I wanted to kill him.

He'd ruined it. He'd taken everything I'd worked for and torn it away from me.

I'm alive and going home.

I'm alive and going home.

The words repeated in my head.

I wouldn't be alive if it wasn't for Jethro.

I'm in love with him.

He'd infected me, and no matter how much distance was between us, that would never change. I was his. And he was mine.

Jethro's eyes locked with me—the golden depths burned with despair and scorching agony. "I warned him. I tried to stop…"

He showed too much.

He *felt* too much.

My diamond collar grew heavier, colder.

You said you'd be the last.

You promised you'd end this.

My stomach somersaulted.

If they're here for you. Leave.

You have no choice.

I ached.

"Warned who? What's happened? Jethro…I'm not leaving. Even if they are here for me."

Jethro didn't move. He looked as if the light in his soul had snuffed out. The peace and openness of last night was gone. Disappeared.

"I'll kill him for this," he muttered.

Unfurling my hand, I looked at my inked finger. I needed him to know that what happened last night wasn't a trick. He needed to know that I intended to stay—even though it might be the worst decision in the world.

My stomach clenched at the thought of leaving.

Facet blurted, "Sir, they're here to take Nila Weaver home."

The words fell like bombs, detonating my last hope.

It's true then.

Cut stood up. He spoke slowly and with the blackest temper I'd ever seen. "You're mistaken, boy. I suggest you get out of my sight. Tell whoever threatened you to get off my fucking land."

"They're—they're in the annex, sir. They said if we don't deliver the girl within five minutes, they'll tear apart the place looking for her."

Jethro fisted his hands. "Tell them she's mine and she's not going anywhere."

Daniel stood. "She's our Weaver now."

In a sick twisted way, the men imprisoning me were now on my side. I was no longer just a betrayer to my ancestors but a betrayer to my father and brother, too.

You would rather stay here than go home.

I would rather love and die young than be empty forever.

"What is the meaning of this screeching inside my house?"

All eyes turned to the raspy voice of Bonnie Hawk as she appeared in the doorway.

Facet moved sideways, giving up his audience to the matriarch of this insane family.

"I see the plot has thickened." Bonnie crooked a finger in my direction, a large ruby glinting in the light. "How did you do this?"

"Me?" I glanced from Bonnie to Jethro. "I didn't do it. I wouldn't."

"It wasn't her," Jethro snapped. "Get rid of the police. She's not leaving."

My arms craved to wrap around him. To thank him for keeping me.

Bonnie shuffled closer, her long skirt dragging on the carpet. Her white hair was curled and immaculate. "She's brought scorn and blasphemy to our name." Her eyes bored into mine. "I've seen what you do, little girl. I know what you want. And you won't get it." Pointing at the door, she ordered, "Get out."

Cut punched the table. "No fucking—"

"She's leaving this house." Bonnie interrupted. "Now."

Jethro moved to stand in front of me, blocking my body with his. "She's staying."

Bonnie smiled coldly. "There is no other way. They're here for her. She's going with them." Her eyes narrowed. "Don't make me repeat myself, boy. You know as well as I do what your obligations are."

I grabbed Jethro's arm, unable to hide my emotions. If I hated the Hawks as much as Cut believed, I should've sprinted out the door, skipping with happiness. Instead, Cut would see that something deeper had happened—something that would be severely punished.

But I didn't care.

Because if I didn't fight, this was over. Here and now.

"Let me talk to them—"

Jethro spun to face me, his temper blazing. "You want to *talk* to them? To tell them what, exactly? The truth?"

"Enough!" Cut yelled. Looking at Bonnie, he frowned. "You want her gone?"

Bonnie nodded, her red lipstick smeared on thin lips. "Immediately."

Cut sighed, his leather jacket creaking as anger wisped off him. "Fine," he said sharply. "Nila Weaver, get the fuck out of my house."

My heart crumbled.

Jethro crossed his arms, still shielding me. His ice slid back into place turning him impenetrable. "I'm the firstborn, and I say she isn't fucking leaving."

Cut moved around the table, his fists clenching. "You dare do this here, son? You know you'll lose—"

"Wait!"

A feminine voice whipped through the aching tension in the room.

"Jaz? What the hell are you doing in here?" Jethro asked, his mask slipping as he looked at his wheelchair bound sister.

She rolled into the dining room with the aid of a blonde-curled maid. Jasmine's bronze eyes met Cut's. "She can't go, Father. It's not finished."

Cut breathed hard through his nose, his temper throbbing beneath his frayed self-control. "Don't speak of things you don't understand. Jethro didn't control the situation. This is his mess. He's failed." Cut looked piercingly at Jethro, sending goosebumps and terror down my spine. "It's over. He's done."

The way he spoke…it sounded like a death sentence.

Jethro gasped, true fear coating his face. "It's not over—"

"Shut. Up." Cut sliced the air with his arm, silencing him. Looking at me, he snapped, "Leave, Ms. Weaver. Your time is up. I won't tell you again."

Jasmine's gaze shot to Jethro's. "Don't let her go, Kite."

Kite.

My soul splintered.

Bonnie shuffled forward. "I see what you're doing, girl. Your family have been clever with their tricks and treachery, but I won't let you spin any more of your filth." Her wrinkly skin furrowed deeper with rage. "Get. Out. *Now.*"

"Was this always your plan, Father?" Jethro looked at Cut, panic and rage twisted his face. "You set me up to fail?" The depth of confusion and agony in his voice broke my heart.

My eyes flared wide. I didn't understand.

"Jethro…he doesn't matter. None of them do." I squeezed his arm. "Believe in us. Believe in me."

"Hush, stupid girl," Bonnie snapped. "You're the same as all the rest. Get out." Pointing at the door, she hissed, "Go!"

The other bikers didn't do a thing. Just sat and watched.

Jethro never tore his eyes off his father—they were clouded and strained. He was a trebuchet straining to release his tension.

"Don't do this," I whispered. "Don't let them ruin what we have."

We were damned to our fates, brought together by a ridiculous vendetta. Yet…something right had come out of something so wrong. We'd somehow found the one person we were meant to find.

I can't go.

"You don't understand, Nila. It's not that easy." Jethro looked at me, running his newly inked finger along the inside of my wrist. "Go, before it's too late."

Memories of the way he'd thrust inside me last night filled my mind. I'd meant what I said—I *felt* him—not just inside me, but what he hid inside *him.*

It was more than truth.

It had been gospel in its legitimacy.

"Jethro…it's too late already. I'm meant to stay. With you."

"She's right, Kite. Tell the police to leave. Find a way," Jasmine said.

I looked at Jethro's sister in her navy wool dress and white pashmina in her lap. Her face was pinched and full of concern. What did she know? Why was she fighting on my side?

Cut slammed his fist onto the table with a resounding thump. "Get your hands off my son and get the fuck out!"

Jethro's face darkened. His gaze sent a brutally painful message.

Leave…at least one of us will be free.

My body wound tighter and tighter.

Tears clogged my throat. "I can't. I won't."

I won't be free without you.

Cut suddenly barked, "Daniel, seeing as Ms. Weaver refuses to leave, escort her off the premises."

Daniel chuckled, his eyes glittering as he moved quickly around the table. "With pleasure, Pop."

"Stop! All of you!" Jasmine shouted, but it didn't do any good.

In a flash, Daniel grabbed my elbow, hauling me away from Jethro, from our bond, from the only existence I ever wanted.

"No!"

Daniel's voice licked into my ear. "Fight me and I'll do something un-fucking-forgivable. Do you want me to do that?"

I tried to stomp on his foot. "You're a bastard."

"Thanks for the compliment."

Jethro lunged, grabbing me and punching Daniel in the jaw. "Get your fucking hands off her." Whipping me behind his body, he glowered at Cut. "I'll get rid of her."

Cut breathed hard. "Good. Then I can deal with you."

Jethro jolted, every inch tight and breaking.

Without a word, he dragged me toward the exit. He trembled as if he'd shatter at any moment, buckling under the weight.

I squirmed, fighting my aching body. "Let me go! I'm not going anywhere."

"You're leaving. If it's the last thing I do, at least I can keep you safe."

I struggled harder. "Safe? I don't want to be safe. I want to be with you."

"Quiet," he choked, his face ashen. "It's better this way."

"You're choosing them over me!" I tried to punch him. "Stand up to them. Leave with me. Don't stay here, Jethro."

He clenched his jaw and didn't reply.

He wasn't strong enough to fight for what we had.

He's choosing his family over me.

I rolled my arm, twisting out of his hold. Scurrying from his hands, I turned to face Cut. "I don't know what power you hold over him, but it isn't enough. He's mine, not yours."

"Nila—don't!" Jethro grabbed me, dragging me backward. "You don't know what you're doing. For fuck's sake, don't make this worse than it already is."

Cut grinned broadly. "Congratulations, Nila. You've successfully just changed the future." His eyes fell frigid and evil on Jethro. "I thought there was hope. But you were just too fucking weak."

The men shifted in their seats. Cut never moved. "Get rid of the girl, Jet. You and I have something we need to discuss."

Life seemed to siphon from Jethro's limbs, growing colder by the second.

"No!" Jasmine screeched, rolling forward. "You can't. You promised!" Tears slid from her eyes, looking at her brother. "Stop this, Kite. I'm sorry. I'm so sorry for making you change, for causing—" She stopped, unable to speak through her sobs.

The worst horror I'd ever felt slithered through my blood.

I'm hollow. I'm hurting. What the hell is happening?

Something darker was at work. This wasn't about me anymore. This was about Jethro. His father.

What would they do to him the moment I left?

I *wouldn't* leave him behind.

Linking my fingers with his, I pulled. "Jethro, come with me."

But he just stood there, rooted to the spot. His eyes wild,

lips parted.

I hovered…waiting. Waiting for one tiny sign that he was still alive beneath whatever fear had struck him mute.

Bonnie sidled up to me, bringing the sickening scent of rosewater and biscuits. "Goodbye, Ms. Weaver. You've earned your freedom today at the cost of another." Leaning closer, she whispered, "You're free, but this is *far* from over, girl. Mark my words; you'll pay for what your family has done."

I stood taller, ready to fight even if Jethro wouldn't. "Stop it, I'm stay—"

Jethro suddenly yelled, "Go! Just fucking go."

The room froze, all eyes pinned on him.

He pointed at the door, shattering my heart into dust. "Leave."

His eyes screamed the truth.

If you love me at all, you'll go.

I need you to go.

"You can't ask me to do this," I said, wiping away a fallen tear.

"I can and I will." Striding forward, he grabbed my face and kissed me in front of everyone. His hands shook, his lips trembled.

He broke me completely.

"Please, Nila. Do this for me. Let me make this right."

Pushing me gently to the door, he commanded, "Go and don't look back."

My world crumbled.

My legs didn't want to move.

My heart didn't want to beat.

His eyes begged me to obey.

Please…go.

Stumbling, I did the impossible.

I didn't look at Jasmine.

I didn't look at Jethro.

I kept moving.

I would honour him.

I would obey him.
Even though every inch of me bled.
Even though every part of me was dead.
I would go home.
I would find a way to fix this.
It wasn't over.
Two seconds later...
...
I was gone.

To be continued in…

Third Debt

Releasing 2015. Date to be advised

Updates, teasers, and exclusive news will be released on

www.pepperwinters.com

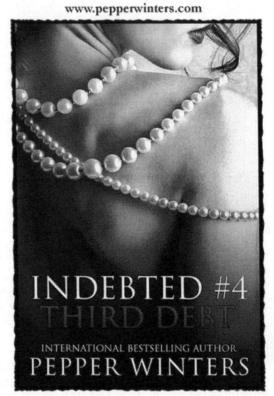

INDEBTED #4

THIRD DEBT

INTERNATIONAL BESTSELLING AUTHOR
PEPPER WINTERS

"She healed me. She broke me. I set her free. But we are in this together. We will end this together. The rules of this ancient game can't be broken."

Nila Weaver no longer recognises herself. She's left her lover, her courage, and her promise. Two debts down. Too many to go.

Jethro Hawk no longer recognises himself. He's embraced what he always ran from, and now faces punishment far greater than he feared.
It's almost time. It's demanding to be paid.
The Third Debt will be the ultimate test of all.

Add to Goodreads

About the Author

Pepper Winters is a NYT and USA Today International Bestseller. She wears many roles. Some of them include writer, reader, sometimes wife. She loves dark, taboo stories that twist with your head. The more tortured the hero, the better, and she constantly thinks up ways to break and fix her characters.

She loves to travel and has an amazing, fabulous hubby who puts up with her love affair with her book boyfriends. She's also honoured to wear the IndieReader Badge for being a Top 10 Indie Bestsellers, best BDSM series voted by the SmutClub, best Dark Romance, best Dark Hero, and recently signed a two book deal with Grand Central. Her books are currently being translated into numerous languages and will be in bookstores in the near future.

Her Dark Romance books include (click for buylinks from numerous online sites):
Tears of Tess (Monsters in the Dark #1)
Quintessentially Q (Monsters in the Dark #2)
Twisted Together (Monsters in the Dark #3)
Debt Inheritance (Indebted #1)
First Debt (Indebted Series #2)
Second Debt (Indebted Series #3)

Her Grey Romance books include (click for buylinks from numerous online sites):
Destroyed

Upcoming releases are (click the link to add to Goodreads)
Ruin & Rule (Motorcycle romance)
Je Suis a Toi (Monsters in the Dark Novella)
Forbidden Flaws (Contemporary Romance)

To be the first to know of upcoming releases, please join Pepper's Newsletter (she promises never to spam or annoy you.)

Pepper's Newsletter

Or follow her on her website
Pepper Winters

You can stalk her here:

Pinterest
Facebook Pepper Winters
Twitter
Instagram
Website
Facebook Group
Goodreads

She loves mail of any kind: pepperwinters@gmail.com
All other titles and updates can be found on her Goodreads Page.

Playlist

My Demons by Starset
Bleeding out by Imagine Dragons
Somebody I used to Know by Gotye
Lost Cause by Imagine Dragons
Monster by Lady Gaga
I like it Rough by Lady Gaga
Point of No Return by Starset
Bad Romance by Lady Gaga
ET by Katy Perry
I Won't Let You Go by Snow Patrol
Run by Snow Patrol
Beating Heart by Ellie Goulding
Silhouettes by Monsters and Men
Weak by Seether
Suffer Well by Depeche Mode
Break Free by Ariana Grande
I like you the way you are by She the Monsters
Angel by Theory of a Deadman
Saving me by Nickelback

Acknowledgements

Seven books and acknowledgements down, and they still don't get any easier. Along with the typical gratefulness, I'm going to answer a few personal questions that relate to the creation of the Indebted Series. First, the acknowledgements.

Thank you to Ari from Cover it! Designs. I'm still awed by the covers for this series.

Thank you to Aussie Lisa and Nina for being so amazingly supportive and awesome friends. I seriously couldn't have done this without you. From our daily PM's to just knowing you're there for my mini-breakdowns. Love your faces.

Thank you to Katrina, Kiki, Mandi, Yaya, Vicki, Tami, Vickie, Ellen, and Natasha for reading the first copy of Second Debt, typos and all. Especially a big thanks to Yaya for being brutal even when she doesn't want to hurt my feelings, Mandi and Tami for inviting me into an incredible friendship, and Kiki for searching the world's music for the best songs.

Thanks to Jenny from Editing4Indies. You have my back and put up with my crazy deadlines and urgent emails. I love knowing you're in my corner.

Thanks to Nadine for running my street team and the amazing girls who help spread the word, and for organising one of the best events in 2015 in San Francisco.

Thank you for my Pepper Pimpettes who do a fabulous job sharing and reviewing.

Thank you to The Rock Stars of Romance for hosting the review and blog tour and for getting me drunk one night so we could finally gossip about the good stuff.

Thank you to my readers who just make me feel so loved and appreciated in all things that I write.

Thank you to hubby for cooking me dinner, keeping me alive, and overlooking the fact I now work entirely in pyjamas.

And finally, thank you universe for making my dreams come true.

Now, onto the questions:

The main question I get asked is: **Where did your inspiration come from for this series?** That isn't an easy one to answer. I've always been a HUGE lover of historical romance and find it brutal, dark, and in some ways beyond the realm of comfortable behaviour in many circumstances. That's because it isn't fiction. That sort of stuff happened. Honour was an unbreakable vow. Tradition was an enforceable law. The Debt Inheritance is so wrapped up in things that happened in the past, that at first it seems unbelievable. How something like that could come about and how it could be guarded and continued doesn't makes sense, but it does if you're steeped in history and family feuds. It's the way of law—the only law. And I hope as the plot is uncovered that it makes a lot more sense why it's so layered.

I also get asked: **Was I worried that Jethro would be unredeemable?** No. I've always known what sort of man Jethro Hawk is. And I've hinted at that in this book. The answers will be delivered very soon and then…it should all make sense. I always knew his affliction and it plays perfectly into his inner conflict of the sort of life he's been made to live.

Right, that's enough. I have to go write the next book. Hope you all enjoyed Second Debt and will continue to follow Jethro and Nila's tale.

Happy 2015 everybody x

Other Book Blurbs & Reviews

Destroyed

This book enticed & enthralled me completely. Pepper's stories are like a fine piece of art. They are profound, unique, raw and beautiful—***Kristina, Amazon Review***

Pepper Winters has a ridiculous level of talent, and I'm in awe of how deeply she delves into her characters. There are not enough stars, seriously—***K Dawn, Amazon Reviewer***

If you like a bit of grey in your romance then you need to get this book because it's one of the best books I've read this year—***Bookfreak***

*

USA Today, #1 Erotica and Romantic Suspense Bestseller.

She has a secret.
I'm complicated. Not broken or ruined or running from a past I can't face. Just complicated.
I thought my life couldn't get any more tangled in deceit and

confusion. But I hadn't met him. I hadn't realized how far I could fall or what I'd have to do to get free.

He has a secret.
I've never pretended to be good or deserving. I chase who I want, do what I want, act how I want.

I didn't have time to lust after a woman I had no right to lust after. I told myself to shut up and stay hidden. But then she tried to run. I'd tasted what she could offer me and damned if I would let her go.

Secrets destroy them.

Buy Now on All Major Online Stores

***

Tears of Tess (Book one of Monsters in the Dark) Book two: Quintessentially Q, and Book Three: Twisted Together, are available now

6 Holy Wow This Author Took Me On A Ride I Never Saw Coming and Left Me Speechless Stars. I've never rated a book 6 stars before so this gives you an idea of just how good I believe this book to be. This story will take you by the hand and show you how both darkness and light exist within all of us. It will ultimately take you by the heart and you will be so glad that you read it—***Hook Me Up Book Blog***

DARK AND HAUNTINGLY BEAUTIFUL....IT WILL LEAVE YOU BREATHLESS!!!!
Pepper Winters is a standout! An absolutely stunning debut!—***Lorie, Goodreads***

*

A New Adult Dark Contemporary Romance, not suitable for people sensitive to grief, slavery, and nonconsensual sex. A story about finding love in the strangest of places, a will of iron that grows from necessity, and forgiveness that may not be enough.

"My life was complete. Happy, content, everything neat and perfect.
Then it all changed.
I was sold."

Tess Snow has everything she ever wanted: one more semester before a career in property development, a loving boyfriend, and a future dazzling bright with possibility.

For their two year anniversary, Brax surprises Tess with a romantic trip to Mexico. Sandy beaches, delicious cocktails, and soul-connecting sex set the mood for a wonderful holiday. With a full heart, and looking forward to a passion filled week, Tess is on top of the world.

But lusty paradise is shattered.

Kidnapped. Drugged. Stolen. Tess is forced into a world full of darkness and terror.

Captive and alone with no savior, no lover, no faith, no future, Tess evolves from terrified girl to fierce fighter. But no matter her strength, it can't save her from the horror of being sold.

Can Brax find Tess before she's broken and ruined, or will Tess's new owner change her life forever?

Buy Now on All Major Online Stores

***

Forbidden Flaws (Erotic Contemporary Romance) Coming 2015

She's forbidden.

Saffron Carlton is the darling of the big screen, starlet on the red carpet, and wife of mega producer Felix Carlton. Her life seems perfect with her overflowing bank balance, adoring fans, and luxury homes around the world. Everyone thinks they know her. But no one truly does.

The silver limelight is tainted the day the couple announce their divorce.

He's flawed.

Raised in squalor, fed on violence and poverty, Cas Smith knows the underbelly of the world. He's not looking for fame or fortune. He's looking for a job to get him the hell away from the danger of illegal fighting, and comes face to face with the woman who ran all those years ago.

Unable to turn down her job offer, he agrees to be her bodyguard and personal trainer, all while she hides her secrets.

He had no intention of letting her back into his heart.

But neither of them were prepared for what happens when forbidden and flawed collide —fracturing the world they know, changing the rules forever.

More Information Head Here

***

Ruin & Rule (Pure Corruption MC #1) Coming 28th July 2015

I love reading MC books but this has to be the best one I've read! I couldn't put it down —***Nikki Mccrae, Amazon Review***

One of the best stories I've ever read. Period. —*Tamicka Birch, Amazon Reviewer*

Ruin & Rule is another dark masterpiece from Pepper Winters. Buckle yourself in for a wild ride that is pure page-turning bliss! —*Rachel, Goodreads*

*

"WE MET IN A NIGHTMARE. THE IN-BETWEEN WORLD WHERE TIME HAD NO POWER OVER REASON. WE FELL IN LOVE. WE FELL HARD. BUT THEN WE WOKE UP.

And it was over . . . "

She is a woman divided.
Her past, present, and future are as twisted as the lies she's lived for the past eight years. She wants the truth, but the one man who holds all the answers is her greatest nemesis of all. Her feelings for the man who worships her in dreams and torments her in nightmares terrifies her. Her unexplainable attachment to the man whose passion and power overshadow everything is her downfall.

He is the president of Pure Corruption MC.
A biker, vengeance-deliverer, and heartless trader.
He lives where no laws or rules apply, obeys no one, and controls everything.
He controls because he must. His ability to trust is gone; his God-given right to love stolen forever. He lives only to reap revenge on those who wronged him.
Until he steals her.

Can a woman plagued by mystery fall in love with the man who refuses to face the truth?

And can a man whose soul is drenched in darkness forgo his quest for vengeance and finally find redemption?

Pre-order Links to Buy on All Major Online Stores

Thank you so much for Reading

xxx

Made in the USA
Lexington, KY
12 September 2017